In 2071, Sergeant Tachikoma leads a Marine combat armor squad. She knows the Corps never promised her a rose garden, only the chance to fight for her country.

Now, she faces her greatest challenge, two terrifying alien pillars that trapped her into reliving the same day again. The day she dies.

Today, she needs every ounce of courage to save her people from annihilation.

Based on cutting-edge theories on the nature of the universe, this white knuckle military SF thriller contains drama and mystery.

"This story is great, with a very firm grasp of the Marine Corps lifestyle."

— Sɢᴛ D. Bᴀʀʀᴏᴡ, USMC

GW00580234

BAD DOG

MILITARY SCIENCE FICTION ACROSS A
HOLOGRAPHIC MULTIVERSE

ASHLEY R POLLARD

TRIODE PRESS

BAD DOG

A Triode Press publication

ISBN:

978-1-912580-00-2 (PB)

978-1-912580-01-9 (eB)

978-1-912580-02-6 (HC)

Copy editing by Inspired Ink Editing

http://www.inspiredinkediting.com/

Cover art by Elartwyne Estole

https://www.artstation.com/elartestole

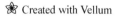 Created with Vellum

To Susan, my Alpha reader,
without whom I would never have written this work.

1. TODAY IS YESTERDAY

You will die like a dog for no good reason.

— ERNEST HEMINGWAY

Sergeant Tachikoma
First Combat Armor Suit Reconnaissance Company
Afghanistan
Thursday, July 2, 2071

It's Big Dog's fault we all died under a mountain in Afghanistan yesterday, and it's my fault we ended up dying again today…

Our Dogs hit dirt as the smoky white trails from incoming rockets target our LZ. Our Thunder Hawks above jink left and right, while launching decoys, sprouting angel's wings of incandescent light as they twist and turn to avoid the oncoming missiles. Our landing has announced the start of hell on Earth as the surrounding broken plain of rocks turns red from the glare of the explosions around us.

Captain Johanson calls out, "Section leaders, give me a three-sixty."

"We should move out now," I say, trying to interrupt him. But it's too late to change the outcome of this day.

The Chinese forces crest the ridgeline, a tsunami sweeping all before them. I kneel and fire, but at four klicks it's unlikely I'll hit anything. As the other Dogs join in the attack, the fire from our guns rises in a roaring crescendo and then crashes as the first of the enemy's artillery shells fall upon us, pinning us in place.

The ground around us shakes as the barrage rips our machines apart.

I'm thrown into the air by the shock wave, and I black out as my Dog ploughs into the ground. I wake up in the open and scream out as the pain from my broken arm and leg hits me. My Dog is shredded. By some miracle I'm free of my machine, strapped into what's left of my seat.

For a moment I lose consciousness, but the screeching agony of my injuries wakes me up. I release the harness, try to roll over, look around me, and I wish I hadn't. I'm surrounded by the smoke and flames from destroyed Dogs, scattered across the landscape like discarded toys.

My flight suit is covered in blood, all mine, which is never a good sign. It's always better for one's general sense of well-being if the blood remains inside one's body, and not leaking out pooling all around me. I giggle.

Still, the pain means I'm alive.

My field dressing is gone, but I remember that blood loss is not a *good thing*, and I'm bleeding out.

Stupid of me, I guess I must be in shock to have forgotten. I forgive myself the stupidity, as I don't think I will live long enough for it to matter. I forgive myself for a lot of the stupid decisions I've made, because in the bigger scheme of things they don't matter. What matters is doing the best you can with the cards life deals you.

Something has poked a hole through the outside part of my thigh.

Blood spurts rhythmically from the hole. A few inches inward and it would've hit my femoral artery. I'd be dead. Given how I feel, maybe that wouldn't have been such a bad thing.

I scream out in pain as I tear a strip of cloth from the ragged remains of my flight suit and push it into the hole. It's the best I can do. I'm operating by rote, trying to survive, knowing I'm prolonging the agony while I'm lying here dying. The sound of my inevitable death approaches as the ground shakes and a wave of darkness descends upon me.

I drag myself back to what's left of my Dog to find the first aid box. As I crawl towards the Dog, my progress is punctuated by cracks and bangs as ammunition cooks off, and the sounds of screaming. The screaming stops, and the silence is worse.

The realization hits me: it was me screaming.

I don't know how long it takes to get back to my Dog. I've lost my PAD and have no way of telling the time. But being alive is good. Except when the pain becomes too much to bear.

Dragging myself along the ground, I eventually get to the cockpit. It's a burned out shell. I count myself lucky not to have ended up trapped inside it, burned alive. My vision grays for a second or two, but the pain is insistent. It calls me back to the land of the living. I'm not long for this world.

My name is Lara Atsuko Tachikoma, I'm a sergeant in the Confederated States Marine Corps, and this is my story.

2. A DAY IN THE CORPS

The aim of every woman is to be truly integrated into the corps. She is able and willing to undertake any assignment consonant with marine corps needs, and is proudest of all that she has no nickname. She is a "Marine."

— COL KATHERINE A. TOWLE, USMC

Sergeant Tachikoma
First Combat Armor Suit Reconnaissance Company
CSN *Hornet*
Thursday, July 2, 2071

I've been aboard *Hornet* for two months, and after ten days at sea all the days start to blur together: cleaning weapons, doing PT on the flight deck, supervising sweeping the ship fore and aft, or having the ship's captain call for all personnel to go to their duty stations for general quarters—which means being confined to this room and lying in my rack.

Don't get me wrong, kicking back and taking it easy is good. But sometimes one can have too much of a good thing. This is such a common experience that sailors and Marines call it Groundhog Day because it sucks to repeat the same day over and over again.

However, one learns to embrace the suck.

The *Hornet*'s a Kearsarge-class amphibious assault ship commissioned by the Confederated States Navy back in '49 before World War Three broke out. My quarters are in the ship's bowels, right on the waterline, with no porthole, and no daylight.

So if someone came along and asked me what living aboard is like, I'd say that every day looks pretty much the same as every other day.

This tour I've got a middle bunk, which suits me right down to the ground. I'm tall enough at five foot eight to access my under-mattress coffin locker without having to either kneel on the floor or stand on tiptoe. Something I've had to do on previous deployments.

There're a couple of pictures stuck on the wall of my rack to relieve the monotony of my space. It's not much, but it's my home on *Hornet*.

I switch on my reading light, pull back the curtains that enclose my rack, and stare at the bulkheads. They're painted in the off-white color the Navy likes to call cream. The color dominates the room, but it makes it easier to see in the dark when the lights go out, as they do from time to time.

So everyone carries a flashlight in case the ship goes dark for whatever reason. Because it's the very definition of not fun to find oneself in a dark room unable to see. The first time it happened I panicked. This was a salutary lesson learnt.

The thrum of the ship's engines vibrating can be felt through the floor. It makes the ship feel alive.

The room is lit by a red strip light in the ceiling. It stays on all the time because people are on different watches around the clock. In the background I hear music playing. Constantly playing so people are not disturbed by any sudden noises caused by anyone entering or getting up and leaving the room.

It's definitely not the Hilton.

My quarters can best be described as a modestly sized room for one at home. It could charitably be called cosy if it wasn't for the fact that I share the space with eleven other women. After a few weeks, life aboard a ship starts to suck. Mostly down to the fact that the noise and lack of space starts to wear on one.

The original POD, plan of the day, had been a joint training mission. The Hound Dogs First Combat Armored Suit Reconnaissance Company were to have had an all-expenses-paid trip outside in the real world to play with the Indian Army.

But last night a fragmentary order had been issued, which changed all that.

This meant I got to enjoy the Corps equivalent of a lie-in and a leisurely breakfast while the rest of the battalion rose at zero dark thirty. This has resulted in rising at our normal 0530. But now I've to get ready to go deal with the Charlie Foxtrot that comes from last-minute changes to our nice, orderly military preparations.

So I swing my sorry ass out of the rack and slip on my flip-flops, not wanting to catch some loathsome foot disease from walking around on the deck in bare feet. I'm up and standing naked in my underwear. Not my best look.

Ignoring the people in the room who are either asleep or reading in their racks, I grab my bathrobe to go to the shower.

I make my way to the women's shared head and start the day with morning ablutions: sitting on the crapper and zoning out. It's really hard to pee when one is embarrassed. But it's been a long time since I was embarrassed by my bowel movements or, for that matter, cared about the smells from people farting around me.

Men might like to think women don't fart, but they're wrong.

We fart all the time. Unlike men, most women don't see farting as being a fun way to make a fatuous comment.

Showering aboard *Hornet* involves wetting yourself all over and turning the water off, followed by rubbing soap all over your body. Once clean I turn the water back on and rinse off, using the traditional Navy allowance of two minutes of water to do so.

All the while listening to the women around me bitching about the temperature of the water or the amount, which seems par for the course for sailors I've met. I'm grateful the water is warm. And it sure beats the hell out of having to wash oneself with baby wipes in the field. Given that a sailor's whole career is spent aboard ship, I guess they've nothing better to moan and bitch about.

Out of the shower I dry and brush my hair, wrestling with my unruly locks, pulling the comb through the knots, and getting it into shape for the day. At last my hair meets the requirements of the Corps.

I complain at the time it takes to do, but after I finish rassling a stray hair into place, I've turned myself from the wild red-haired mess into a Marine. Personal grooming is more than doing it by the numbers. It's about taking pride in one's presentation and appearance.

During recruit training, I'd cut my hair right off because it was more trouble than it was worth trying to maintain it while under the tutelage of my drill instructors. Especially Swinton, who used to deride us all for enlisting and trying to spoil her beloved Marine Corps.

Since then I've let my red hair grow back down my back. Improvise, adapt, and overcome has long been the motto of the Marine Corps, where you learn what that truly means if you want to maintain any sense of one's self as a woman.

Not that we don't have our fair share of women who don't care for how long their hair is, but it's my best feature. I've got what my mom calls a runner's build, which is a nice way of saying I'm not very curvy. Being in the Corps means I'm not likely to put on any weight to fill out my natural assets anytime soon.

The other trouble with being a redhead Anglo-Japanese woman is getting noticed when out on liberty, where I tend to attract the jerks.

By jerks I mean men who want to get their leg over. The kind of men who seem to think you're giving them the come-on message when you are only being friendly by talking. It's something you can't win, because if you do give in and sleep with them, they tell all their friends how easy you were to get into the sack.

Even today, in the Corps, if you're a woman who is seen as friendly to everyone, then people will see you as being easy and a slut. Being seen as a slut is a bad thing. It's the equivalent to being seen as lying in the gutter with all the other garbage.

I'm so not big into jerks, which leaves me with the only other option a woman has when she is in the Marine Corps; be professional and reserved at all times. But the downside to being professional and reserved is you will be seen as a bitch by all the swinging dick-jerks when you refuse their advances. However, on balance, being seen as a redheaded bitch is better because it cuts down on a lot of the static.

I'm pretty much my own person anyway, never being the kind of woman who needs a man to feel secure about herself. The weapons the Marine Corps issued to me make me feel secure because sex with a man doesn't always match up to the satisfaction I get from getting paid to blow shit up.

Back at my quarters it takes me a few moments to find a clean sports bra to put on. Next I pull on the special underwear we use when going out on a mission, as you can't really stop to drop your pants for a piss inside the cockpit of your Dog.

The Corps has been hinting new technology will take care of

the problem in the future, but like most things in life, change takes time. When change does come, it's in your face. Though in this case, perhaps not in your face, come to think about it, but it will be great when new materials can be used to process and remove waste in the future.

With that done I pull on my Dog suit and make sure the vent tubes can be plugged when I get in the cockpit. The insulated environmental suit has a heap load of sensors built in. Making sure everything is working, I run through the standard diagnostic checks from the sensors, checking my PAD. All the telltales show green for once.

Putting my boots on means I'm now dressed and ready for the day ahead—ready to kick ass, chew gum, and take names.

Our mission today will likely involve hurrying around doing stuff, then doing nothing while waiting for other stuff to happen, before going off somewhere else to repeat the same thing all over again. It's a routine you learn to either love, hate, or plain put up with, because whatever you might think, nothing changes to make stuff go faster.

Except being shot at, which is all kinds of fun and games until the screaming starts.

Breakfast is the best meal of the day. I make my way from my quarters forward and up to what the Navy calls the dirty-shirt mess, where you can go eat before or after a mission. It used to be only for aviators. Nowadays we combat armor-suit operators get to use it too. It's also *Hornet*'s mixed mess where officers and enlisted can eat together.

Who says the military never evolves in the face of change?

I take my place at the back of the line because whatever time you turn up, there's always people waiting to be served. It's the biggest thing I can complain about, as the food, while not haute cuisine, is freshly cooked and hot. Not only that, but you get to point at and choose what you want from a selection, rather than having to eat what you're given.

Being given a choice is always a good thing in my book.

Then I go sit with the Marines of Second Platoon, who greet me with the chorus, "Good morning, Sergeant."

They've left a space at the table for me opposite Lieutenant McCarthy, who is a stocky dark-haired man. He can sit with us today, as it's considered good for morale for the officers to fraternize with the enlisted on the day we all go out on a mission together. Alpha Squad sits to his right, Bravo on my left.

No one in my platoon stands over five foot nine in order to fit inside their machines. So they're all shorties who are nothing special to look at, but they carry the spear into battle with me.

McCarthy stops eating his food to speak. "Morning, Sergeant, sleep well?"

"Morning, Lieutenant. I slept like a log."

Someone whispers on my left, "What's 'slept like a log' mean?"

The general hubbub at the table increases as Private First Class Vosloo starts recounting a story, so I don't catch the reply. He's telling everyone about the time he and his friend were trekking in the Rockies and met a sleeping bear in the woods. The denouement of Vosloo's story being that he ran faster than his friend, who got eaten by the bear.

Laughter breaks out; they're all very young and impressionable.

Sitting on my immediate left is Private First Class Rodriguez from Texas. He's swapping components of his breakfast with Private First Class Jackson who is also from Texas, who notices me staring.

"It's a Navy breakfast, Sergeant," he says, as if that explained everything, which it kind of does, if you are a hungry young Marine.

"So the Navy's not feeding you enough?"

"Not that, Sergeant. It's just we get more of what we like best if we swap. Ain't that the truth, Rodriguez?" says Jackson.

"Truth for sure," replies Rodriguez as he shovels food into his mouth.

"The truth is that beans makes you fart," says Lance Corporal Kowalski.

"You should know, you're the fart master here," says Jackson.

"Outstanding Marines," I say.

Next to them is Private Jones, who is sitting upright, and he appears distinctly uncomfortable at the banter. Jones is straight out of Dog MOS training, and this is his first rotation. He has the tendency to act as if he's still a recruit, where sergeants are like gods.

"Hey, Jones, why you eatin' shit-on-a-shingle for?" says Jackson, exaggerating his Texan drawl, while winking at Rodriguez.

"I like SOS, it tastes nice," says Jones. Betraying his ancestry with his Welsh accent. "It reminds me of home. What's it to you?"

"'*It reminds me of home.*' Is that where you learned to speak like that?" says Rodriguez.

"What's wrong with the way I speak?"

"Nothing I guess," says Jackson.

"It's just that you're not from around here, are you, Jones?" says Rodriguez, drawling out the words more than normal.

"Leave him alone, you two," says Lance Corporal Delgado from Alpha Squad. "I like his English accent, it's classy." She says *classy* as if it rhymes with *sexy*.

"You like everyone, Delgado," says Kowalski.

"I keep telling you, I'm Welsh—I'm from Wales. I'm not bloody English."

Jones had enlisted with the Corps to get Confederation citizenship. When I asked him why, he replied, "Have you ever visited Wales, ma'am?" After I ripped him a new orifice for calling me *ma'am*, I had to agree I had no idea that Wales was like the boonies.

"So I can see," says Rodriguez, smiling. "Only the finest quality ground beef in a rich cream sauce on a thin white slice of the Navy's finest white toast for our young Welsh *gyrene*."

"Anyway, more importantly, where the fuck is Wales?" asks Jackson.

"I had to get a map to find out where Wales is," says Rodriguez.

"What's a gyrene?" asks Jones, interrupting the flow of banter.

Lance Corporal Kowalski, sitting beside Jones, speaks. "We're gyrenes, Jones."

Kowalski is the only man in Bravo Squad who looks old enough to shave. It's because his beard shadow shows even when freshly shaved. Like most lance corporals, he thinks he has the answer to everything, and if the Corps would only listen to him, we could all kick back and take it easy.

He's a muppet and a pain in the ass, but it's a phase all lance corporals go through. I continue listening as I sit and eat my ham and eggs. I enjoy watching my squad josh each other over inter-Corps rivalry between us recon jocks and the line battalion.

Corporal Knight from Alpha Squad cuts in, "Gyrenes are the Spam in the can, the chunky salsa of the Corps, Jones. It's your chance to shine. Show the hard chargers you don't need to be seven feet tall and weigh three hundred pounds to be a badass Marine."

Knight is a wiry string bean of a man who likes to run all day long but still has energy left over to party through till dawn. He continues with his spiel. "Even the Corps knows power armor levels the playing field, so luckily for you, Jones, you don't have to be built like a brick shithouse to pull your weight in the Corps."

However, as the saying goes: "There's the right way, the wrong way, and then there's the Marine Corps way." As far as the Corps is concerned, new doesn't mean better, in spite of the fact that powered exoskeletons have been standard issue for over forty years.

Jones asks, "Don't we nickname our rides Dogs because of the BigDog prototype?"

He's referring to the old United States Department of Defense and DARPA project from sixty years ago. It riffs off the tradition started when the Germans called the Marines *teufelshunde* or Devil Dogs after the Battle of Belleau Wood in World War One.

Kowalski replies, "Jones, the sergeant needs to square you away. Everyone knows we call our combat armor Dogs because they appear as if they're begging when racked for storage…"

"Cut the crap, Kowalski, we've got a long day ahead of us," I say, butting in.

Both of them are talking shit. The acronym Dog comes from Dispersed Operation and Guidance, which is the virtual interface system that allows us to drive our suits over any terrain with ease.

"Yes, Sergeant."

3. CHINA

He who is prudent and lies in wait for an enemy who is not, will be victorious.

— Sun Tzu

Shàngwèi Looi
Commander Special Operations Force Falcon
Democratic People's Republic of China
Xinjiang Province, China
Tuesday, June 23, 2071

Looi Kin-Ming sweeps his hand through his receding hairline while he considers the orders he'd received. HQ had commanded him to take his *lián kuijiǎ*, an armored suit company, into the Spīn Ghar region of Afghanistan, where he is to engage an American Special Forces team. His mission is to prevent the Americans from achieving their objective. Something that was easier said than done.

Like it or not, as his father had always told him, "Ni wúfa bìmian de shìqíng, huanyíng." *What you cannot avoid, welcome.*

Looi has called in his three *shàowèi*, junior commissioned officers, to his office, and they now stand in front of him looking nervous.

"We've received orders to undertake a mission in Afghanistan, the details are on your slates. Your thoughts and suggestions please?"

No one's told him what the Americans must be prevented from finding, only that high command doesn't want them to find it. His superiors emphasized the fact that it's not in China's national interests for America to gain control over what's under a mountain there. Underlined by being told he is authorized to use a nuclear demolition charge to bring said mountain down.

If burying the thing under the mountain meant burying the Americans with it, then so be it. Obviously, the Chinese government would express regret if any Americans died due to a *terrorist* incident. But Looi has to wonder what he did in a previous lifetime to deserve this opportunity to further China's national interests.

Shàowèi Zhan Daliang rubs his prominent nose. He's finished reading the mission orders and glances up to speak first.

"Our orders tell us we're the closest readily deployable unit. But we're a special forces reconnaissance unit unsuited to this type of mission. Shàngwèi, it will be difficult to get there within the expected time frame before the Americans arrive. Therefore we need a contingency plan to face this eventuality."

Looi studies Zhan and wonders what had inspired the young man to be so bold in expressing his thoughts. He'd interpreted the orders as saying: since you're not currently fighting on the front lines, your command is the right choice for the task. In his own mind he hears his father's voice, *Are you sure this is wise?*

"A good point, Shàowèi, but what might we want to do in this contingency plan of ours?" He watches Zhan squirm as he's put on the spot.

"The land route takes us over some of the poorest roads in the world and through some of the highest mountain passes in the region. I doubt we can get to the mountain before the Americans unless we fly there, Shàngwèi."

"And pray tell me how we will hide an unscheduled military flight from China across Afghan airspace without calling American attention to our movement, Shàowèi Zhan," he says, wrong-footing the young officer.

On paper his lián has seventy-two men, split into three *pái*, with each platoon consisting of twenty-four men, each under the command of one of his shàowèi. The reality is he has forty-nine effectives in his command. However, he'd been told in no uncertain terms that he had more than sufficient resources to deal with twelve American Special Forces personnel being sent to investigate the mountain.

Shàowèi Wang Xiang interrupts his thoughts. "Sir, I disagree, there's no need for us to fly. I think its inevitable we will need to destroy the mountain, burying the Americans under it. Our contingency plan should be based on how the Americans respond to this act."

The sharp-faced young man juts his chin out as if to emphasize the determination in his words.

"That's a very good point, Shàowèi Wang. Any suggestions on what the Americans might do, and how we should prepare if we do have to fight them?" Looi tries to remember when he'd been so naive.

China was already engaged in a dispute with the Russian Commonwealth in Mongolia. His unit had only returned last month from a six-month deployment fighting a guerrilla operation against the Indian Army in the Jammu and Kashmir Province. He really needs six months to refit and rebuild his unit, but orders are orders. He also has to complete his mission without starting a war in Asia.

Wang shakes his head no in reply. Looi looks at Shàowèi Li Dongfeng and ponders how a young man with movie-star looks, attracting all the women he meets, ended up in the Army. He bids Li to speak with a nod of his head.

Shàowèi Li says, "Both of my colleagues' observations have merit. I also disagree with Zhan about needing to fly. However, we should reassess our assets and work to our strengths. I agree with Wang about the need for a contingency plan, but we need several such plans to account for the obstacles that we might face, Shàngwèi!"

"Two very good points, Shàowèi Li. Please continue."

He remembers his father had told him an old proverb as a child: If something seems too good to be true, it probably is too good to be true. What has become clear from the intelligence operatives reports he's read is that the Americans are expected to land in Afghanistan in the next forty-eight hours.

"We also need to discuss the conditions that will define the successful completion of our mission. If, for instance, we are delayed in delivering the nuclear device to bring down the mountain, it will be difficult to not reveal ourselves to the Americans. They're not stupid, they'll know someone supplied the nuclear mine. We should take that into account when making our plans."

"Again a very good point, Shàowèi Li. However, the pressing problem is how to get across Jammu and Kashmir Province and into Afghanistan in the same time frame as the Americans. My intention is to transport our lián kuijia by using trucks acquired from civilian sources."

He pauses and pinches his chin. "I estimate if we drive continuously, we can cross into Afghanistan, and reach Spīn Ghar region with enough time to deploy the nuclear mine. Then leave before the Americans arrive. However, it would be wise to plan on being delayed, and work through various scenarios. I think it's best we make these contingency plans while we are traveling though. Any questions?"

"Are there any specific things we should consider, Shàngwèi?" asks Shàowèi Zhan.

Looi steeples his hands, his fingers fluttering, pausing before speaking. "The enemy of my enemy is my friend, but our friends in Afghanistan abide to their ways, which are not ours. We shall need to tread carefully to keep their actions in line with the needs of the mission."

"I understand, Shàngwèi," says Zhan, which Looi seriously doubts.

"I want you all to go now and get the men and their machines ready for transportation. Command has informed me that fifty civilian trucks will arrive by the end of the day. Any further questions?"

"No, sir," reply his three young officers, who are about to learn a hard lesson from another old adage: "No plan survives contact with the enemy."

His young officers had stated the obvious: "Wèi àn jìhuà jiùshì jìhuà shībài." *Failing to plan is planning to fail.* But they'd missed the thing that was obvious to him; they were going in blind, which was the same as planning for failure.

He would query his contacts higher up in the chain of command. Perhaps he could learn more, but now there's the paperwork to do, hours of work before they can depart. The nagging lack of details about the mission smells like a *pidan*, century eggs, a delicacy whose enjoyment is an acquired taste outside of China.

4. ON THE UP AND UP

Leadership is the art of inspiring people to enthusiastically take action toward the achievement of uncommon goals.

— Col John R. Boyd, USAF

Captain Johanson
First Combat Armor Suit Reconnaissance Company
CSN *Hornet*
Thursday, July 2, 2071

Johanson knocks on the door of Colonel Philmore's cabin and hears, "Come in."

The colonel stands over six and a half feet tall and is close on to a hundred pounds heavier than Johanson, all of it muscle. Despite the colonel being on the go since zero dark thirty, he looks focussed and squared away. Even sitting down, the colonel dominates the room with his presence.

"Reporting as requested, sir."

He sees a tall lean looking civilian sitting next to the colonel, who acknowledges his presence with a nod of his head. With the three of them in the cabin, it feels even more cramped than usual.

"Ah good, I'd like to introduce you to Mr Anderson from the Agency, who came aboard *Hornet* last night. He has a rescue mission he needs our Marines for. Mr Anderson, this is Captain Johanson, whom I spoke to you about earlier. He may look like a bantam weight, but trust me, he's the Marine for the job."

He inwardly sighs at the colonel's bantam comment. Johanson is a wiry man in his early thirties who is going gray at the temples. He only scrapes under the mandated five foot nine inches maximum height to be a combat armor reconnaissance suit operator.

The Corps could be somewhat schizo at times, with a credo of being a macho gung-ho hard charger on one hand, and facing off against affirmative action policies on the other. The changes in ethos seek to bring the force up to speed with civilian sociocultural attitudes.

Anderson rises from his chair and offers his hand out to shake. "Good to meet you."

Johanson shakes the proffered hand before replying to the colonel. "Very good, sir, but as you say, it's always unwise to judge a Marine by their size, sir."

The colonel stares at him for a moment before speaking. "He's right, Mr Anderson, size isn't everything, because there's also intestinal fortitude and skill, and Johanson's Marines have both in abundance."

"Sir, may I ask about the progress of Exercise Flying Sparrow?"

The Amphibious Readiness Group, carrying the Thirteenth Marine Expeditionary Unit, had been prepping for the last three days for this joint training operation with the Indian Army and US Navy. But Johanson's company had received a FRAGO pulling them from the operation. The fragmentary order had changed his command's plans for the day and had malleted their preparations.

This operation was meant to demonstrate what joint cooperation can achieve in reducing piracy on the high seas of the Indian Ocean. Another equally important component was sending a message to both the Russian and Chinese governments that America and India are now working as allies in this region.

A rather pointed message of, *OoRah* and *Hell yeah, America!* Waving the colors, for the first time in twenty years, to show everyone America is back on the world stage.

"The rest of the battalion is away and our birds are back and being prepared for your SAR mission. The Agency has been given priority by order of the president, and Admiral Buford has been fully briefed on what changes in the planned operation are required by the ARG. Is your team ready to see some action?"

There is only one answer to this question: a strong affirmative while projecting a totally positive mental attitude. "Yes, Colonel!" Any other answer would be considered at best nonsensical. At worst, it would have required his unit to be incompetent at carrying out their assigned orders.

"Good, your unit has been assigned to recover an Army Special Forces Alpha Detachment that was working under the auspices of the CIA to reconnoiter an area of interest in Afghanistan."

"I see, sir."

For the relevant meanings of *asked* and *assigned* that amounted to orders given, which could then be denied as never issued if something went wrong.

"The Army Alpha Detachment has failed to call for pickup at the end of its assigned mission envelope," Anderson says. "So I need your people to undertake a tactical recovery of aircraft and personnel for the CIA."

Johanson looks at Anderson and says, "You can count on us, sir."

"I need you to understand that this mission is of the utmost importance, but there're things you're not cleared to know, as they're above your security grading. All I can say is that you will be doing the greatest of services for your country."

That was spook doublespeak for you. *We can send you somewhere, but not tell you why.* This was like telling him: *Don't ask me why because the answer will be don't ask.* This was often followed by something like: *If we told you, we would have to kill you.*

It's all utter bullshit, because sending us somewhere to do stuff means we will get to see what it is we aren't cleared to know, thought Johanson.

"Captain Johanson, it's time for the 1st CASR Hound Dogs to earn their pay. I shall leave Mr Anderson in your capable hands. Dismissed."

Johanson comes to attention and indicates to Anderson to follow him out of the cabin. He tries not to think about the blood his people might spill today to earn their pay.

5. LIMITATIONS

The present is big with the future.

— GOTTFRIED WILHELM VON LEIBNIZ

Mr Anderson
CIA Analyst
CSN *Hornet*
Thursday, July 2, 2071

Anderson follows Captain Johanson out of Colonel Philmore's cabin into the ship's narrow corridor. In his short time aboard *Hornet* he's picked up on the sailors and Marines referring to the floor as the *deck*, which seems to him to be an unnecessary obfuscation. But the Navy has its traditions. And by God they'll keep those traditions alive whatever the cost.

Everywhere he looks, any spare space is occupied.

The ship is crammed full of equipment hanging off the walls, which he keeps catching on as he squeezes his way past the people they meet. The sense of being trapped in a tiny space is made worse by having the deck divided in half with a line of tape on the floor.

Two sailors are cleaning the floor, and they stare at him as he stops to squeeze by them. They look bored. He sees Johanson is disappearing ahead of him in the labyrinthine corridors of the *Hornet*. Not wanting to fall behind, he starts walking faster to catch up.

Johanson turns and sees him struggle to climb through yet another hatch and asks, "So, Mr Anderson, are you surrogate qualified?"

Anderson wonders whether Johanson stopped to ask the question because he sensed that he was falling behind and to give him time to catch up, or whether he'd been thinking of the mission.

"No, I'm not. I thought that would be obvious since you've read my jacket."

He is also far too tall to meet the mandatory height requirement for CAS-C4P combat armor. That and the fact that he didn't come from a security forces background.

"Didn't think you were, but I don't assume, because in my experience it makes a fool out of me and you. Besides you never know with the Air Force what crazy idea they'll come up with next to extend their operational remit. Those SF operators don't seem to realize that stomping around in their overly large combat armor suits doesn't make them hard asses. They'd be better off sitting in the comfy couches the rest of you Air Force types are used to working from."

"Couldn't possibly comment, I ran ORPs myself. Nowadays I do analysis, and honestly the chairs aren't that comfortable."

He resents Johanson's implication. But having knocked his shins on the edges of the hatches and banged his head for his trouble, he gets the impression that an ergonomic operating area is not high on the Marine officer's list of considerations. This gives him a whole new perspective on how the Marines view the world around them.

"Figures you'd say that. So you really are a back-room chair jockey then. I'll make sure you get the permissions to access the CYCLOPS feeds. You'll feel right at home watching everything from an aircraft circling the LZ."

"If you say so," he says.

Anderson had never been involved in low-altitude operations circling over a landing zone, so he isn't sure what it would feel like. All his service experience had been with Orbital Reconnaissance Platforms high above the Earth, his job being to manage the limited windows of opportunity polar orbits provided. Mostly by making sure that the information handovers didn't result in information overload from cascading feeds.

"Thank you," he says.

"Besides, you'd only get in the way if you were attached to us in a HOS."

Anderson wonders where this conversation is going, apart from making him feel even more like a third wheel on a hot date.

"I had no expectations in that regard."

"Is this your first field assignment, by any chance?"

"It is. Why…does it show that much?"

"Well, it makes a refreshing change from the usual 'I want to be part of the boots on the ground' requests we get from Agency operatives. A man ought to know his limitations; it seems you're one of the rare ones who does."

"Thank you—I think."

Johanson had clearly formed an impression of him, and he wasn't sure whether he should be flattered or insulted. Maybe both were the intent.

"May I ask a question of you?"

"Sure, fire away, Mr Anderson."

"Do you ever get used to living inside a ship all day?"

Johanson chuckles. "You get used to it, though it does get a bit tiresome after a while. Still, it motivates people to get up on deck for training, and the view off the back of the fantail is good."

In Anderson's mind being inside the *Hornet* is what it must be like to live inside a termite nest, with all the workers serving the Queen. He doesn't imagine that Admiral Buford would take kindly to being described as the Queen of the flotilla.

One thing for sure, a sailor's life is definitely not for him.

Flying is his thing, but finding himself coming on board the carrier in the middle of the night could be described as one of those career highlight moments; as in, landing in the dark on the deck of the *Hornet* had been terrifying.

6. ARIES

To be a sergeant you have to know your stuff. I'd rather be an
outstanding sergeant than just another officer.

— SGTMJR DANIEL J. DALY, USMC

Sergeant Tachikoma
First Combat Armor Suit Reconnaissance Company
CSN *Hornet*
Thursday, July 2, 2071

After breakfast I head up to operations for the 0800 briefing,
walking in with Lieutenant McCarthy to take our seats. The
briefing room, like all the other rooms on board *Hornet*, is the
standard cream color the Navy paints everything in. I can hear my
mom crying out for pastels to alleviate the tedium of everything
painted the same color.

Still, with the rest of the battalion off elsewhere we have
plenty of room to sit where we like, which makes a change.

The overhead is a tangled mess of ducts and cabling with a 3-
D projector stuck in the middle of it. We take our places in the

fold-down seats. They're bolted to the deck to prevent them from moving when the ship is pitching around in rough weather.

Second Lieutenant Perez and Sergeant Thompson from Third Platoon had gotten in before us and grabbed the seats at the back, and are talking together about today's upcoming mission. When I'd first met Perez, I'd taken his attitude as typical of all new lieutenants who want to make a good impression but end up trying too hard. And he's a bit full of the righteousness of his opinions for my taste.

It's a good thing Sergeant Thompson is a lot older than Perez and keeps the lieutenant on track.

Thompson's a down-to-Earth likeable guy. I only recently made sergeant, and he's been giving me pointers to help me settle in to my new role. At first I thought he was hitting on me, but he's a committed family man who really only talks about his wife and children.

Second Lieutenant Beckford arrives after us with Sergeant Washington by her side. He's been tasked with getting the lieutenant up to speed after she dropped the ball during the last training assignment. Over the next few minutes the rest of the officers and NCOs of the company trickle in, with Gunnery Sergeant Locklear, the senior NCO, the last to enter before our commanding officer arrives to brief us.

Captain Johanson enters the room with a civilian by his side, who must be six foot four, as he towers over us all. His appearance distracts me until Gunnery Sergeant Locklear calls out, "Attention, officer on deck!"

Johanson scans the room. "OK, people, take your seats! As of now we're tasked for a new mission called Operation Clean Sweep. Mr Anderson is here from the CIA to brief us."

Anderson affects a beard, his light brown hair pokes out of his *tacticool* baseball cap, and he appears to be in his early thirties. He looks fit for a civilian, dressed in what passes for military-geek chic. He wears a black multipocketed field vest, coyote brown BDU trousers, and Gore-Tex boots.

Obligatory shades tucked into his jacket pocket.

Everything is brand spanking new and from all appearances has never been worn near anywhere where such clothes would be required. Still, it makes a difference from the usual suits spooks wear. No one has informed the agent that wearing a cover indoors marks him out as not belonging here. And who says Marines don't have a sense of humour?

Everyone turns their eyes towards Anderson as he starts speaking, and, in true Corps fashion, we all stare into the space above his left shoulder.

"Some time ago reconnaissance satellites picked up a magnetic energy pulse coming from inside a mountain in the Spīn Ghar region of Afghanistan. But our HUMINT assets were unable to throw any light on the indigenous activity occurring in the region. We know Yeshua bin Yussuf is the local warlord of the area. He's not exactly what you would call friendly to American interests, which means we've been unable to get anyone into his organization."

The history of Afghanistan is one of invasion and war. And it sucked to be them, but Anderson isn't telling us the whole story. This is all mundane knowledge.

"Our orbital assets observed activity as the various local forces moved into the area, then left. However, whatever is happening is unclear at this time. The fact remains, there is an intermittent magnetic energy pulse emanating from deep underground, and no faction is taking credit for it."

It's the usual spook snow job to describe the chaos and confusion in Afghanistan as something that remains unclear.

Anderson clears his throat and repeats the information regarding the magnetic anomaly. He looks around meaningfully, as if he's told everyone the most important thing ever and we should be grateful for being allowed in on such secrets.

Johanson asks, "Mr Anderson, should we infer that the Agency has made further attempts to uncover more intelligence from the site?"

"Yes you should, I was about to get around to that. A week ago the Army launched an Aries suborbital transport from our Colorado AFB to insert an Army Special Forces Alpha Detachment PACE suit team to recon the site. Unfortunately, they crashed on landing and contact was lost shortly thereafter. We would therefore like your company to go in, secure the landing site, retrieve the lost team, and hopefully not start a land war in Asia."

Just like that, easy to say, so much harder to do. PACE stands for Power Armor Combat Environment. This is the standard Army battle rattle. Similar to our MARPACE suits, except less waterproof.

The big question is what's so important about a magnetic pulse coming from under a mountain in Afghanistan, which requires an orbital insertion of an Army Special Forces team? Both the Chinese and the Russians had to have tracked the flight, so this is hardly a stealthy mission operating under the radar.

Johanson replies, "Thank you for summarizing the current situation, Mr Anderson."

He turns towards the screen and pulls up the flight plan. It has the latest weather forecast for the area overlaid on top of it.

"As you can see from the table, Admiral Buford transited our strike group from the Indian Ocean into the South Arabian Sea early yesterday. We're currently headed towards the Pakistani coastline. Our mission is cleared to fly across Pakistani airspace into Afghanistan."

You could've heard a pin drop in the room as everyone stopped what they were doing.

Johanson continues. "Our mission is to secure the landing site to retrieve any surviving Army personnel and equipment."

He puts up pictures on the auxiliary screens hanging from the overhead, which show the fuzzy outline of the crashed space-plane. People nod as they upload the new tactical data for the mission onto their PADs.

"We will then recon the area for any intelligence we can find about the unknown energy source Mr Anderson has alerted us to. The situation on the ground shows no clear signs of enemy activity at this time. That does not mean there're no enemy forces in the area, only that it's unlikely we will encounter any during our time on-site."

Johanson pauses before continuing with the briefing. "However, it's highly likely we will meet noncombatant inhabitants indigenous to the area. They're to be treated as nonhostile unless they act in a manner that's likely to impede the success of the mission. Remember, we're there to retrieve friendly forces that may be in bad shape."

A euphemism for *dead*, because if they're wounded, I would bet the soldiers would've signalled for pickup by now. Even standing around in the open and lighting a fire would be enough to draw the attention of a CIA reconnaissance UAV to them.

Johanson stops to fiddle with the screen display. "There's a MULE diverted from Air Force theatre assets en route as an attachment to our force for the retrieval of the downed insertion vehicle."

How convenient there's one in the area that can be tasked for the mission we're being sent on today.

"Execution of the operation is by rapid deployment by vertical insertion to secure the crash site," says Johanson, pausing to let his three junior lieutenants make notes on their PADs.

All the NCOs are sitting easy, gauging from the tone of the orders what the mission entails.

"Once our first goal has been achieved, Fourth Platoon will provide an all-round defence until the Air Force MULE departs with the retrieved Army space-plane."

An estimated time line appears on the screens.

Second Lieutenant Beckford of Fourth Platoon sounds decidedly unhappy as she acknowledges her orders, "Yes, sir."

I can't blame her for being nervous. The Air Force's idea of an ETA is at best a bit hit and miss. MULEs are great for lifting and getting loads moved, but headwinds and weather fronts really impact on the time it takes for them to arrive in a timely fashion.

Johanson addresses Second Lieutenant Perez. "Third Platoon will screen the crash site and act as a Quick Reaction Force to slow any unaccounted for forces that might want to interfere with our mission."

"Aye, aye, sir," says Perez, nodding.

It's easy to tell he's all gung-ho for the opportunity to be seen as a hard charger rising to the challenge of putting the beat down on the enemy.

The lieutenant hasn't seen what happens when the meat meets the metal yet. So if the shit does hit the fan, he will be addressing his experiential shortfall via the traditional steep learning curve called "coming under enemy fire."

"Once the site's secured, First and Second Platoons will advance to the area where the energy source is emanating from. We will search for and find the Alpha Detachment, then retrieve them," says Johanson, pointing at the area on the map marking the crash site.

People are comparing the distance between where the plan shows us hitting the dirt and the location of the energy source under the mountain. The figures flash on the screen with time intervals for each stage of the mission objectives.

"Service and support will require us to carry stretchers, medical supplies, and body bags. As we're going in by ourselves, we'll be relying on the Dogs' corpsman AIs for the treatment of any wounded personnel."

I hear breath whistle through people's teeth. If the shit hits the fan, we'll be breaking Dogs down so as to carry pilots out in their retrieval cocoons. *So not good.*

Johanson continues speaking. "Evacuation of personnel and equipment will require their weapons and equipment be distributed amongst our platoons' personnel. In the event of any enemy personnel being taken, they're to be disarmed and secured for Lieutenant Bergeson for processing."

Lieutenant Bergeson says, "Yes, sir!" Excited that Johanson has given him the S2 Intelligence ball after Beckford so spectacularly dropped it during the last training mission.

"The chain of command is as follows: First Platoon will be under Second Lieutenant Bergeson and Sergeant Ramirez as his second in command, with company Gunnery Sergeant Locklear and myself attached. Company call sign is Cerberus. I'll be using Big Dog on the platoon leaders' channel. Gunny will be Growler. First platoon is Hellhounds…"

A murmur of oorahs punctuate the moment.

We don't just rely on our FREAK and crypto to prevent the enemy from knowing what we're talking about. We are also given call signs and phonetic shorthand to maintain OPSEC because it's best to assume that all calls are being monitored by the OPFOR.

"Second Platoon will be under First Lieutenant McCarthy, with Sergeant Tachikoma as his second in command. Call sign Fenris. Third Platoon will be under Second Lieutenant Perez with Sergeant Thompson as his second in command. Call sign Wulfgang. Finally, Fourth Platoon will be under Second Lieutenant Beckford with Staff Sergeant Washington as her second in command. Call sign Lobo. Any questions?"

"Sir, what are our load-out requirements?" I ask.

The company's combat armor suits can be configured with

different ordnance packages according to mission-specific requirements, which is what makes them so flexible.

Johanson looks at me, "Let's keep them light, Sergeant Tachikoma."

We've all trained hard, so we can fight easy. But some missions require us to be loaded for bear. Others for every bear in the woods.

But light means fast, and fast is always good when there's ground to cover. Judging from the maps, there's a lot of ground to cover on this mission. Of course if we meet any serious opposition, our only recourse will be to shoot and scoot.

Usually if we need serious firepower, we can call for artillery support. And the Navy gives good artillery support because there's nothing like an incoming hypersonic shell to ruin an enemy's day. However, this mission is out of the range of our ship-based artillery, which will suck big time if serious shooting begins.

"Remember, this is strictly a search and rescue to snatch and grab our people out of trouble, not an opportunity to bring hell down on the locals," says Johanson.

"It's also important to retrieve any information on the source of the magnetic energy pulse the Army Alpha Detachment may have acquired," says Anderson.

This gets him a look from Johanson I wouldn't want to be on the receiving end of. The spook has sold us today as a simple retrieval mission. Though in my experience nothing is ever simple if it requires a company of Marines in combat armor to put boots on the ground.

After we're dismissed I go to spread the word to the rest of my platoon. I make my way from the aft briefing room forward to the bow where our combat armor suits are stored. My passage is slowed by sailors cleaning the passages along my route.

I arrive to see the rest of the company standing around waiting for the news on what's happening.

They're of course totally overjoyed to find they will be retrieving some Army Snake Eaters who screwed the pooch by crashing their shiny new space-plane. The air turns blue with a symphony of F-words. But they're less unhappy with the load-out orders for their Dogs.

"Move your asses and elbows people. Get your battle rattle together and check out your Dogs one more time."

My platoon replies, "Aye, aye, Sergeant."

We're Marines, and we make do with old stuff. Rather than going in high and fast in a shiny new hypersonic space-plane, our Dogs will be going in low and slow in our old V-32 Thunder Hawk tilt fans. The Thunder Hawks are informally known as Chickens because they look like they're about to lay an egg.

We ride into battle in our Dogs, but the suit sensors turn it into an extension of our bodies, making it seem like we're wearing battle rattle rather than driving a vehicle. Our combat armor had been developed after the Chicago massacre of '37, when power armor infantry had been chewed up by combat androids. The One-Zero-One hack has made the deployment of fully autonomous combat androids a no-no ever since.

The tech crew has brought out the M41-AC230 autocannon and affixed it to the right arm of my Dog, locked in place by a combination of the hand actuator and autolocking bolts in the arm itself. My PAD confirms the connections are good.

As my Dog is running light this mission, it only leaves the inbuilt M240LC machine gun and the three-tube smoke dispenser to sign off on. Unlike aviators, Dog jockeys have a more hands-on relationship with their ride, so along with the rest of my platoon I recheck my Dog's readiness, working my way through the checklist with the systems flagging everything as copasetic. I make sure the first aid box, my survival kit, and my weapon are secure.

Without power, the dormant ChameleonFlage panels on my Dog are a dull silvery-green color. Using the system takes power, and when the Dog is moving it can still be seen as a ripple. Like most camouflage systems, it works best when the Dog's stationary.

There's also the fact that the individual panels will stop working when damaged. But by the time this usually happens, you're generally in some sort of furball with more pressing things to worry about. Usually recon units, like ours, are meant to set up and observe before blazing a route. In this role the ChameleonFlage serves its purpose well enough.

Once finished I walk along the deck checking on the progress of the rest of my platoon. My way of showing a keen interest in their personal well-being and all.

Kowalski is talking to Lance Corporal Eversmann, one of our mechanic technicians. Eversmann in turn is advising Kowalski not to tell him how to do his job. Their exchange of F-words demonstrates their cunning linguistic skills.

"What are you swearing about, Kowalski?"

"It's the leg actuator on my Dog, Sergeant. It's now due for replacement."

"You've had three days of prep and you're bringing this up now?"

The Corps keeps everyone busy. So along with going to the armory every day to stand in line, pull your personal weapon, and clean it routinely, we run daily maintenance and diagnostics checks: all part of our preventative maintenance schedule. So if something is not done one day, it certainly gets done the next.

"It meets specification," says Eversmann.

I check the status of Kowalski's Dog on my PAD and give him

a look. "Seems Eversmann is right on the button here. What's your problem, Kowalski?"

"I know what it says, Sergeant, but it don't feel right when I'm in her."

"Can you be any more specific than 'it don't *feel* right'?"

"No, not really, Sergeant."

"OK, I'll make this simple for you, Lance Corporal, this isn't the time to be bringing up problems. There's a fine line between concern over something wrong with your ride and expecting unrealistic levels of perfection. Do I make myself clear, Kowalski?"

"Yes, Sergeant. No complaints, I hear you loud and clear."

I leave Kowalski to get on with his preparations and go check on Privates Rodriguez and Jackson. I find them working on the left shoulder of one of their Dogs. They're loading its three-tube smoke dispenser.

"Switch the ChameleonFlage on and see if the dispenser is keyed in," says Jackson.

"On," replies Rodriguez.

Jackson's Dog displays the words *fart dispenser* as an exploding graphic across his combat armor. Kowalski is stifling his laughter behind me.

"Can that ass-hat shit now!" I say, trying not to laugh.

Private Jones is working by himself. I make a note to remind Kowalski that he should be buddying with the new guy.

"How's it going, Jones?"

"I'm good, Sergeant, but can I ask something about the mission load-out?"

"Sure, go ahead, Private. What's on your mind?"

"I was wondering why the standard load-out for the CASE-2X is the M41-AC230 long recoil 20 mm autocannon with five shot 40 x 53 mm underbarrel grenade launcher, because it seems to me that we would be better off going with a 7.62 M134…?"

I interrupt Jones's recitation before he can give me full readout on the rotary cannons' specifications. "Jones, I'm sure your weapons instructor at Marine Combat Training would be delighted to hear you're able to quote the official nomenclature of your assigned equipment. However, we haven't got all day to jaw on all the details. *Dog* and *autocannon* are sufficient to convey with clarity what you're talking about."

"Sorry, Sergeant. While prepping my Dog, I was thinking about how we can swap our primary weapon because of the weight we could save. It struck me we are only carrying six magazines with ten rounds each on this mission. Four magazines with tungsten-steel penetrators and two magazines of high-explosive dual-purpose HEAB smart rounds for soft targets. It doesn't seem like enough to me."

"Sure, a rotary cannon is lighter than an autocannon, Jones. Until you account for the supporting backpack. And while carrying five thousand rounds is a good thing, the weight of so many rounds, not so much. Then there's the weight of the feed chute and extra powerpack to drive the feed mechanism to account for on top."

"Sorry. I should've thought it out before asking, Sergeant."

"It's easy to forget these things, Jones. Besides, your Dog has an inbuilt M240LC in the left arm, with two hundred rounds of 7.62 if you need to lay down suppressive fire. In the worst-case scenario, you can even pick up and use stuff as field-expedient weapons."

"Thank you, Sergeant."

"Remember, there're no stupid questions, Jones. Keep it up."

This got a total puppy-dog expression of gratitude from him for not bawling him out.

Then it is time to get the Dogs into their drop sleds. Built-in tracks on the soles of the feet allow the Dogs to cruise along roads at speed, or in this case be used to reverse them into the drop sled. Once in place the Dog is folded down, so it sits back on its heels.

Once the Dogs are ready to be loaded onto Chickens, I make sure everyone goes to the head. Our combat utilities are plumbed for that eventuality. But truth be told no one likes to sit in the cockpit of their Dog with that special damp feeling that comes from an unscheduled leak.

Our combat utilities share a lot in common with zoomies' flight suits. They've got inbuilt cooling and a network of sensors that augment our ability to control a Dog. With our helmets on, the sensory feedback from the machine itself makes it an extension of our bodies. I imagine it must be what it feels like to be a cyborg. But we get to return to being human once we get out of our Dogs.

With Bravo Squad in their cockpits, I walk over to talk to Lieutenant McCarthy, 1st CASRs acting executive officer. He's talking with Corporal Knight about last-minute details.

"How's it going, Sergeant?"

"We're good to go, Lieutenant. Everything is set for the vertical insertion." He goes a little green in the face. "We've done this before, Lieutenant."

"First time I've done it for real though."

We all climb into our cockpits where we'll get to experience the luxury of being strapped into our Dogs for the entire flight. Corporal Knight gives me the thumbs-up indicating it's time to get our Dogs loaded aboard the birds. We button up and I sit and watch the prep from inside the virtual reality environment of my cockpit.

The hangar deck crews, dressed in blue, maneuver each of the sleds in turn, loading them one by one into the waiting bays of the

Chickens. Turning us into waiting eggs ready to be hatched at the drop zone.

Each bird holds up to six Dogs arranged in single file. A full mission load. Today we have eight birds to lift the forty-two Dogs of our understrength company. On paper we're meant to be able to field fifty-six Dogs, including a command team of four, but the days of thirteen Dogs to a platoon are long gone. Much to outrage of old Marines everywhere.

Still it means that one of birds is traveling light and can loaded up with ordnance to support our mission.

The Dogs completely fill the interior of the tilt fan. Once inside, I switch over to the hangar deck feeds, which allows me to see the hatch closing on the back of the bird, sealing us in. With my helmet on I can hear the warning sirens warbling and see the flashing lights as the hangar crew maneuvers our birds onto the elevator to take us up to the flight deck. Turning my head allows me to see the deck beneath my Dog or look around is there was nothing between me and the rest of the ship.

Over all the noise comes the command, "Sweep the ship fore and aft for commencement of flight operations."

The crew are doing the prelaunch FOD walk-down to clear the deck of any foreign objects, things like small nuts or other debris, which fall off the aircraft and vehicles used to move the aircraft around. It keeps the flight deck clean, tidy, and safe.

Nobody wants anything sucked into an engine or blown at high speed by the force of a tilt fan at full power.

I follow the progress as we're handed over to the flight deck crew and switch from the hangar deck feed over to those on *Hornet*'s island with my usual interest entering a hazardous environment. The bridge's feeds give a complete overview of everything that's happening on deck.

All the while I get to sit inside the hermetically sealed, air-conditioned interior of my Dog. A luxury the deck crew doesn't enjoy.

Outside on deck it's the typical scene of Navy hustle and bustle. Sailors move around doing final checks, combined with a lot of hurry up and wait as our aircraft are lined up for take-off. Every movement on the flight deck is coordinated with a precision to make even the most hard-hearted drill instructor cry with joy.

Then it's time to go, and the engines of the bird in front screams as it lifts off.

Our bird follows suit, and as the tilt fans spool up to full power, there's a slight wobble as we lift off the deck. I track the rear view from our bird, watching the birds for Third and Fourth Platoons take to the air after us.

Below our flight are four of the ships in our flotilla.

CSN *Hornet* is a Landing Tilt-Fan dock amphibious assault ship. Or to put it in simpler parlance, a Big Gray Boat surrounded by other BGBs of the ARG. She's sailing at the head of an echelon with CSN *Denver*, a San Diego-class amphibious transport dock ship, off her starboard side.

Off our port side is the CSN *Tortuga*, a Seattle-class dock landing ship. Trailing astern of *Hornet* is CSN *Forrest Sherman*, a Zumwalt-class guided missile destroyer. Our ships are part and parcel of what's necessary to get the embarked Marines onto land during an amphibious assault.

Hidden from sight, below the surface of the ocean, is the CSN *Texas*.

She's a North American Confederation-class fusion-powered attack submarine acting as the ARG's underwater escort. To the bubbleheads below, everything on the surface is a target, which is why they're there. She's here to protect our flotilla from possible interference by hostile navies that don't want American warships returning to this region.

Like the Russians and Chinese who've been shadowing the ARG for the last few days with their spy ships.

Our flotilla disappears into the distance. The ships growing smaller with every passing moment until they're swallowed up, lost in the vastness of the Arabian Sea, as we climb to our cruising altitude of fifteen thousand feet. Levelling off, the birds throttle back to a steady three hundred knots.

The platoons settle down inside their Dogs. Everyone distracts themselves by doing something to cope with the boredom of being cooped up during the flight. I pull the feeds from each member of my platoon.

On my screen I arrange Bravo Squad below Alpha taking advantage of the flight time to test the comms-system.

With the platoons' Dogs in line of sight of each other, the laser-net autotalk system identifies each speaker by briefly zooming in their image as the platoon engages in some trash-talk banter.

The laser-net is less than good when dealing with a large number of people or when you want to talk to one specific person in private. Then the Corps insists on using time-proven radio voice procedures to maintain clarity of communication. Lieutenant McCarthy is checking his PAD, reviewing the mission and updating the flight plan, when Jones interrupts me.

"Permission to ask a question?"

"Go ahead, Private."

"What happened to the Army team? Why wait a week to retrieve them?"

"They're Snake Eaters, Private, they don't like to ask us for nothing. When the Army goes out on a mission, they're on the clock. If the mission timetable says a week, then by god the Army takes a week."

Jones grins at me and gets back to work. This assumes

everything had been going according to plan though, and that didn't add up with what we had been told by the spook.

After I get a sense that nothing is adrift with my people, I close my eyes and doze, letting the conversations float over me. You never know when the next chance to rest might come.

I wake up a few hours later.

We've reached the border of Afghanistan airspace, where the birds drop from cruise altitude to fly nap-of-the-Earth for the rest of the journey. We fall off the locals' airspace radar as we hug the ground with the aircrew using LIDAR to avoid hitting anything that might ruin our day. Flying low, we get a fair bit of buffeting from air turbulence, but I've always found this quite comforting and doze off again.

I'm awake by the time the crew chief gives us the ten-mike heads-up, and I check the platoon readouts as the remaining minutes count down.

As the birds approach the crash site, the rear ramp opens up. The whoosh of the air rushing past muffles the whine of the rapid vertical deployment rails extending out back. All the Dogs' systems are locked into the bird's navigation tracking system, and we'll be released as we reach our drop spots.

The timer counts down the last few seconds. My Dog shoots out the rear of the bird. There's a *whoosh*, followed by a *snap* as the drogue chute pulls the main chute out, catching the Dog as it falls to the ground.

Even though the Chicken has slowed to forty klicks for the drop, my body is snapped back into my seat as the chute catches hold. My restraining harness automatically pulls tighter, compensating for the g-force from four tons of decelerating drop sled.

Then there's a *crash* as the momentum of our descent bleeds off with all the subtlety of a sledgehammer hitting a wall. This is followed by another *bang* as the base of the drop sled crumples from the impact with the ground. These are all good noises, as it means my fatal fall has turned into a mere bruising as my Dog grinds along the ground with a *screech* before it comes to a halt.

Our Chickens fly in a low circle around us before heading back to the bird's nest on *Hornet*.

My autochute blows away, detaching as my drop sled comes to a halt. The crumple zone has done its job and been crushed by the force of landing, dissipating the energy. Then the restraining bolts fire, releasing my Dog, and I stand up.

"Fenris, sound off by squad, over," I say, waiting for the platoon to confirm that all the Dogs are on the ground five by five. "It's time to make sure we can't be seen, out."

The Dogs ChameleonFlage changes us from standard Marine Corps green—because as far as the Corps is concerned, green is the only color a Marine can be—into translucent shadows. Moving around fast will overload the system, so not being seen is still best achieved by not moving.

Standard operating procedure is to wait a bit because waiting is what happens to fill in the time between doing something or being shot at.

The lieutenants each confirm their platoons' successful deployment to the captain, and we move forward to the line marked on the map that is on our heads-up display. Anyone looking at us would probably see the movement from disturbances on the ground as a rippling shimmer as the Dogs move across the terrain.

Of course we still made a big enough racket to wake the dead, but while that would give a direction to look in, most people are poor judges of how far away a sound is from them.

Apart from our movement, all is quiet. Probably because all the noise we made has scared any local fauna away. You'd have to be deaf or dead not to have heard us landing.

The lack of any response is down to the fact that this part of

Afghanistan is hardly a thriving metropolitan area. Rather, it's a desolate wasteland. Once we reach the marker on our map, we stop and wait, monitoring the feeds from the drone on our screens.

It's as quiet as a morgue. Too quiet if you ask me.

7. YAWM AD-DIN

Keep your friends close—hold your enemies closer.

— ARABIAN PROVERB

Warlord Yeshua bin Yussuf
The White Mountain, Afghanistan
Wednesday, June 24, 2071

Yeshua bin Yussuf sits on a stool in the entrance of the cave, staring at the mountain across the valley as darkness falls, questioning his faith in all that is holy in his world. He finishes drinking his tea while his people eat and chat amongst themselves in the flickering light of the camp fire.

"Some more tea?" asks Abdi-al-Hazred.

He scratches at the mole on his face. "Yes, please, Abdi, I would very much like some more tea. Thank you."

Churagh-Ali, one of his leftenants, asks, "Guided One, how can anyone who has heard the words of the Qur'an turn their heart away from Allah?"

"As a young man sitting at my father's feet, I was told about people who studied the Qur'an without understanding what it meant or doing anything even if they did. One cannot move the mountain."

His followers chuckle at the allusion to the Prophet.

He'd seen jealousy consume people who lived in fear of being murdered for what they owned. Yet they could not see they already lived in a world where their parents would outlive them because of the greed that filled its heart.

Someone says, "Tell us more."

"I live my life trying to understand what I see. What I've learnt is, to truly understand Allah's will, one must listen to one's heart. I heard the call to jihad and chose to live my life as a warrior of Allah. Now I fight against Shaytan's agents, the Gog of Magog."

The devils who whisper evil in the hearts of men and women, leading them into sin that would destroy all that is holy in the world. Now in his own heart he hears the whisper of Iblis, Shaytan, the leader of the shayateen, and despair fills him.

"Allahu Ahkbar," says his followers.

"Allah is testing our faith with the khurafa we uncovered under our former home."

There's a murmur of conversation, and the words "the Afrite in the pillar" are spoken out loud. What he once thought was an improbable fantasy. A story meant to entertain men, to scare women and children, had been found under the White Mountain.

"For sixty years we've been digging, shaping the natural caves into a hidden fortress to hide from the strange noiseless drones that spy upon us, and to stand there when Yawm ad-Din comes."

A voice by the fireside asks, "When will Yawm ad-Din come?"

His father had taught him to see the approaching signs of the day of judgement.

"Soon. We have seen objects that speak, sold by businessmen

to defraud their customers with false promises of happiness. We have seen the wise men of the community speaking, and having their words ignored, being told they were old and know nothing of the ways of the modern world. All this and more we have seen."

There are nods of agreement.

"The Afrite must be stopped from entering our world," says Abdul-Baser, the first of his followers to complain in any situation.

"What Allah wills, happens," says Churagh-Ali.

"This is not the will of Allah. I've seen the ways of the modern world when I was a young man sent to study at a university. The Americans call their country the land of the free, but in their land only wealth earns the respect of others. I've seen farmers' crops fail despite enough rain falling during the year to grow plenty. I've watched as the bankers foreclosed on their loans to the farmers. This is an evil we must fight."

The debts seemed to him to be worth less than the long-term value of the land. Such laws were wrong.

One of his followers asks, "What can we do?"

"Be faithful to Allah and be happy with his blessings. We live in a world full of wealth. Do not complain about lacking possessions, because owning things does not make you happy."

Murmurs of agreement and nods of heads acknowledge his words. How can people who have so much be so unhappy with their lives, and yet still want more?

He continues speaking. "Respect your family, marry, and bring children into the world."

Yeshua bin Yussuf is appalled that people no longer care if their children are illegitimate. He can understand, and forgive, those women who bear children from fathers who've died in wars. They were fighting for what they believed in, but to deliberately father an illegitimate child is a sin against Allah.

The sound of thunder in the distance rolls around the fire-lit cave and echoes in the darkness.

"Follow the laws of the Qur'an," he says.

In the West he'd been disgusted by seeing men wearing silk clothing, dismayed by laws allowing men to marry other men. This was as nothing to what he'd seen lying under the mountain across the valley—the Afrite.

"Thank you for your words of wisdom, Guided One," says Abdi-al-Hazred.

His people had dug too deep under the mountain revealing a greater evil than the evil of men. He'd seen it with his own eyes. Had felt his body gripped by the Afrite in the pillar. The faces of his men are lit by the firelight of the cave; the shadows flickering catches the fear in their eyes. They seek his counsel, reassurance that all will be well.

"We must do something," says Churagh-Ali, "because it's a sign the Yawm ad-Din has begun."

"Fear not when the Yawm ad-Din will come. Allah will guide us," he says, using his voice to calm his followers.

Yeshua bin Yussuf had watched as the Afrite showed them scenes of Yawm ad-Din: the unnatural movement of the sun rising in the West, mountains that moved, and oceans that came and went without rhyme or reason he could understand. He'd watched helplessly as one of his followers had been gripped by the Afrite, drawn to the pillars, and had died when he touched them.

They were an evil that must be destroyed.

"Listen to the Guided One," says Abdi-al-Hazred. "He will tell us what to do."

Now he'd been told the Americans are coming, who don't care that what is under the mountain is evil. The memory of the Afrite had been forgotten in time like grains of sand blown in the wind.

"We will not allow the Western shayateen to unleash this evil into the world. Even though they've made the waters rise, caused lands to be lost, and try to hasten the end of time itself." For Yeshua bin Yussuf, if Allah allowed, this thing would not happen. He would see the Afrite destroyed.

"But how? We don't know how," says Abdul-Baser.

"The shayateen of the East came to me. They've pledged themselves to bring the mountain down on top of the Afrite."

Churagh-Ali speaks. "How do we know we can we trust them? What do they want from us?"

"We can't trust them, but if Allah wills it, we can trick evil into destroying evil. As for what they want, they've asked us to help them prevent the Americans from getting to the Afrite," he says.

A ripple of movement as the shock of what he says is taken in and understood by his followers.

"The Guided One has spoken," says Abdi-al-Hazred.

"The thought of working with the shayateen fills my heart with dread. But, we must not let our fear of being tricked stop us now. We will prevent the Afrite from being let loose upon the world. It must be hidden from the sight of man forever."

His words raise a small cheer of, "Allahu Ahkbar."

"Allahu Ahkbar," he says, knowing they have little time to prepare.

But his people know how to fight those who would invade their land and drive them off. This is their land, right or wrong, and by Allah they will defend it from the infidels, from all those who try to come here and lead them away from the word of Allah.

Just like all the other times they had driven off those who tried to impose their foreign rule over Afghanistan.

8. A LONG WALK IN THE SUN

Everything that is possible demands to exist.

— GOTTFRIED WILHELM VON LEIBNIZ

Sergeant Tachikoma
First Combat Armor Suit Reconnaissance Company
Afghanistan
Thursday, July 2, 2071

The ragged ridges on the hill ahead are covered in loose rock, which slows our progress. The platoons are Oscar Mike, but we're only managing to average five klicks per hour. At this rate we won't reach the designated target until 1800 hours, which puts us well behind schedule.

This is ideal ambush country. There are hundreds of places that would make good spots to set up kill zones, without having to try at all. A shit load of bad guys could disappear here and never be seen until after they fire.

It's too quiet. Apart from us, nothing else moves. I focus on the feed from the reconnaissance UAV looking for movement. Still nothing.

Ahead of us is what passes for a road around here.

On any reasonably smooth surface the Dogs can skate along on the tracks built into their feet at up to fifty klicks per hour. So we take advantage of our good fortune to make up some time getting to our destination. Despite traveling the rest of the way on the road, I've been overly optimistic in estimating how long it will take us to reach our destination.

We don't arrive at the cliffs until 1845 hours. By then the mountains are starting to cut off the sunlight, leaving us in a twilight setting as we move through the lengthening shadows.

Lieutenant Bergeson's platoon leads the way up the slope. The UAV's circular holding pattern has brought it over us again. From up there the enhanced image of the ground below makes our Dogs look like small toys.

As the darkness increases, my Dog automatically switches modes and superimposes a thermal image over what I'm viewing. The screen shows an enhanced composite image of everything outside, which appears hyper-real, but with tags where the Dog scan shows black processing artefacts.

This makes it easy enough to see where I'm going, for flexible definitions of the word *easy*. Dog jocks sense their surroundings from the screens and HUD. But it's easy to lose a proper sense of depth and distance when everything you see is made of pixels generated by some computer's algorithms.

The formation snakes around the edge of a sheer rock face, forcing us to adopt a conga line to traverse the narrow path upwards. Sergeant Ramirez from First Platoon finds an opening in the cliff face, but it's way too small for our Dogs to use. So the captain issues orders to keep searching for an entry site into the mountain.

A little while later we stop again when the front of the

formation finds a wide cleft we can use to get in. The ground has been churned up from vehicles passing through here. It's confirmation we've found a way inside the mountain.

The route ahead of us narrows where rocks have fallen. This results in our Dogs being metaphorically nuts-to-butts as we shuffle past the constrictions in our path. We go from slow to moving at a snail's pace.

The speed of our progress is frustrating. Made worse as we hit yet another choke point where more rocks obstruct our route. A fresh fall judging by the lack of tracks. This forces us to stop and twist to slip through the narrow gap.

Private Lopez is bad-mouthing spooks who order the deployment of Dogs where a Force Recon MARPACE team would be better suited. This earns him a reply from Sergeant Ramirez, who tells him to un-ass his situation and get with the programme.

Getting past the choke point, we enter a large cave. This means our thermal signature will now be a dead giveaway. Even with our ChameleonFlage on, we've just become much easier targets. But nothing stirs as we walk further into the darkness ahead.

We get a break when we pick up a ping from a transponder left by the Alpha Detachment PACE suit team.

That's the good news. The bad news is there are two passageways leading out from the cavern. But we can't tell which route the Snake Eaters took, as we can't pick up any signal from any other transponders they might have planted.

The captain comes over the company comms-channel.

"All section leaders, this is Big Dog. I intend to search both routes simultaneously. I'm designating this as our rally point—Romeo Victor One. Am I understood? Over."

A chorus of "aye, ayes" answers him.

Lieutenant McCarthy then says, "Big Dog, this is Fenris Six, I just had a thought. If we plant our own transponders on the same frequency the Army Alpha team used, then we build up a sensor map of the route we take. Not only that, but we can link into their network if it's still up, over."

I wish I'd thought of that. Doing so will increase our chances of finding the source of the magnetic pulse and being able to report back what was generating it too.

"OK, make it so, people, and let's get this show on the road, out," says Captain Johanson as First Platoon takes the left-hand tunnel, while we go right.

Lieutenant McCarthy orders Corporal Knight to take point for Alpha Squad and puts Lance Corporal Kowalski on point for Bravo. I bring up the rear to make sure none of the Dogs became separated by any unforeseen difficulties from what might lie ahead: like getting lost or turned around from taking the stupid pill.

The tunnels take us further into the heart of the mountain.

When the signal from the transponder behind us starts to fall off, I pop one of ours up on the ceiling. I then send a ping back to the first transponder, which carries the message to First Platoon's tail-end Charlie. A few moments later I get a ping back, confirming that the net is up.

The beginning of a line-trace map appears in a window on my screen.

Even if this tunnel leads nowhere, we'll be able to build up a picture of where the tunnels under the mountain go. I pop another transponder up as we get further along the tunnel and see that First Platoon has done the same. Clearly neither route is easier than the other to move through.

Other than the first Army transponder we've picked up, there's nothing else to indicate they made it this far.

Thinking about it, though, Private Lopez was right, this operation would be a whole lot easier for a MARPACE team.

Their smaller suits would have more room for maneuvring in here, which would be easier than us getting down on all fours to get past the parts of the tunnel where the roof lowers. The delays makes for slow progress.

"Fenris Four, we've come to another branch. I'll take Fenris Alpha left, you go right, over."

"Solid copy, Fenris Six," I say, repeating the orders back to Lieutenant McCarthy before saying, "Out."

I plant another transponder to maintain the tenuous link to the rest of the company. The map is enlarging as both platoons progress, but after going about four hundred meters, we come to a dead end. We're all bunched up and have stopped moving.

Kowalski, being his usual helpful self, states the obvious over the radio.

"Fenris Four, the tunnel has gotten too small to go any further, over."

I bring up his feed, and I can see a small hole leading downwards in front of his Dog on my screen. It is so small even a MARPACE team would be unable to climb through it, which is good news I suppose. The bad news is turning the Dogs around in the confined space to retrace our route.

I piggyback a SITREP message over the transponder network notifying the lieutenant of our progress.

I lie my Dog flat on the ground, roll her over, get up facing back the other way, and begin making my way back to where we started. Jones is complaining over the laser-net about how bone this all is, and getting told, "Shut up, Jones," from Jackson and Rodriguez.

The squad are on edge, nerves taut, hence the chatter.

"Can it, people," I say, mostly to reassure them and let them know they shouldn't be slacking off on the job. Unsurprisingly enough, it takes us longer to get back to where we started. By the time we do, the transponder map is a couple of points bigger too.

First Platoon has also come to a junction where they've had to split up into two squads. The mountain is a maze of tunnels, which are dividing the party into bite-sized chunks. If this carries on, we will need to double back to search tunnels we can't cover in the first pass.

I put the worry to one side. We have room at the junction to reorder our order of march. So I get Kowalski back on point with Jones behind him while I bring up the rear again.

If anything, the route the lieutenant's squad has taken is even harder to traverse. The size of the tunnels constrains our speed as we crawl through eight hundred meters to link back up with McCarthy. I ping a message to that effect up to him and get a confirmation back five mikes later it had been received and understood.

Checking the mission timer, I'm hit with the realization that we've been inside the mountain for over an hour. The tunnel opens out a bit, and I'm able to get my Dog up off the ground and into a crouching walk. This allows us to quicken the pace from dead slow to slow.

The lieutenant pings me, *Contact Alpha Detachment.*

"Fenris Bravo, pick up the pace. Fenris Six has found the Army team, out."

"Fenris Four, there's weapon fire ahead of us, over," says Kowalski, again stating the obvious, as the sound of firing echoes in the distance.

Damn it, just as things were starting to look up.

I ping the lieutenant for a SITREP, wishing we were close enough to talk over the laser-net. Then I pass the contact message from the lieutenant with Kowalski's report back along the transponder network to the captain. Not that First Platoon can help us anytime in the foreseeable future. Now it's up to me to assess the situation and earn my pay.

"Bravo Sierra One, move forward. Get me a picture of what is going on ahead of us, over," I say to Kowalski and Jones, and hear, "Roger that, out," in reply.

As we traverse the tunnel I keep an eye on Kowalski's feed. There's an opening ahead, which appears to lead into a large cavern. We're close enough now I can hear from inside my suit the sound of individual cannons firing.

Kowalski crawls his Dog up the slope to the opening and deploys his shoulder sensor mast up to peek over the ridgeline into the cavern ahead.

Linking to his feed, I can see two of our Dogs are down and the other three are on the right-hand side of the cavern behind some cover. They're exchanging fire with five Chinese ATSs, nicknamed Fatties, their equivalent to our Dogs. Damn, so not what we need.

We're bunched up all together, so I open the Bravo Squad's laser-net channel.

"OK, we're going to stack up, pack in and take the Fatties down. Kowalski and Jones go left, Jackson and Rodriguez go right, and I'll take center. I've set up an autosqueal to Alpha to let them know we are coming in. Your targets are designated on your HUDs. Let's do this, Marines."

I hear their replies, and time seems to slow down as we get it on and the data streams across my heads-up display.

Kowalski and Jones slide left as they go over the ridgeline, surprising a Fatty and blowing it away before it has a chance to react. It goes up in an impressive display when the fuel ignites with a satisfying *whoomph*! Jackson and Rodriguez go right, taking fire as they do, but catching another Fatty in their crossfire, which flops to the ground.

From the feeds I can tell that the drop off the ridge is only two meters. So I take my Dog straight over the top, firing on the move. The boom from my autocannon reverberates around me. I smash into the ground, which causes my Dog's legs to automatically cantilever to take the strain of the impact.

It gives me the edge, and I surprise a Fatty as it turns towards Kowalski and Jones. My Dog slides along the floor, and I fire off another two rounds; *boom, boom!*

The first shot hits the Fatty's arm, which parts company from the suit, and ricochets off the cavern wall, bringing down rock in the process. The second misses, and the Fatty pops smoke, but I'm already locked on. I fire another two rounds, and both of those hit it in the body, causing it to collapse like so much dead weight.

The final Fatty is bugging out.

As it runs for cover everybody fires. The Fatty literally disintegrates in front of us, as both the fuel and the ordnance blows up, causing its powerpack to short out and emit a charge of electricity that crackles in the air. The blast throws all of Bravo Squad's Dogs backwards, the force of the explosion slamming us into the ground.

"Sound off, people, over," I say, relieved when everyone in my squad reports in as fine. Ordering Jackson and Rodriguez to move up to the front past where the last Fatty had fallen and take up guard at the other entrance into the cavern, I call, "Bravo Sierra Two, take up positions in the tunnel ahead of us. I don't want us getting bounced, over."

Standing up, I survey the situation; nothing moves.

Checking my autocannon's magazine, I realize that it's empty. Could've sworn I'd only fired eight shots, but in that last exchange I must've loosed another two rounds in all the excitement. I dump a SITREP over the transponder network to Captain Johanson while my team checks out Alpha squad's surviving Dogs.

Lieutenant McCarthy and Corporal Knight have been taken down in the initial ambush. Their suits are both holed with nothing but an irretrievable mush inside to indicate a person had been in control of them. The electronic logs tag them as dead, and all that's left to comfort me are my memories of them.

I'm shocked, devastated by their loss. I will grieve for my dead friends later.

Now I need to deal with the good/bad news, which is that Hernandez is alive, but his Dog has lost a leg. He's therefore combat ineffective. Leaving Vosloo and Delgado from Alpha Squad still in the game. I signal people around me to switch over to the laser-net so we can talk and do what's necessary.

"Kowalski, strip the spare magazines off the lieutenant's and sergeant's Dogs." I pause to think what I want to say next. "Jones, go check on the six PACE suits." The remains of which the Chinese used to bait the ambush.

Captain Johanson pings me back, confirming I'm now in charge, which formalizes the chain of command. He orders me to take Bravo Squad further into the mountain and send the survivors of Alpha Squad back out. It's all well of him to give me an order, but getting Hernandez's Dog fit to move to fulfil it is going to be a bitch.

"Vosloo and Delgado, I want you to strip a good leg off one of our two downed Dogs to get Hernandez's up and running. All the Chinese Fatties are toast, but we might still be able to download data from the hulks. Hernandez, get your ass over to the Fatties and see if you can retrieve anything from them."

It would do everybody good to keep them focussed on a job.

Hernandez speaks. "But, Sergeant, that means popping them open too."

"Keep your helmet on and suck it up, Marine. Just count yourself lucky that you aren't the chunky salsa in the can," I say as I scan the carnage around us.

There are eight destroyed enemy all-terrain suits, which were probably part of a Chinese Direct Action Squad. They usually deploy in three groups of eight, so there could be sixteen others waiting in reserve to counterattack us. If we're lucky. In the worst-case scenario we could be facing a whole damn lián, a company-sized formation with sixty-four more suits, in which case we would be well and truly screwed.

But there's no way of telling what lies ahead of us.

Jones speaks. "Sergeant, all the PACE suits have had their memory cores removed, but one of the operators did a data dump into the comms-buffer before he died. I'm copying it now."

"Good catch, Private."

Without the memory core codes, we won't be able to access the PACE suits' mission logs, but I'd class it as better than a kick in the teeth.

"Lance Corporal Delgado, once you get Hernandez's Dog operational, I want you to cocoon our dead and then lead the remains of Alpha Squad and rendezvous with Big Dog at Romeo Victor. The captain wants the INTEL from the Alpha Detachment PACE suits and anything we can get off the Chinese suits back to the *Hornet*. Understood?"

"Aye, aye, Sergeant!" says Delgado.

She seems pleased to be in command. She will soon learn better. It's now 2130 hours, and the mission is far from over.

"Bravo Squad with me. The captain said we're to follow the tunnel the Fatty was trying to exit through; he wants us to find out where it leads."

I take point, heading further into the mountain. I can't imagine it's going to get any easier the further we go in, because so far, today has been full of unpleasant surprises.

9. CRASH SITE

The two enemies of human happiness are pain and boredom.

— ARTHUR SCHOPENHAUER

Second Lieutenant Beckford
Commander Fourth Platoon
First Combat Armor Suit Reconnaissance Company
Afghanistan
Thursday, July 2, 2071

Beckford scans the site around the downed Aries space-plane, searching for the cause of the crash. She sees the culprit is an inconvenient gully on an otherwise featureless plain. This had changed the Army's nice, smooth deployment into a tipped-over, nose-first, shit-hard landing.

Beckford sympathizes with what had happened here. Unexpected crappiness can totally mess up anyone's plans.

The crash reminds her of the training mission when she'd first joined the platoon. A stupid accident during deployment, and things turned to crap. Shit happens. The death of one of her people had knocked her back, and she'd made a bad first impression with both Captain Johanson and the rest of the Marines under her command. Not her fault it had happened, but it was her responsibility.

Speaking over the platoon laser-net, she says, "Lobo Four, take your squad in and search the plane."

"Roger that, search the plane," comes the reply from Staff Sergeant Washington.

Beckford hears Captain Johanson requesting updates from her on the company command channel. It's annoying because he can monitor both her and Washington's Dogs' feeds and must've heard her previous transmission. She sends an autoconfirm to him with the message, *Wait one*.

"Lobo Six, we've found two dead operators inside the cockpit of the plane. Looks like they died on impact."

Beckford scans the feeds from Staff Sergeant Washington's Dog. From the mess, she can see the crash was the most likely cause of their deaths.

"OK, leave them in place and see if you can download the craft's record of the landing." Switching channels, she speaks to Captain Johanson over the radio. "Big Dog, this is Lobo Six. We've found two dead in the cockpit, no signs of the rest of Alpha Detachment, over."

"Lobo Six, good work. Secure the crash site and wait for the MULE to come in and do the pickup. Once the package is away, link up with Wulfgang and await further orders. Any questions? Over."

"Big Dog, is there anything you want us to do while waiting? Over."

"Just follow Wulfgang's Six's orders, out."

For a moment Beckford wonders whether she's done something wrong. Is Johanson's decision to put her under Perez's command a message about her performance? She mutters to herself, "Remember it's nothing personal, it's just the chain of command."

Beckford alternates between scanning the horizon and checking the readouts from her platoon; listening in to background chit-chat across the laser-net, mostly small talk, irrelevant to the job at hand, mixed in with people pointing out movements to each other; confirming something is wildlife, and not a hostile force advancing towards them.

Beckford lets it flow over her.

She could order them to can the chatter, but it would gain her nothing useful. She didn't issue orders because she could, she gave orders because something needed doing. Sometimes what needed doing was standing still and waiting. She's bored, but being bored means nothing bad is happening. The time passes slowly.

It isn't good enough to follow orders. You have to understand your commander's intent behind the order.

She'd failed to parse Captain Johanson's intent properly the last time, and it had led to a fatality. Too much haste, not enough action. It makes her all too self-conscious about her performance on this mission. Everything she does will go towards her next appraisal. After screwing the pooch, she's keen not to get another ass-chewing from the captain. Another strike, like the last, will mean the end of her career.

Distracting herself from the worrying thoughts, she monitors the feed from the UAV, tracking the progress of the rest of the company. First and Second Platoons are now at the base of the mountain, beginning to make their way up a narrow path towards the top.

And the beauty of the landscape surprises her. But it has an edge to it, a bleak harshness waiting to catch the unwary. The weather can be unpredictable, and without the proper gear you would be exposed to extreme temperatures, which would kill you.

Of course that's assuming the locals didn't kill you first, either for being a foreigner or because, in her case, being a woman not in the company of a male relative. The rules women have to obey here are alien to her, and she can't begin to imagine living here with her partner.

The UAV catches sight of Lieutenant Perez's Third Platoon. They've circled around the perimeter of the crash site and are now spiralling out, swinging away from her position and heading to secure the entrance site where the company had gone inside the mountain.

Then the crew of the Air Force MULE updates their ETA to under an hour out. They've been delayed by unexpectedly strong headwinds slowing their progress. This is an inconvenience for the aircrew. If anything kicks off here before they arrive, it could end up being downright unforgiving for her Marines on the ground. She tags each member of her platoon, speaking a few words to each to get a handle on their mood.

"Lobo Four, what do you think about our situation?"

"Platoon's a bit bored, but you already know that. They're good with it, they know their jobs."

"Am I missing anything?"

"You're doing fine. If I think you're about to drop the ball, I'll tell you." She appreciates the positive feedback from her staff sergeant and settles back for the long wait.

10. HURRY UP & WAIT

Leadership is solving problems. The day soldiers stop bringing you their problems is the day you have stopped leading them.

— Gen Colin L. Powell, USAR

Second Lieutenant Perez
Commander Third Platoon
First Combat Armor Suit Reconnaissance Company
Afghanistan
Thursday, July 2, 2071

Perez curses under his breath. He's on the clock to complete his assigned task according to the schedule. Unfortunately, the rough ground is not cooperating with his plan to advance in orderly military fashion. At this rate they will miss hitting their marker on time.

He sees Privates Jackman and Schwartz lagging at the back of the formation. The two Benny boys are pissing him off big time. They're dragging the platoon's performance down, and he orders Sergeant Thompson to deal with them.

Searching around him, he sees that if anything kicked off here, it wouldn't be easy to conceal the Dogs in this terrain. There's too much open ground with clear lines of sight, and he knows all too well that concealment isn't hard cover. His platoon would have a hard time of it because they'd be easy targets.

However, he'd joined the Marine Corps to fight.

So far there had been little opportunity to do so. He wants to see action and dish out pain, but to win out here you'd need to play hardball. A message from the captain interrupts his train of thought—the other half of the company are about to enter the interior of the mountain and will therefore be out of contact for the duration.

Perez acknowledges the captain's message, and as far as he's concerned it's all good. For one, it means he'll get the opportunity to show his ability to command and be seen as a Marine Corps hard charger—a natural leader of men, well suited to combat. So bring it on if you think you're hard enough.

As long as Beckford's platoon doesn't screw the pooch by misinterpreting their orders, then everything is looking good. What's he thinking? Of course Beckford will screw up, just like she did last time.

11. ENTANGLED

Fortune favours the bold.

—— PUBLIUS VERGILIUS MARO

Sergeant Tachikoma
First Combat Armor Suit Reconnaissance Company
Afghanistan
Thursday, July 2, 2071

As we move down the tunnel, another ping comes in from the captain. His squad has been engaged by the enemy, thereby officially exceeding today's quota of all kinds of good news. I pass the word along to the rest of my squad to stay tight.

So far the tunnel has been clear of unfriendly Fatties waiting to pop us a new one. But piloting the Dog through the interior of a mountain isn't like driving down a road. There's a lot of ducking under obstructions with the uneven ground and loose rocks underfoot making it difficult to stay upright.

It would be easier to drive a four-by-four truck through here.

As the tunnel turns, light appears ahead of us but then cuts off as we walk up to the opening into another large cavern. I signal my squad to halt and order them to alternately go left and right as we enter. This will make it harder for anyone waiting to shoot at us, as it will force them to track us individually and give us a chance to return fire.

We're close to each other, so I use the squad laser-net to talk.

"OK, Marines, time to make yourselves a hard target. On my mark, move. Mark!"

At my command the Dogs move quickly into the cavern ahead. I tense in anticipation of enemy gunfire, but all is still except for our movement. The squad works their way around and out from the entrance, searching everywhere that can provide cover or conceal the enemy's position.

The cavern seems to disappear into the foreboding darkness with nothing but the Dogs' own IR sources lighting up the way forward.

"OK, people, let's fan out and make like we have a purpose. The Corps is not paying us by the hour, let's move it," I say.

"Aye, aye, Sergeant," comes in reply.

The floor seems designed by nature to trip us up. To add insult to the day injuries, my Dog slips on the loose rock.

Jones breaks the silence. "This reminds me of the time I went caving in Wales as a kid."

"And you thought this would be a good time to tell us now why, Private?"

"Sorry, Sergeant, I was just thinking out loud."

"OK, Jones, keep the chat to stuff we all need to know about."

Our squad's line morphs into a rough arrowhead formation as we progress further.

The going becomes easier as we move into the central area of the cavern as the roof rises above us. Standing ahead of us in the center of the cavern are two stalagmites—free-standing pillars that tower over the Dogs.

We approach cautiously. Four PACE suits lie on the ground destroyed from the damage taken during a firefight. But where had the light come from?

"Give me a three-sixty now," I say, getting my squad to form a defensive position around the stalagmites.

In front of me is part of one of the Army PACE suits lying face flat on the ground directly between the two stalagmites. The only thing is, the suit had been cut in two with surgical precision. I don't know of any portable weapon that can do that to a suit. I call, "Sound off."

"Kowalski, all clear."

"Rodriguez, clear here."

"Jackson, I've got nothing."

"Jones all clear, Sergeant."

This is way above my pay grade, so I ping a message to the captain. *Found the rest of the Alpha Detachment. All PACE suits combat wrecks, condition of corpses suggests action several days in past.* The captain sends orders to retrieve the bodies and rendezvous back with him when done.

"OK, let's scan the area for anything the Army Snake Eaters might have dropped around here."

My squad spreads out and starts searching.

The remains of the body lying on the ground between the pillars are from someone's head and shoulders. I go over to try and identify who it was. Putrefaction has set in, and I'm glad I can't smell it.

One thing for sure, we aren't going to pull any information off the suit. As I kneel down, the space between the two stalagmites to my right shivers like a chameleon screen shifting.

"Contact! My right!" I shout, turning to fire at the shimmer.

My shot disappears into the distance. I'm now looking at somewhere outside the mountain. I blink and do a double take, because I don't believe what I'm seeing.

Shouts from my squad interrupt me.

"No contact and I can't seem to move. I'm stuck," says Rodriguez.

"Where's the contact? Where is it? I can't move!" says Jackson, the sound of panic rising in his voice.

No one else has fired. Ahead of me is the other half of the PACE suit. It's lying on the ground on the other side of the stalagmites.

"Check fire, people, stand easy."

I stand up and walk between the stalagmites into the light ahead of me.

The inside edges are smooth. It's as if they had been sliced apart. A rush of excitement courses through my body. I lean over and grab the leg of the PACE suit with my left hand and haul it back through into the cavern. The suit is frozen solid, and unlike the other half of the body, it's in remarkably good shape.

What did I just do? How can the body not be in the cavern?

I turn to look through the shimmer and walk back between the two pillars, and realize I'm standing outside in the open. The sun is beginning to drop down behind some mountains in the distance, and I'm standing in shadow.

Do what? How can the sun be setting again when it's already night-time? This is nuts. How can I be inside a mountain cavern one moment and then outside the next?

I turn back the way I came, then turn back around and stare out across a plain. Ahead, the ground rises up in one direction, and the beginning of a jungle stretches to the horizon. In the sky are birds, except they're not birds, but something like large bat things flying up from the jungle canopy, and I notice two moons.

Clearly I'm not in Kansas.

Goddammit, this makes no sense, so I walk around the stalagmites and peer between them, seeing two of the Dogs in my squad standing with their backs towards me. I go back to where I started. The two halves of the PACE suit are still lying on the floor of the cavern.

If I was mystified, my people are even more confused.

I hear Jackson say, "Where did the sergeant go, man? She's dropped off the squad net. Shit, what's happening to me?"

The alien jungle in the distance is dark and forbidding. I imagine it would be a world of pain and hurt for anyone to try to traverse it. Having seen enough, I walk back through the stalagmites into the darkness of the cavern.

My Marines are frozen in place.

"What is it, people?"

"You just disappeared off our screens, Sergeant, and I can't move my arms and legs," says Jones.

"Sergeant, you walked between the stalagmites and didn't come out the other side," says Rodriguez.

"It was like one of those magic tricks you see in shows when they make people disappear in front of your eyes," says Jackson.

They're not making any sense.

"Let's keep a lid on it and stay calm. Less jawing. Kowalski, take Jones and go through the pillars and see if I missed anything. Be quick about it."

"I can't do that, Sergeant," says Kowalski.

"Didn't ask; that's an order, Corporal," I say.

"No, I mean I can't move," he says.

On my screen I can see the fear in his face. In all their faces. They're petrified by what's happening to them.

The shimmer between the pillars stops, its disappearance signalling the return of darkness to the cavern. It's as if normality is restored, and the people in my squad unfreeze.

Jones asks, "What was that?"

"I don't know, but I'm glad it stopped. I felt like I was being controlled. I've never been so frightened in my life before," says

Kowalski, followed by Jackson and Rodriguez saying together, "Amen to that."

Whatever *it* is, it's certainly the most likely cause of the mysterious magnetic energy pulse our Mr Anderson from the CIA sent us here to collect data on. I put the problem to one side; we're on the clock.

"OK, the easy bit is over. Let's check out the rest of the cavern."

During the ten minutes it takes to confirm the cavern is empty, Kowalski kvetches and moans about the place giving him the heebie-jeebies. He also finds another tunnel that leads out of the place. Jackson and Rodriguez bag the two halves of the sliced-up PACE suit, and they strap one half to the back of each other's Dogs.

With the other three PACE suits we've found, it looks like mission accomplished. We're good to go.

As we're about to leave, the shimmer thing happens again, but this time there's water and a beach with daylight bursting into the cavern. No plain rolling out into the distance and no sign of a jungle. I can't believe what my screen is showing me.

I pop my cockpit's hood and climb out of my Dog, compelled for some reason to walk towards the pillars. There's a perfect red sun rising over the ocean. As I try to walk between the pillars I brush one and am thrown backwards as if I've been hit by an electric shock.

In that instant I'm caught by something and see my whole life in a moment of perfect clarity, all the choices I've ever made.

It's like I'm staring at reflections in a multifaceted crystal, with thousands of different me's, all moving and doing different things. Some sequences are clear, others are clouded, caught in midmotion and juddering between two choices of what to do. Then everything goes black.

When I awake, the smell of putrefaction greets me, and I look up to see Kowalski's Dog kneeling over me.

"You sure scared the shit out of us, Sergeant."

"What happened?"

"You got out of your Dog, walked towards the stalagmite, and just fell over."

"Good thing you fell backwards, Sergeant."

"Why's that, Jones?"

"'Cause if you had fallen forward, you would've been stuck on the other side of that thing, and we couldn't move and go get you."

"Or worse, cut in half when the shimmer stopped," say Jackson and Rodriguez together.

I have a momentary urge to check my fingers and toes and count them, as I'm rather attached to my various appendages. The idea of being sliced into parts by the pillars is not the most appealing thought in the whole wide world.

"I get the picture. Were you two separated at birth or something?"

"I don't know how you even pulled that shit off, Sergeant," says Kowalski. "The rest of us were frozen in place, unable to move, and scared shitless."

"So I gather. OK, I'm truly grateful for your help here, but this doesn't mean that we're going to be sharing warm showers together. Let's get this gaggle-fuck on the road, people, that's an order."

We're Marines, we break things for a living. Investigating crazy weird-ass pillars that shimmer and freeze people is way outside of our remit.

12. ANOMALY

All war is based on deception.

— SUN TZU

Mr Anderson,
CIA Analyst
Langley, Virginia,
Monday, June 22, 2071

Anderson prepared for the morning meeting with his boss. His office has a window that gives a view out on to the inner courtyard of the annex. A luxury he's grateful for, as it allows the morning sunlight to brighten the drab corporate gray decor of the place. His friend and coworker Ben Pantoliano walks into the room.

"Hey, Glen, good morning, how's it going?"

"Hey, Ben, working my ass off preparing for a presentation this morning. You?"

"I had a great weekend."

"Rub it in why don't ya."

"So Moss is on your back?"

"Yep."

"Sucks to be you I guess."

"Could be worse, I could be you."

"You're just jealous of me and mine," says Ben, stifling a laugh.

"Think again, sucker. I don't see what she sees in you."

"Up yours too. You want coffee?"

"Yeah, that would be good."

Ben leaves the room, and Anderson continues checking for mistakes, pressed for time.

"Here you go. Don't say I never get you anything."

Anderson looks up to see a cup of hot black coffee held out for him. "So you and your woman had a good time then?"

"Sure did. You know Rosie wants to set you up with a friend of hers."

"Tell her thanks, but no thanks. I'm not looking to hitch up with anyone."

"So, what you working on?"

"The Chinese mining operation."

"That? I thought it was nothing."

"So did I, but go figure." He blows on his coffee and then sips some, scalding his tongue.

"I'll leave you to it. Want to have a game of squash later?"

"Sure, it will cheer me up to whup your ass."

"In your dreams, pal," says Ben, sitting down at the desk opposite.

Anderson continues working, pulling in files, tidying up the details, and polishing up the summary. Once he's finished, he drinks the remains of his now tepid coffee and then shuts down his workstation.

"Catch you later," he says, walking out of the office.

"Good luck," comes the reply.

He makes his way down the broad corridor towards the elevators. It could be any office anywhere, but the lack of corporate logos mark it as governmental property decorated by the lowest bidder. He has to go up several floors to get to Moss's office, where he finds her waiting for him.

"I've booked a room for the presentation," she says. "Follow me."

Moss leads him back to the elevators taking them down to the basement to a secure room with no windows, and soundproofing material covering the walls. As the door opens he's greeted by the sight of a two-star general accompanied by assorted military officers, and a number civilians from other agencies, all sat waiting for the meeting to start.

"I wasn't expecting..."

Moss interrupts him. "You'll be fine. Start setting up."

Anderson goes to the head of the table, where he logs in to the room's secure standalone workstations and brings up the display.

"Good morning, everyone, this is Mr Anderson, who will be making today's presentation," says Moss, sealing the door to the windowless room.

He puts up the first summary.

"As you can see from the map, the Chinese mining operation is north of Akekule Lake, here in the Tian Shan Mountains on the border with Mongolia." Pictures of stunning mountain landscapes give way to a satellite view showing earth ravaged by mining. "At first we logged this as a scientific venture, but these shots here show military equipment being moved underground," he says as he runs through the presentation.

Some of the people already appear bored.

"Our initial investigations were aimed at finding out why there was such a significant military involvement in this project. Given that the Chinese don't differentiate between the government and the military, the former are often retired military officers, this makes such assessments a difficult proposition at the best of times."

He stops speaking to take a sip of water.

"Orbital geological analysis of the area showed nothing worth mining at this site. There are no rare earth minerals or other resources coming out of the operation. Given China's current economic situation, I was asked to liaise with NCS resources."

This is the CIA's National Clandestine Services. He pauses as he realizes this meeting means he's stepped into a bigger arena.

"Please continue, Glen," says Moss.

"The question was why the attempt at secrecy? It's not possible to hide a mining operation, and during my research, I discovered the costs of its construction were nowhere to be found. Why bother hiding the cost of doing something you can't hide from sight?"

He takes a moment to change the picture and look at the notes on his PAD before continuing with his presentation.

"On revisiting the GEOINT data, I noticed that the site of the mine is on top of a magnetic anomaly. This led me down a different path when I came across some published papers researching this subject."

One of the civilians interrupts him. "Ms Moss, why have you brought Mr Anderson in to present this information to us?" The man wears a suit marking him as someone from one of the TLA services that make the CIA look like a bastion of freedom of information.

"Glen already knows 90 percent of what's happening, and for me to bring someone else in now would only expand the number of people on the need-to-know list. Besides he has the right background to take this to the next stage and meets the clearance requirements."

Moss pauses, then looks up from her PAD.

"Is this going to be a problem? Glen, close your mouth, it's most unbecoming, and carry on."

"Yes, ma'am. As I was saying, I started researching geophysical magnetic anomalies that result from chemical properties of the rocks. The obvious connection is the ability to monitor seismic activity, which after the big quakes of '30 and '31 has been a global concern. But the research indicated applications to do with the detection of submarines. It was at that point I flagged up the military aspects of this operation to my boss."

"Very good, Glen. Sit down now, you may want to take notes. Mr Smith from the DIA will now fill us in on the rest of the details about this Chinese operation."

Smith stands up to speak. "Thank you, ladies and gentlemen. If you will pay attention to what I'm about to run on the screen, you will see something rather intriguing, which should make what the Chinese are studying clearer."

The agent plays a short video clip.

It shows the inside of a mine with two pillars standing in the middle of a large open area with the air shimmering in the space between them. A robot walks between the pillars pulling a cable while a man in a white lab coat stands by monitoring the process.

He's repeating something in Chinese, which is unintelligible.

Then the shimmer between the pillars stops, and the cable attached to the robot drops to the ground. The robot can no longer be seen. People run into frame to assist the man who has fallen to the floor.

The clip then repeats the sequence.

Anderson wonders what sort of world Mr Smith from the Defense Intelligence Agency lives in where a clip of video with garbled Chinese is described as making things clearer?

"We have to thank my opposite number, Mr Jones from the NSA, for enhancing the image and audio quality of the clip. Let me now play the clip with a translation of the recovered audio."

Jones specialized in SIGINT analysis. Anderson met him a while ago when they were working on another case together. The National Security Agency was commonly referred to as the No Such Agency, on account of the habit of their operatives denying they existed. Something that was comical in these times, which only goes to show that the NSA has a sense of humour after all.

A man is screaming, "Bangzhù wo, wo dòng bùliao, wo de xiongkou téng." The translation is, *Help me, I can't move, my chest hurts*, repeated over and over again. There's a thump as the man falls to the ground, followed by silence.

"I'll leave the clip running with the sound off," says Smith. "As you can see, a robot walks between the two pillars pulling a cable and then disappears. The man has been identified as a scientist called Dr Chao Xing. We concluded he died as a result of this experiment. Our current theory is that the Chinese are developing a new weapon system that can create seismic tremors."

"I assume this clip was procured through DCS agents?" asks one of the Army officers.

The Defense Clandestine Service is the overseas espionage arm of the military. The lapel name badge and rank insignia identify the officer as General Wayland.

A search brings up his bio on Anderson's PAD, which indicates he works out of the Pentagon's E-ring. Everybody and their dog was twitchy about the degree of seismic activity around the globe. Earthquakes had been steadily increasing over the years without any explanation that all scientists could agree on as the cause.

"It was, General. And the point of your question is, sir…?"

"Well, Agent Smith, provenance is everything. How do we know this isn't some Chinese intelligence operation to uncover our assets working undercover?"

"Without going into any details of how the clip was acquired, we are able to corroborate the authenticity of the recording from both the embedded image data and SIGINT from the NSA."

Anderson sits back to listen to Wayland and Smith lay into each other's respective services. It is like watching some vaudeville act where two comedians exchange insults, but without the popcorn.

"How do you know that the Chinese Ministry of State haven't leaked this as some kind of canary trap to identify a spy within their project?"

"Well, General, I can reassure you that our foreign national source remains in contact with their handler, and there's no evidence to suggest any other versions of this clip exist. It's as good as it gets."

"Contrary to your assertion, in my experience it's better to assume everything is part of a disinformation scheme designed to hide the truth. Basing one's conclusions off one HUMINT source is too soft for my taste."

"I can't speak to your elaborate conspiracy agenda, General. We too prefer hard intelligence from objective-based sources where the reality of the evidence can be tested. But we live in an imperfect world. However, it seems unlikely the Chinese would expose one of their top scientist's to something they knew would kill him."

"You can say that, but how did we find out he didn't die of natural causes?"

"Because he's not the first worker to die. All autopsies of the victims show the same thing. Brain haemorrhage. One worker suffering a brain haemorrhage may be regarded as unfortunate. More than two starts to look like a trend," replies Agent Smith with a smile on his face.

"More like carelessness," says General Wayland.

"May I interrupt?" Anderson waits for the two men to acknowledge him, pausing before speaking. "Do we have any idea what the purpose of attaching a cable to the robot during this test was?"

"That remains unclear at this point, Mr Anderson," says Agent Smith. "As does the reason why the Chinese are hiding the project from their own population, unless it is, as we suspect, a special weapons project."

"That was going to be my next question."

"So what do you think, Mr Anderson?" Smith asks.

"If we wanted to hide something, we would sandwich the truth between two layers of lies, so as to make it seem implausible. Then we would dissemble by answering with a lie sandwiched between two truths. But the Chinese are all about maintaining the status quo until they can leverage an advantage. So the question is what advantage is there here for them?"

"I can answer that," says a woman in a smartly tailored suit who stands up to interrupt the exchange. "If I may, Mr Anderson has the right of it."

He nods at her to thank her for acknowledging his contribution.

"My name is Dr Scott, and I'm the lead scientist and manager of the Magnetic Anomaly Project. I work as part of the Geological Survey studying the phenomena as part of our Earth survey operations, which is cofunded in conjunction with the Air Force."

Dr Scott pauses as all attention in the room focuses on her.

"Since the Great Quake of '31 and the near collapse of the global economy in the ensuing crisis, we've been studying the link between magnetism and seismic activity. There are many things that can cause magnetic anomalies. These range from natural magnetic sources generated by geological processes or chemical reactions in the ground, to remnants in the Earth's crust recording changes in its magnetic field over geologic time."

"And your point is, Dr Scott…?" asks General Wayland.

"The point is that we found a set of pillars when digging at one of our Washington State facilities, and we've been studying them for some time. Our research has allowed us to identify the unique magnetic signature of these anomalies. We think we can show they're correlated to the increased seismic activity around the globe."

"Very interesting I'm sure, Dr Scott, but what's the bottom line here? Are we talking about a new weapon?" asks General Wayland.

"Please let me continue. As I was saying, the source was unlike anything we could've imagined. We found two pillars made of some sort of iron, which had glassy, smooth inner faces but rough edges on the outside."

"Uhm, fascinating. Are they natural, and what makes them so important?"

"We don't know what the pillars are. We've not come across anything like them before. And don't ask me how they operate. But what we do know is that they will allow us to connect between two places."

A ripple of motion, like a wave at a sports match, travels around the room as the import of the statement is taken in.

"Say again?" asks Agent Smith.

"The magnetic pulse occurs when the pillars connect to other pillars we think are on other worlds. We don't understand the mechanism of the connection yet. However, people caught in close proximity to the pillars when this happens are unable to move."

Anderson admires her ability to speak quietly while making her points heard. It is a trick he needs to learn.

"This disrupts the person's homeostasis systems, causing amongst other things their blood pressure to spike, which can be fatal for those who are not physically fit. We're still gathering data and developing the physics and mathematics behind the process," says Dr Scott.

There's a moment before anyone reacts to her statement. Then the room is overwhelmed by the sound of voices as people start speaking to each other.

General Wayland interrupts. "All right, people, calm down." He waits for the hubbub to lessen. "It might have helped if you had told us this first, Dr Scott."

"Possibly, but I needed to be sure you had independently discovered the pillars before disclosing my information, and I have your attention now. As a result of our studies, we recently discovered what we think is the location of another set of pillars in Afghanistan. We want confirmation that the third magnetic anomaly in Afghanistan is generated by a pair of pillars."

"For what purpose, Dr Scott?"

"To advance our scientific knowledge, General. We can't just send a probe through our pillars and hope they go to Afghanistan. Every time these things open, they go to different places."

"I see. Can these things be used as a weapon? And what does the Chinese involvement mean?"

"Not a weapon, General, more a force of nature, and I imagine that if the Chinese are aware of this third site, then they'd want to investigate it too. All we want is confirmation that the site is what we think it is," she says, sitting down.

"Securing permanent access to the Afghan site would likely be impossible in the current political climate. However, it would be possible to send in a Special Forces team for a look-see, but we would need authorization for such an operation to proceed, Dr Scott."

"General Wayland, the president and Joint Chiefs of Staff are in agreement as to strategic need to gain more intelligence on this phenomenon. Did you not receive the memo?"

The general shuffles in his seat and whispers with his aide.

The aide nods while accessing a PAD before whispering in the general's ear.

"It appears I have received a memo to that effect with authorization to deploy an Alpha Detachment into Afghanistan. We will be able to land them on-site forty-eight hours after I issue the order, which I will do as soon as this meeting is over. Ms Moss, do you have anyone in mind to run your side of the operation?"

"I do. Mr Anderson has all the right qualifications that make him eminently suitable to act as liaison officer for this case. Glen, please speak to Colonel Booley after the meeting."

Anderson takes a moment to process the news of his new assignment. Colonel Booley is the commanding officer of the Twenty-Fourth Special Tactics Squadron, who operate the suborbital insertion teams.

"Glen, did you hear what I just said?" asks Moss.

"Sorry, I was thinking through the implications of what we're looking at."

"Meeting closed, and, Glen, here's a copy of the RED SLIPPERS file. What are you waiting for? Get a move on." Moss stands up and leaves him to think about all the things he needs to do and worry about all the things that could go wrong.

As career opportunities went, this is one where he doesn't want to drop the ball.

13. TIME TO DIE

We can't all do everything.

— Publius Vergilius Maro

Sergeant Tachikoma
First Combat Armor Suit Reconnaissance Company
Afghanistan
Thursday, July 2, 2071

I send a brief SITREP updating our progress to Captain Johanson, including the incident of me touching the stalagmite-pillar things. Having found the source of the magnetic anomaly, we have achieved our mission parameters.

But it has cost the lives of two members of my platoon. And I feel a mix of sadness and anger. I'm more than a little concerned when I get no return ping.

"Kowalski, take point; Jones, follow him. Rodriguez and Jackson, support them. I'll bring up the rear," I say, hearing the affirmatives confirming my order has been understood.

I put my grief aside, as I need to concentrate on getting the squad back out in one piece and in a timely manner.

Moving back along the tunnels takes all our concentration to scrabble safely while traversing loose rocks. I'm faintly surprised to find we've gotten back to the site of the original ambush without realizing it. Delgado and the others are gone, taking the dead with them.

That's good. It was at least a gesture of respect for those who died. More respect than had been shown by the Chinese when they'd used the dead bodies to bait their trap.

We move on and continue climbing back up the tunnel, which we'd passed through what seems like an eternity ago. The ground is treacherous underfoot. We have to stop every time we come to a spot where the tunnel narrows to remove and then reattach the PACE suits we're carrying. It slows us down.

The desire to scream *move faster* is an attractive urge but one that will not help us in our current situation.

Finally, we get back to Romeo Victor, and I know we're on the home stretch. I try connecting to the captain again but get nothing on the company net.

"Listen up, the transponder net is down, and I'm not picking up anything from the rest of the company. Kowalski, move forward and have a look-see. Everyone else stay here in the cleft," I say, hearing the order acknowledged as he scoots out from the cover of the rocks into the open ground.

Kowalski says, "Sergeant, you've *gotta* see this."

I move past Jones, Jackson, and Ramirez, shocked at what I'm seeing from Kowalski's feed. The ground is strewn with the wreckage of Dogs and Fatties. Captain Johanson's platoon must've been ambushed as it came out of the mountain.

"Jackson, Ramirez, Jones, come out and circle up."

In all likelihood the platoon had charged through the ambush and then been caught by the Chinese backstop squad, who had shot the remaining survivors caught by the surprise attack. We could be faced with the prospect of being overrun by the remaining Fatties waiting to jump us.

Kowalski asks, "What's that smoke over there to our left?"

"Looks like more burning Fatties," I say. Zooming in, I can see the remains of a lone Dog that had taken a last stand against the attackers. Whoever it was had been one hell of a Marine.

"Somebody from Perez's or Beckford's platoons, I guess?" says Kowalski.

"One of Beckford's, judging from where the Dog fell. Look over at the crash site, you can make out the remains of Beckford's platoon. They must've been hit by artillery fire."

Though that rather begged the question of how Perez's platoon had been taken out.

I get through to *Hornet*'s CIC and talk to Colonel Philmore. He confirms that some enemy bright spark had probably disassembled towed artillery pieces and hauled them up into the mountains. They'd preregistered the crash site coordinates and taken out Beckford's and Perez's platoons.

A clever enemy. I make a note to kill them at my earliest convenience.

Not being in the open on the mountainside while waiting for pickup to come seems like a very good idea right about now. The colonel informs me the birds are on the way for us, ETA ninety minutes. The Navy has missiles en route and will bombard the emplaced artillery before the Thunder Hawks arrive. So the extraction should go by the numbers.

"OK, take cover back inside the mountain. Birds Nest says there's enemy artillery zeroed in on this area. We're Oscar Mike."

The squad moves back past the cleft into the mountain as the ground starts shaking beneath our feet.

"Holy crap what's that?" asks Jones.

"Do they have earthquakes in Afghanistan?" asks Jackson.

The mountaintop above erupts, and a wave of blackness envelopes us.

14. ATTACK

Beware of false knowledge; it is more dangerous than ignorance.

— GEORGE BERNARD SHAW

Mr Anderson
CIA Analyst
CSN *Hornet*,
Thursday, July 2, 2071

Anderson is standing next to Colonel Philmore in the muted light of *Hornet*'s CIC listening to the officers talking around him as he watches the feeds from 1st CASR, the First Combat Armored Suit Reconnaissance Company, nicknamed the Hound Dogs. The screen above his head updates the status of the mission, showing the position of the UAV as it passes over the crash site and circles back to head north.

One of the CIC officers speaks. "New picture! Incoming fire detected aimed at crash site Alpha-Bent, designated as Bogey One. Wait one! Correction: two incoming artillery strikes, second designated Bogey Two. First track aimed at the crash site, the second track at targeting Cerberus Three Papa."

The plot on the screen shows the artilleries' trajectories with two thin crimson-red lines, one heading towards the crash site, the other towards the entrance to the caves on the mountain.

"Confirmed: rounds have hit crash site Alpha-Bent, confirming point of launch. Splash on Cerberus Three Papa, second tracking trajectory now being traced," says another CIC officer as two more tracks form on the screen indicating the enemy artillery batteries firing again.

"Hostile ripple on both targets. Lost contact Cerberus Three and Four Papa, Blue-Ceased. I repeat Blue-Ceased. We're blind on both platoons." Reporting the loss of contact with the two platoons who were no longer transmitting any signals.

As the first line of tracks disappears after hitting the ground, a third set of lines indicates more rounds have been launched. The cold, clinical trace of lines on the screens in the CIC means dead Marines on the ground. Anderson knows the ground has turned red from the blood of the dead and the dying, as if crimson rain had fallen on the land.

Colonel Philmore turns to him and speaks. "So much for there being no hostiles on the ground, Mr Anderson."

Anderson feels the icy tones in the man's voice accusing him.

"That's not my fault, Colonel. We developed the best picture we could from the intelligence resources we had."

"It may not be your fault, but those are my Marines dying out there," says Colonel Philmore. "About the only good thing I can say now is that the artillery must have been dragged into the mountains and dug in to have avoided being detected by our surveillance UAV."

"How's that good?"

"It means they're not going to be moving them anytime soon."

Anderson can see the icons on the screen for each of the Dogs has turned from green to red, with text next to each indicating they had been rendered combat ineffective by the enemy fire. The two platoons caught by the artillery barrages are destroyed.

Time seems to stop as his mind races with questions. Who did this and why now? What has agitated the locals so much that they are prepared to use the scarce assets they have, knowing they'll will be destroyed in a counterstrike? Then another platoon comes up on the screen.

He hears the flat monotone of: "Birds Nest, this is Fenris Four, over."

"Solid copy. This is Birds Nest, over," replies Philmore.

Anderson listens as Sergeant Tachikoma updates the colonel on the mission status and reported she'd found the source of the energy pulse. If it wasn't for the horrendous loss of life, the mission would be an unqualified success. The responsibility for losing forty men and women is down to him because he's underestimated the importance of what was hidden under the mountain.

Then the camera aboard the UAV catches the sight of the top of the mountain disintegrating. It has to be from a nuclear explosion. *This can't be happening.* General quarters sounds out over *Hornet*'s tannoy. He's too stunned to say anything as the destruction plays out on the screen.

He slumps down into a chair as misery engulfs him.

15. FORLORN HOPE

Courage is endurance for one moment more…

— Unknown USMC Second Lieutenant

Sergeant Tachikoma
First Combat Armor Suit Reconnaissance Company
Afghanistan
Thursday, July 2, 2071

I wake screaming in pain, with the cockpit lit by the emergency backup light, indicating the main power has failed. My leg is broken, and the pain sweeps over me with the insistence of a sledgehammer.

None of the controls are responding.

There's nothing I can do to restart my Dog's systems. I bang on the cockpit hatch trying to open it and but can't get out. Even if I could open it, I doubt I can climb out with a broken leg. My suit creaks around me. My Dog must be buried under tons of rubble.

The air tastes stale, smells bad, and panic begins building inside me as I bang futilely on the hatch. Then I try to turn on my emergency oxygen reserve, good at best for thirty minutes, but there's no response. Gasping for air as my chest tightens, my pulse rises as my heart starts to race faster, which is only going to kill me sooner.

Don't want to die like this, but today isn't looking so good on the what-I-want front.

Shoten. I focus on the moment, narrowing my awareness to my breathing, and my feeling of panic slowly drains away. Accepting the inevitability of my death, I become calm, because by now the crews of the Thunder Hawks would've found me and dug me out.

I get the emergency kit out from underneath my seat, which I never thought I would have to use. I break open the first syringe, stabbing it in my thigh. The drug starts to take effect as a rush of coldness flows along my leg, and I inject myself with the second dose.

The warning label reads "Do not administer more than one dose every two hours."

I haven't got two hours, and I think about Mom, and how she was when Dad died.

"Sorry, Mom, I didn't mean to upset you like this," I say, knowing I'm going to die alone, fearing my body will never be found and returned home to be buried next to my dad. I start hallucinating, points of light streaming across my vision as I lose consciousness.

16. DÉJÀ VU

*No man ever steps in the same river twice, for it's not the same
river and he's not the same man.*

— HERACLITUS

Sergeant Tachikoma
First Combat Armor Suit Reconnaissance Company
CSN *Hornet*
Thursday, July 2, 2071

I wake disorientated, and my sight is blurred. Shadows move
across my field of vision, and for a moment I wonder where I am.
The last thing I remember is injecting a syringe with painkillers
into my leg in the cockpit of my Dog.

My chest tightens, and the panic of being trapped rushes over
me. I pinch myself to make sure I'm awake and not dreaming I'm
awake. My arm hurts, so I must be awake.

I feel so stupid when my PAD tells me it's 0530 hours,
Thursday, the second of July, 2071.

That was one very vivid nightmare, and I'm compelled to

pinch myself again to reassure myself that I really am awake. My arm still hurts. I've learnt when you're are in pain it means you are alive. Also, in my experience, it's better to not keep reminding yourself that you are alive by causing yourself pain. It's not clever, and it's surely not funny.

Seeing the pictures on the wall are reassuring.

The first runs through a series of Mom in her nurse's uniform standing next to me, taken the last time I was on leave Stateside. Next to it is an older still of me with my dad, taken before my thirteenth birthday, shortly before he died in a car crash. Mom has never remarried.

It has been twelve years since Dad died, and she still hasn't gotten over him. Though she told me she was thinking about dating again the last time we talked. But it would be good for her to move on with her life. She's not getting any younger and complains about being lonely.

Thankfully, I'm never alone, because being in the Marines is like being a member of a very large family. OK, it's often a highly dysfunctional family, but a family all the same. Everyone in my platoon would lay down their life for me and me for them.

You can't beat having family like that, which is one reason why once you're a Marine, you're always a Marine.

Still, that has to be the worst nightmare I can remember ever having. Usually they only happen when I'm suffering from sleep deprivation. The first time I ever dreamed I'd woken up, only to wake up and find I'd been dreaming, happened during my thirteen weeks of recruit training at Parris Island. Our drill instructors used to wake us up in the middle of the night to motivate us.

I can remember having a nightmare where Drill Instructor Swinton was chewing my ass and telling me what a disgrace I was, wearing the uniform of a Marine. This was followed by a few choice, colorful epithets as to my sullying her beloved Marine Corps with my unworthy sorry self. I had then been woken up by Drill Instructor Swinton to face her storm of F-words for real.

She used to scare the hell out of me. But after I completed the Crucible, she smiled, saying, "Well done, Marine." Hearing her say that was the best thing ever.

After I pull myself back into the here and now, I go get washed and dressed, then make my way to breakfast. The servers load my tray with my favorite ham and eggs. They're meant to be sunny-side up, but in the Navy this means a hard yolk, because the Navy says they can't be done sunny-side up and runny. Allegedly we'd all get salmonella poisoning if eggs were ever served undercooked.

We're Marines; we're more likely to die from being on the receiving end of a kinetic penetrator than food poisoning.

While I'm at it, I also grab an orange juice, toast, and an obligatory cup of coffee to kick start the day with. Then I make my way over to sit with my platoon, who've all gotten here earlier than me. How they managed to do so I can't rightly figure. I must be losing my touch, or something.

I'm greeted with a chorus of, "Good morning, Sergeant!"

A space has been left for me to sit opposite the lieutenant, like we always do when we are going out on a mission. It's a Second Platoon tradition. Still, it's a total déjà vu moment as I see everyone is looking at me. This is quite disturbing because they're all sitting in exactly the same places as in my dream.

The weirdness increases as the lieutenant repeats the exact greeting as well.

I reply, "Didn't sleep well, rough night." McCarthy raises an eyebrow at me, so I smile back and shrug at him. But what can I say that won't make me appear odd?

I notice Delgado as she turns to whisper to Hernandez, but miss what she says as Vosloo starts telling the bear in the woods story and everybody laughs. A weird tingling sensation sweeps over me and for a moment I feel like I've fallen down a long tunnel of light.

"You all right, Sergeant?" asks Rodriguez. "You look like you've seen a ghost or something."

"Nah, she always looks like the pale rider," says Jackson. People laugh at the pun.

"Don't mind him, Sergeant, you just need to eat more iron. It will put the color back in your face."

"Rodriguez, stop brown-nosing the sergeant. Want to swap your hash browns for my beans?" asks Jackson.

Rodriguez raises his tray to make the swap. "Hell yeah, beans keep me regular, and it's always good to stay regular, if you know what I mean."

"Let me guess, it's a Navy breakfast, you get more if you both swap?" I say.

Jackson says, "You took the words right out of my mouth, Sergeant."

"See I told you that sergeants know what you're thinking before you think it," says Rodriguez, and they both laugh and high five each other. They shovel the food into their mouths like there is no tomorrow, as Jones sits eating his SOS, ignoring everyone around him.

Rodriguez starts to josh Jones, but I interrupt before Jones can reply. "He likes it because it reminds him of home, doesn't it, Jones?"

The conversation unfolds around me, and I marvel at knowing what they're going to say before they open their mouths to speak. It's also obvious that Delgado is going to need to change her tack if she wants to get anywhere with Jones.

"So we can see," says Rodriguez. "You like all the gyrenes, Delgado, don't you?"

Which makes her blush, and I relax as the exchange goes off script.

Then, as if on cue, Jones asks, "What's a gyrene?"

Lance Corporal Kowalski, sitting next to Jones, butts in. "We're gyrenes, Jones."

And then Corporal Knight cuts in after him, going through the whole "gyrenes are the Spam in the can" spiel.

I'm seriously starting to think I'm going nuts. I take a mouthful of OJ and force myself to eat. My ham and eggs has managed to turn into a less-than-nourishing-looking mess on my plate. As I chew my food, my platoon joshes each other, replaying the scene in my dream word for word.

I must be losing the plot with every day seeming like every other day on board the ship. I tell myself it's the sucky feeling from doing the same old thing each day, and I'm not going stir-crazy from being cooped up inside a tin can.

Having finished eating, not really having tasted the food going down, I swig the last of my coffee. A cup of strong, thick black Navy Joe. I'm grateful for the jolt it gives me, which brings me back to reality.

At 0800 I walk into the briefing room with McCarthy and take my seat. Then it's déjà vu all over again seeing Perez and Thompson having already snagged the best spot in the room. I sit and watch the exact same events unfold, but I notice more. Little things like how much pleasure Gunnery Sergeant Locklear takes in calling out, "Officer on deck!"

When Captain Johanson enters, I instantly recognize the man beside him. Johanson signals the start of the meeting as my heart pounds in my chest.

"Lieutenant, have we met this guy before?" I whisper to McCarthy, who grunts back a negative.

I stare at the man, whom I've never met yet already know.

Johanson goes through the briefing with my colleagues around me listening intently to what's being said. Anderson starts to ramble on, explaining what our CIA-sanctioned operation entails. My chest tightens, and my hands begin to sweat as I realize I've heard this all before.

This must be what going crazy feels like.

Again Johanson follows news of Mr Anderson's black op's fiasco by telling us how this mission is to proceed. He gives us orders on how he wants us to deploy. I still can't imagine that the Pakistani government are pleased with us flying through their airspace though.

This can't be happening to me.

I pinch myself again to make sure I'm not dreaming, but sure enough, it hurts. So, if I'm not dreaming, what's going on? Then I weigh up my options, and none of them appear very good for my long-term career prospects. Keep calm and carry on. If I wait and see what happens next, perhaps I will learn something.

The alternative is to go and see the shrink and be certified as insane.

Johanson brings up the latest weather forecast for the area, and it's a perfect day for flying into trouble. Whatever the reason why this is happening, the only thing I can do is try to make a difference.

Johanson asks if there are any questions. It's in that moment I think perhaps I'm here to change what happened to us during my dream.

I speak up, "Sir, what about load-out requirements?"

"What about them, Sergeant Tachikoma?"

"Sir, Mr Anderson told us the local warlord is somehow involved with what's going on at the mountain. I inferred several of them have met in this area. It seems to me this might be an indicator of local cooperation. If so, they might be planning an offensive, which would mean they'd want to build up their assets in this area. This could mean our force is facing heavy-weapon systems."

"Mr Anderson, what's your opinion of Sergeant Tachikoma's points?"

"All I can say is we've not spotted any movement of military forces, other than the usual trucks with men. However, given the history of the area, I would expect the locals to react negatively to your presence."

"Marines are used to negative receptions, Mr Anderson," says Johanson.

"Sir, if we go for a mixed load-out for the deployment, we can have First and Second Platoons armed for speed, with Third and Fourth Platoons loaded out with a mix of indirect fire support and anti-armor options. This gives us a more flexible force with which to respond to any increase in local force concentration. I've downloaded my suggested weapons mix to the system, sir."

"Looks like you've given this some thought, Sergeant. Anything else you would like to add?"

"I suggest we drop Fourth Platoon closer to the crash site with the rest of the company closer to the mountain. Also, it would be useful to task the UAV to circle north of its present holding pattern. We can use it to check out the reverse slopes of those mountains within eight kilometers of the crash site."

"So you expect us to come under fire from artillery then, Sergeant?"

"Yes, sir, I do. I think there's a high chance of that happening. And it's also likely we will be facing armored forces too, sir."

"And all this is based on what exactly?"

Ah, the what-do-I-tell-him-now moment.

"It's my opinion we're heading into an ambush, sir. I'd want to capitalize on an enemy trying to retrieve their forces after an operation had gone wrong. It's what I would do if an enemy came into my zone of control, sir."

"So I see, I'm glad they don't have you on their side, Sergeant."

Several people laugh at Johanson's comment.

You wouldn't be laughing if you knew what I felt. But I could hardly tell them I'd dreamed that I'd lived through this day already. Because then they would really laugh at me or, worse, think I'm insane.

"Right, I've authorized Sergeant Tachikoma's suggestion. If nothing else, it will be good practice for Third and Fourth Platoons to deploy with heavy-weapon packs. Sergeant, please come and see me in my office in fifteen. Meeting dismissed."

At least my suggestions for arming the Third and Fourth Platoons with support weapons had been agreed to by Captain Johanson, but I wonder why I'm being called to his office now?

Both Washington and Thompson mouth I owe them one as we leave the room, while Lieutenants Perez and Beckford look less than impressed by the extra preparation my suggestions will entail.

I take a minute to ask Corporal Knight to keep an eye on Bravo Squad until I get back from meeting with the skipper. On my way there Lieutenant McCarthy catches me in the gangway and tells me he is most impressed by my performance. He'd be less impressed if he knew why I'd said what I had.

Captain Johanson's office is the size of a broom closet, one deck below the hangar bay in the aft of the ship. I stand outside in the gangway, quickly checking that my appearance is satisfactory. At the designated time, I rap on the hatch and announce my presence.

Then I hear, "Come in, Sergeant." I enter the room to see Johanson sitting at his work screen.

"At ease, Sergeant Tachikoma."

"Thank you, sir."

"That was quite some performance, Sergeant. So tell me what made you speak out like that?"

"It was a gut feeling, sir."

"Some gut you've got there, Sergeant. I've been reviewing your permanent record. You originally enlisted with the Navy as an officer candidate but had some trouble in a brawl, which led you to us."

He pauses as he reads through the incident. "However, your performance since has been exemplary. I see I've rated you as an excellent NCO who would make a good candidate for officer training. So I want to ask you again, will you consider accepting a commission to become an officer?"

"Sir, as I said at the time, I'm very happy in my role as an NCO." I'm realizing what my being summoned was all about.

"It's not just about being happy, Sergeant, it's about stepping up to the plate when called. I think that you find it very comfortable being an NCO, but it's time to move out of your comfort zone. Where do you see your career with the Marines heading?"

"Not given it much thought, sir."

"Well, I would like you to. After your performance at the briefing, I would like you to consider it an order, Sergeant Tachikoma."

"Yes, sir!" I said because there isn't a lot else I could say in this situation.

Oh joy, I get high enough up the chain of command to have some real authority only to find myself facing the prospect of sliding back down the pecking order again. The idea of having to reverse rolls and start again as a junior officer is not all that appealing. I wonder if I could keep my sergeant insignia in case I needed to motivate some grab-ass short-timer?

"One last thing, Sergeant, why do you think we'll be ambushed?"

I've gotten to the end of the meeting without looking like a crazy woman, and he goes and asks the one question that will guarantee it.

"I dreamed about it, sir."

"Just like the dreams Lieutenant Backsight Forethought had in *The Defence of Duffer's Drift* then, Sergeant?" he replies, referring to one of the recommended books the Marine Corps makes all its junior NCOs read, which gives me a way out.

"Yes, sir."

"When we get back I'll put a recommendation in for your commission."

I remember reading the book back when I made lance corporal. It's about a young lieutenant who has to stop the enemy from crossing a river ford. The book is how he goes about following his orders. Each time he thinks he has gotten it right, he has a dream where he finds out the errors in his plan. Then he gets to go through the same day over again, doing things differently, until he gets his plan to work.

Certainly dreaming about the mission the night before was interesting, but I hope I don't get to experience my nightmare again anytime soon.

Still it could be worse, I could be actually dead.

———

In the kennels my company is busy prepping their Dogs, changing their weapon load-outs. So I run through the CASE-2X checklist while I go over a plan of what to do in my head.

After finishing I have time to spare and walk over to talk to Sergeant Thompson from Third and Staff Sergeant Washington from Fourth Platoon. They've finished talking to their respective lieutenants, who are both in the last phase of checking their Dogs.

"Hey, Tachikoma, you come to smirk at giving us all this extra prep to do?" asks Thompson, who seems like he's about ready to start an argument with me.

"I thought I'd come and see you do some work for once." I grin at him.

"Hey, cut the woman some slack, Thompson," says Washington.

"Seriously, sorry to give you guys extra prep and all. But better to have stuff you don't need than need stuff you don't have. Trust me when I tell you, I've a feeling you guys will need to be loaded for bear on this mission."

"Well, next time your gut tells you something, Tachikoma, why don't you volunteer your scrawny ass for the job? At least you've got a first lieutenant leading your platoon."

"Hey, who made you in charge here?" says Washington, interrupting Thompson. "It's not like you're having to hump the extra gear yourself. Besides, it was Captain Johanson who gave us our marching orders. Seriously, Tachikoma, what's up? It's not like you to be jittery."

"I can't rightly explain but I had this dream, and everything in the dream seemed really, really real."

"Do you remember this conversation in your dream then?" Thompson asks.

"No, I don't, which is a good thing. In my dream we all died."

"That's some bad dream to be having just before a mission," says Washington.

"Ain't it just?" I say. "But I'd rather look silly about having a bad dream, than have it come true. Our combat armor has pretty impressive protection, but once a round gets inside it's not a pretty sight."

"That's pretty morbid, Tachikoma," says Thompson.

"I don't think it takes much imagination, Thompson, to know what happens when a round penetrates a suit and rattles around inside."

"You're as bad as she is, Washington. You both trying to spook me before the mission?"

"It's so easy," I say.

"Remind me why I took you under my wing?" Thompson asks.

"For my stunning wit and repartee."

"Dream on, woman. More like redheads are dangerous," says Washington.

"Because red is the same color the inside of a Dog becomes when everything is turned into chunky salsa? Could be worse though. Imagine flame grill specials if the Dog's fuel is ignited," I say.

"You're right, Thompson, she does have a morbid imagination."

"It's her special skill."

"Don't encourage her."

"Listen to him, I'm on a roll here. Anyway, it's more likely your ordnance will cook off."

"Still ever the optimist, Tachikoma."

"Seriously? You both need to get out more. At least if the ammunition explodes, it takes place outside the suit. And your Dog will protect you from the overpressure."

"You've taught her well, Thompson."

"Why, thank you, Staff Sergeant Washington."

"If you two bozos have finished ragging on my sorry ass, all I'm trying to do is make sure everyone gets back alive. Better to listen to my gut telling me something bad is going to happen and be prepared for the worst, than the alternatives."

"I agree you're *trying*," says Thompson, smirking at me.

"So how's it going?"

Washington replies, "We looked at your suggestions and chose to go with an M21-A8 Gauss rifle for both squads of Third and Fourth Platoons. This will give us four heavy shooters in case the locals decide to deploy any tanks."

"Of course this means they'll be relying on their buddies to carry the extra powerpacks to keep them going," says Thompson, stating the obvious.

"Yeah, and...?"

"I decided we ought to add missile packs to the other Dogs in the squads. And we've decided that we need some GECALs with grenade launchers as well," says Thompson.

"Let me guess: you've both gone for those on your Dogs?"

"You got it in one. What's not to love about some fifty cal rotary cannon action backed up by being able to pop some grenades?"

"If I may interrupt you two in your mutual appreciation of all things rotary for a moment," says Washington, "we decided to arm both the lieutenants with an antitank missile launcher to make them feel special."

Then Thompson cuts in, "It might keep them out of trouble for a little while longer too. Meanwhile we've fitted one Dog in each squad with a heavy-indirect-fire missile pack."

"Sounds like a plan to me." I grin as I say, "Are you sure you've got enough firepower?"

The heavy-indirect-fire missile packs are a bitch to carry on a Dog but pack one hell of a punch and are able to saturate an area with high-explosive rounds.

"Sure as we can be, given that we're going to all this effort based on a gut feeling from you dreaming about stuff that hasn't happened yet," says Thompson, giving me a stare with one eye pulled down by his finger.

"Besides, we all love it when a plan comes together," says Washington. "And whatever the reason, going in prepared to face the worst is better than going in unprepared. I wish I'd thought of your suggestions."

"Yeah, me too, but don't let it go to your head, Tachikoma," says Thompson.

I wish them good luck, reassured to know I've done my best, as I leave them and go finish prepping my Dog. After talking to Lieutenant McCarthy again, I get into my cockpit. The rest of my platoon are being processed by the hangar crew, who are closing the lids on their Dogs.

Then it's my turn. My screens become my window on the world as the hangar crew slides the Dogs into the waiting birds.

My Dog shudders slightly as the elevator takes us up to the flight deck where we wait for the deck crew to finish the FOD check prior to launch. Time passes soon enough, the pilots open up the throttles, and our birds leave *Hornet* behind.

As we level off for the four-and-a-bit-hour cruise to our destination, I check on my squad again to pass the time.

People are recording those in-case-I-don't-come-back letters on their PADs. Since I had dreamed this mission was going to get real serious, and the chances are I won't make it back, I decide to record a letter to Mom. It will be uploaded into the bird's system, tagged for release if I'm reported as dead.

A morbid thought that causes me to become hot all over as I tell her I love her. I tell her I chose to do what I am doing, and it wasn't her fault I died.

Private Jones interrupts my thoughts and asks what's happened to the Army team. I change tack with my answer, asking him what he thinks.

He replies, "They're Snake Eaters, Sergeant. Who knows what they think? I guess if it were us who had screwed the pooch, we wouldn't want to ask the Army to come and save us."

Uncannily like the answer I gave him in my dream. "Good answer, Jones. Remember, the Army likes to stick to the schedule like clockwork. So if the mission timetable says they stay out for the whole week, they do. Marines, once we've done the job, we move on to the next one." I see Jones nod.

"Thanks, Sergeant."

Still, it kind of assumes the plan had gone by the numbers for the Army, which according to the spook, it hadn't. I doze off, tired from the stress of what has happened so far today. No point in wasting an opportunity to catch some Zs.

17. MELMASTIA

The best weapon against an enemy is another enemy.

— FRIEDRICH NIETZSCHE

Shàngwèi Looi
Commander Special Operations Force Falcon
Democratic People's Republic of China
The White Mountain, Afghanistan
Wednesday, July 1, 2071

Looi and his company had been invited to eat with the warlord's men. Zhongzhi Wú had conveyed the invitation to him and also noted that to refuse the Afghan's offer of hospitality would be seen as a grave insult. He'd thanked his sergeant for the advice and made arrangements to secure the unit's kuijia out of sight with a *bán* of men to guard them. Not that he expected any trouble, but his command was not inside a secure perimeter, and protecting his assets was both good military practice and prudent.

The warlord Yeshua bin Yussuf greets him. "As-salaamu 'alaykum."

Looi uses the reply Zhongzhi Wú had coached him to say. "Wa 'alaykum salaam."

He wonders at the irony of the exchange wishing peace to his host in a time and place where peace is in such short supply.

Once they've exchanged greetings, Yeshua bin Yussuf introduces his three senior leftenants: Abdi-al-Hazred, a wiry man who he judges to be about the same age as the warlord; Abdul-Baser, a stocky man with a patch over his left eye; and Churagh-Ali, who glares at Looi and his people before forcing himself to smile as the warlord says something Looi doesn't quite catch.

After the introductions, his lieutenants and his men find themselves sitting around a fire in a large cavern.

A chill goes down his spine from a draft of cold air as the sparks from the fire waft towards the holes in the ceiling, and above he can see the night's stars twinkling overhead. Some of those stars are man-made, but there is nothing here to draw any unwanted attention from prying eyes. Everyone is electronically black, and the area had been swept.

He now has to enjoy his host's hospitality before they could discuss his more pressing concerns, the arrival of more Americans.

"Are you enjoying the food, Captain?" asks Yeshua bin Yussuf's senior leftenant, Abdi-al-Hazred, in broken English.

It takes him a few moments to parse the meaning before he can reply. "Aywa jayyid, jiddan shukran."

The man smiles at him, which he takes as meaning he hadn't mangled his reply.

Yeshua bin Yussuf speaks to him in his impeccable English. "Thank you, Shàngwèi Looi, for your respect and kindness in replying to my leftenant. It's not often he gets to practice his English on others, apart from me." He then turns and speaks to his leftenant. "Yak team wahed."

"Laa afham. Laa atakallam 'arabi jayyidan," Looi replies,

apologizing that his Arabic is not good enough to understand what is being said.

"Ah, that is because I was speaking to him in Dari, Captain Looi," says Yeshua bin Yussuf as Abdi-al-Hazred sneezes. "Afiat bashad."

"How many languages do you speak?"

"Just four. As we say, one language is never enough, yawa zhaba heskla bus nada," he says, laughing with his men. "Most of my people speak Pashto as their first language, apart from Abdi, for whom it's his third language."

"It must make things difficult at times."

"Masha Allah, as Allah has willed, so it is." Yeshua bin Yussuf's followers make gestures and repeat "Allahu Ahkbar" in reply.

Looi holds a piece of bread in his right hand to scoop up some of the food in front of him and starts to chew. The Afghans sitting with them start to eat as well. They may live like medieval peasants, but these men aren't ignorant, nor stupid for that matter, and he needs their help.

Looking back at the progress of the mission, over the days there'd been one setback followed by another that started with the delay in setting off. All of which had been beyond his control after they'd discovered that almost half of the civilian trucks they'd been given were not fit for purpose.

"Law samaht, mihtaaj musaa`da law samaht." *I need your help*, he asks.

"Laa afham, we have helped you. What more do you require of us? Have I not given you melmastia? Is everything not as it should be?"

Laa afham exactly described the lack of understanding between them. "The Americans are coming, and my command cannot stop them from taking control of the White Mountain without your support."

The warlord speaks with his leftenants, explaining to them, Looi imagines, what he'd just said. The exchange is voluble and fast, far beyond his meagre means to follow.

Zhongzhi Wú acknowledges the conversation with a silent nod and shrug. The sergeant had been tasked with learning the local language and customs but is clearly as lost as he is in understanding the mores of these people.

"Nì jìng chuu rén cái." *Adversity makes a man wise, not rich.* Looi turns and speaks to Shàowèi Wang sitting next to him. "What do you make of the warlord?"

Shàowèi Wang rubs his finger on his jaw, which juts forward. "Bú shàn shi zhe bù shàn zhong." He agrees, *A bad beginning does indeed make for a bad ending.*

When he'd decided to split his force into two, he'd chosen to send Wang ahead in the working trucks while his men got the rest serviceable. The lieutenant's pái kuijia had faced a challenging problem of preventing the American Special Forces team from achieving their mission.

By a stroke of good fortune, the American space-plane had crashed on landing. This accident had both reduced their numbers and delayed their deployment. Wang had made the most of this opportunity to catch up and eliminate the American force before they could transmit any data they'd recorded.

But it had cost men's lives, two dead and two seriously wounded, with two others unable to operate their suits until their injuries healed.

That was the good news. The bad news was that they were still waiting for the bomb to arrive. He'd been promised it would arrive two days ago, and now he's been told it would arrive tomorrow. No time as to when, just that it was on its way, delayed in transit and will arrive tomorrow.

Looi wishes he could believe that.

Shàowèi Wang speaks. "Feeng wú cháng shùn, biing wú

cháng shèng." *A boat can't always sail with the wind.* An old proverb to be prepared for difficulties and setbacks. "The man is a formidable force in this region; he's integrated tribes who think of him as the Mahdi even though he denies that he is. He's very secure and won't be easily swayed, Shàngwèi."

When did the young shàowèi become so wise? The loss of his men during the fighting here had obviously tempered him.

Looi remembers reading in *The Art of War* about considering the terrain an army had to cross. Sun Tzu said this was the third most important factor to consider when planning for war. The enemy in this case hadn't been the Americans, but the time it took for them to drive here.

"La hawla wala quwata illah billah," says Yeshua bin Yussuf interrupting his thoughts. "So, Captain Looi, what more do you want from me and my followers?"

"Use of your tanks and artillery, which we could use to fight the Americans. The Americans will send in Marines in heavier combat armor than ours. Without your support we will be unable to stop them from taking control of the mountains and the pillars of fear."

The cavern becomes silent as he speaks, his men listening to what he says. The Afghans pick up on the tension and now listen to what their leader is about to say in reply.

"Precious commodities that I can ill afford to lose, Captain. What do you offer in return?"

"What do you need?"

The warlord grins and turns to his men and jabbers away at them. An exchange taks place with more gestures and exclamations of "Allahu Ahkbar" from amidst the warlord's followers.

Abdi-al-Hazred speaks. "In bimani ast!"

Looi looks at the warlord, who replies, "Kaan suu' tafaahom. Sorry there's been a misunderstanding, Captain. Our tanks are not here, and we only have limited ammunition for our artillery."

"But you have ammunition for them?"

"We do, but only four shells for each piece, and I'm reluctant to use them, as we haven't been able to find more. It's a subject of some embarrassment to me, ana aasif."

He hopes that the expression of being sorry means he has a good position to bargain from. "What if we were able to replace the ammunition you used, would that be sufficient to guarantee your help when the Americans come?"

The warlord speaks to his leftenants before replying. "We would be left without the means to defend ourselves until your supplies came. That would make us vulnerable. We would want guarantees too."

"I understand, I can promise you this on my own authority. It would be a matter of arranging for a third party to deliver the shells to you. It will happen if I say so."

"I believe that you are a man of your word, Captain, and can even understand that this is a matter of little import for you or your masters, but I will want six shells for every one we fire."

Looi blanches inside. Resupplying the warlord is one thing; increasing his stocks would empower the man, unbalancing the stability in the region.

"Two for one sounds fairer to me," he replies, hoping he's judged the situation correctly.

Churagh-Ali speaks. "Hal tazon anani ghabi?"

"Kaan suu' tafaahom," says the warlord to his leftenant, smiling. "Four for one would be a fairer deal, Captain."

"Ghayr maqbuul," says Churagh-Ali, the anger in his voice obvious to all who hear him speak.

"Kha sehat walary," says the warlord, raising his glass in a toast. "Khub'ast, yak team wahed."

Looi knows he has the man's agreement. "Three for one, my final offer."

"Done, and well bargained too," the warlord replies, holding out his hand to shake on the deal, which surprises Looi. Churagh-Ali scowls at him.

"Khub'ast. Yak team wahed," says Abdi-al-Hazred.

"We will work together as one. My Disciples will rain steel death upon the American shayateen for you."

Looi knows that when they are gone the Afghans will call him and his men shayateen too.

The enemy of his enemy didn't make them friends, but a bombardment from the warlord's so-called Disciples, ancient Russian-made artillery, will still do the job well enough when the Americans send the inevitable retrieval force. Americans are, if nothing else, predictable when it comes to such matters.

Having access to artillery will allow him to secure the success of the operation.

"I will order Shàowèi Li and Zhongzhi Suun to liaise with your artillery crews."

"As you wish, Captain, but I thought we would be working with Leftenant Wang and Sergeant Wú, who we've gotten to know over their last few days with us."

"I have other plans for them, sorry."

"No apology needed, Captain, I understand the need to make the best use of one's trusted people."

Now he has to trust the people above him in his chain of command to deliver on their promises.

There are no doubts about getting the shells for the artillery because it isn't time critical for the success of the plans. But the decision by the Ministry of State Security Intelligence to provide them with a Russian-made nuclear weapon via a third party could put their mission in jeopardy.

Given what he now knows, courtesy of the delay in setting

off, the Americans cannot be allowed to challenge China's lead in studying the pillars of fear that promised new worlds for the taking. However, if the Americans are able to land before he's able to plant the device, then he risks losing his force.

Looi knows nobody will be sent to retrieve their bodies. It would be considered a loss of face to his government to admit his men were ever here.

18. A DIFFERENT WAY

Observe, orient, decide, and act.

— Col John R. Boyd, USAF

Sergeant Tachikoma
First Combat Armor Suit Reconnaissance Company
Afghanistan
Thursday, July 2, 2071

I wake a few minutes before the Chicken's crew chief gives us the ten-mike drop warning. The telltales for the platoon are green across the board as the ramp opens. The wind whines past the rear as the deployment rails are extended.

A few moments later we're shot out of the rear of our bird. My restraining harness pulls me back tight in my seat to protect me. The terrain slides past with my sled grinding along the ground, with the rest of the platoon following suit behind.

Above us our Chickens turn one after another and head back towards *Hornet*. Then I call out over the squad net, "Sound off," as the bolts on the chute and the sled blow. The chute immediately begins to disintegrate, dispersing in the wind.

I hear affirmatives from my squad and check to see if the other half of the platoon is in the clear too. Everything's five by five.

"All Fenris Dogs, turn on your ChameleonFlage now. Let's not be seen, people, over," I say as I wait for the lieutenants to confirm their platoons' successful deployment to the captain.

Third Platoon had been dropped close to the site of the crashed space-plane as per my suggestion. The rest of the company has dropped a couple of kilometers away from them, closer to what passes for a road in these parts. The coordinates for our destination are up on the HUD. Captain Johanson orders us to sit and scan the area around us for any signs of hostiles waiting to give us a hot reception.

If I'd been waiting here to ambush us, I would've shot the living crap out of us during the drop. I wonder why they hadn't done so in my dream. Oddly, this thought is reassuring.

The officers conflab for ten minutes to confirm our bearings and check the UAV feeds before the platoons start moving.

We walk across the treacherous loose rock towards the road where we convert into glide mode exposing the tracks, and we start rolling along the road making our way towards the mountain. It's 1600 and we're running right on schedule as we get to the edge of the mountain. Here we must stand up and walk the rest of the way in a line to traverse the narrow path leading upwards.

Uncannily, as in my dream, Sergeant Ramirez finds an entrance to a cave. It's way too small for our Dogs to enter. So we keep moving forward and try to find another way into the mountain.

A short while later, we do, and a sense of dread comes over me. We're in front of the same three-meter-wide cleft that leads inside the mountain. A shiver of fear runs down my spine.

Standing near Lieutenant McCarthy, I talk to him over the laser-net. "Sir, would I be right in thinking you're going to suggest to the captain we use our remote sensors as a transceiver net to map the inside of the mountain?"

"If I didn't know better, Sergeant, I would suspect you were either hacking my system or reading my mind. How did you know I was going to suggest that?"

"Sir, I didn't get to be sergeant on account of my good looks. It was more of a thought that dropping one outside here would keep a line of communication open to the rest of the company, sir."

"It's a good idea, Sergeant. I'll tell the captain."

No doubt he'll also say it was my suggestion, and I feel really bad that I would get the credit for the idea. Somehow it seems wrong to be taking advantage of something that happened in my dream. I'm making myself appear better than I really am. It doesn't sit right with me.

The captain orders a transceiver beacon dropped where the cleft opens up. Johanson then sends a test text message to Third and Fourth Platoons. A short while later a reply comes back.

The transceivers aren't designed to maintain real-time communications. Not enough bandwidth. However, they can be used to pass short messages along and maintain a low-signal signature when observing an enemy position.

The two platoons leave the daylight as we walk past the cleft and into the passageway and darkness.

Then another moment of déjà vu happens as Private Lopez says over the company laser-net conference channel, "Good-for-nothing spooks should've sent a MARPACE Force Recon team."

Followed by Sergeant Ramirez saying, "Lopez, we don't have all day to wait on you to get your sorry ass into gear. Move it, Marine."

My dream is coming to life as we see two passageways

leading out from the first cavern. So now the captain has to make a choice. Predictably he splits the party into two to search both routes simultaneously.

I remind myself that dreaming this happened before doesn't mean anything. It's SOP for a recon company.

But parts of the day are unfolding differently. Still it spooks me by how much it feels like I'm repeating the same events. A loud chorus of "OoRahs" break me out of my fugue. I rationalize my misgivings and reassure myself I'm not reliving my dream as something I don't remember happens.

"OK, you heard the captain, Oscar Mike, let's move it, Marines. Time to get this show on the road," says Gunnery Sergeant Locklear.

First Platoon moves down the left-hand tunnel while we head down the right.

Our tunnel leads us deeper into the mountain. The mountain I dreamed would collapse on top of us. The weight of the rock hanging over us seems to be pressing down on me. Then an image of being crushed under the weight of the roof as it caves in on me flashes into my head.

All of a sudden I'm frightened, distracted by the idea of being trapped inside my Dog. I lose my footing as my Dog's foot catches on a protrusion, which knocks a bit of rock loose. The jolt brings my attention back to what I'm supposed to be doing.

I bring my Dog to a halt and take a moment to adjust my machine's orientation. The tunnel is asymmetrical, and I turn sideways to make the most use of the limited room and avoid hitting any more bits of rock that are jutting out from the walls around me.

This mission is turning into my worst nightmare. I push the cheery thought out of my mind. Now would not be a good time to kick back and take things easy, so I take a moment to pause and check on my people's readouts.

It's reassuring to find everything looks good, as in, we're all alive. Though this is not a permanent state of surety given the nature of any mission in hostile territory.

Lieutenant McCarthy orders Corporal Knight to take point for Alpha Squad. Meanwhile, I order Lance Corporal Kowalski to take point for us. I'm bringing up the rear as we follow the route leading us into the heart of the mountain.

I keep popping up transceivers on the ceiling as we progress deeper inside the mountain, repeating my actions in the dream, which is making the day more spooky with each passing minute. Private Lopez's comments take my mind off my dream.

If we do meet the Chinese Fatties, then we're far better off being in our Dogs than the Army Alpha Detachment would've been in their PACE suits. By comparison they would've been torn apart by the Fatties' guns if the Chinese had given them so much as a hard stare.

My train of thought is interrupted by Lieutenant McCarthy telling me to take my squad right. That's my cue to change events.

"Wait one. Can I make a suggestion that you take the right-hand route?"

"Got a reason there, Sergeant?"

"Just a gut feeling that it would be better for you to go right, and I'll go left, sir."

"Humph, well if it will make you happy, Sergeant, we'll do that."

I call my squad to a halt and reorganize our line of march at the junction.

I take point with Jones behind me and Kowalski to bring up the rear. I get him to take over the job of planting the transceivers.

We move through the tunnel until an opening appears. This leads into a large cavern.

Like the one I'd seen in my dream.

Time to find out if I'm really stupid, crazy, or even both. I crawl along the floor to the cavern entrance as quietly as I can with the rest of the squad following behind me. When I reach the ridgeline I pop up the sensor mast on my Dog's left shoulder, peep into the cavern, and wait.

The scan shows eight Chinese ATSs hiding in ambush.

No doubt they've picked up our advance along the tunnel from the noise we made. I can only hope they haven't realized we know they're there waiting for us. Ahead are the six PACE suits left in the open as bait.

I'm shaking as I realize I really am reliving yesterday all over again. Up to now I could pass everything that has happened today as a dream, or at least make myself believe it was a figment of my imagination. But I can't for the life of me see how I could've dreamed this situation up in my wildest nightmares.

I take a deep breath and let it go; whatever's happening to me will have to wait until later. I don't want to die here today, so I need to come up with a plan.

The lieutenant messages me that his squad has come to a dead end and he will make his way back to rendezvous with us. I message him back about finding the PACE suits and the ambush that had been set to greet us, and I tell him we will wait for his arrival. He sends back a confirmation, and I set about bringing my squad up to speed by downloading the data from my scan.

This has to be done securely—so I turn to Jones and touch the shoulder of his Dog. Over the connection I download the image files, and the target designation order, with the instruction to pass this along to all the Dogs by hard link.

When the lieutenant catches up with my squad he will get the download too. Hopefully he'll follow the suggestions I've given him and pass them on to his squad before coming to join me. Fortunately, when Lieutenant McCarthy arrives he's done exactly what I've asked. He comes alongside me to join the assault stack.

Over the hard link, McCarthy asks, "Where are we with the plan?"

"Stacked and packed, ready to take the Fatties down, sir. Kowalski and Jones will go left, followed by Jackson and Rodriguez going right. I'll take center with you, sir. We'll be followed in by Knight and Hernandez, who'll go left, with Delgado and Vosloo bringing up the rear and going right, sir."

"Outstanding plan, Sergeant. Anyone would think you had done this before," he says, sending the order to the platoon confirming my plan. "Let's do this."

We start our assault and catch the Chinese by surprise.

They've held their fire, waiting for us to enter the kill zone, but we're inside their decision cycle, and our heavier Dogs outclass their Fatties.

We hit them, and we hit them hard.

The cavern is filled with exploding ordnance cooking off. The overpressure from the back blasts causes my Dog to start skidding across the cavern floor. As I fall, I continue firing as the last Fatty tries to escape by exiting the cavern through a tunnel at the rear. I fire a short burst from my autocannon, ripping the Fatty open, killing the pilot.

Despite finding myself lying on the ground, I think that went well all things considered.

"Sound off, people," I say.

Everyone but McCarthy and Knight report in.

"What's happened to McCarthy and Knight?" I ask, rolling my Dog over onto its face to stand up.

"They're both down, Sergeant. They were hit during the assault," says Jones, pointing behind me.

From where I stand I can see McCarthy's Dog had been

caught in crossfire. Three Chinese Fatties had been able to move in close before they were taken down. His armor has been breached.

Then I check his suit's telemetry, replaying the last two minutes to find out how he died. It's not a pretty sight when armor-piercing rounds ricochet around inside a suit. What I see only goes to prove the adage that suits are only bulletproof from the inside.

"Sergeant, it's Delgado, I'm with Corporal Knight. His suit is KO, but he's alive."

I go over to her. Corporal Knight's Dog has taken a real beating and lost a leg in the firefight. Knight himself has been knocked out, which is some good/bad news—better than being dead.

"Hernandez, Vosloo, and Delgado, stay here. Delgado, get Knight's Dog working again, strip the lieutenant's machine for parts. Hernandez, I want you to pull what you can from the remains of our Chinese friends' Fatties, and find out what they're doing here. Vosloo, go see what you can pull from the PACE suits. I suspect they've been stripped already, but you never know, we may get lucky. Then retrieve our dead."

I hear three sets of "aye, ayes" in reply as I send a message to the captain. His reply confirms I'm to take command and continue with the mission. I give my people the heads-up on Johanson's orders, and then I lead the way into the tunnel the Fatty had tried to use to escape.

I've been able to change some things that happened, so this isn't a dream, but something else. My best bet is to try to make the most of whatever *it* is.

Finally, we get to the part where the tunnel starts widening before it opens out into another cavern. I can see the light from the pillars' opening, which cuts off as we approach. I bring my squad to a halt and give the order for them to peel off to the left and right as we enter. On my signal the Dogs work their way round and out from the entrance.

"Fan out, people, and let's make like we have a purpose. The Corps is not paying us by the hour, let's move it."

For a moment I see all my people as mindless automatons going through the same motions as before. Every action they've taken is predictable, the result of causes and effects determined from the moment of the Big Bang. I try to remember something I learnt about causality and free will in a psychology class, but the thoughts elude me.

The squad creeps slowly across the unchanging treachery of the floor.

Then I wait for Jones to speak. On cue he says, breaking the silence, "This reminds me of the time I went caving in Wales as a kid."

"Any more insights you want to say out loud, Private?"

"No excuse. Sorry, it won't happen again, Sergeant."

Our Dogs move through the cavern taking up a rough arrowhead formation as we advance. There's a faint glow on my screen ahead from where the magnetic energy pulse spikes are coming.

"OK, looks like we've found it. So let's go and check it out," I say, as I remember the thought.

If everything we do is the result of an endless chain of causality, everything is determined. If this isn't the case, then everything we do is random. I put the idea aside to concentrate on the task at hand.

Ahead of us stand the two pillars of rock, and my squad follows me as I go towards them.

"Squad, three-sixty and roger up," I say, ordering them to get into a circular defensive position and sound off.

One of the Army PACE suits is, like it was before, full of putrefied person. My squad sounds off. I text a message to the captain, and as I get the same answer back, a wave of coldness flows over me in my Dog.

"The captain wants us to scan the area for anything the Army Snake Eaters might've dropped around here. So start searching."

19. A WALK INTO DARKNESS

Although the whole of this life were said to be nothing but a dream and the physical world nothing but a phantasm, I should call this dream or phantasm real enough, if, using reason well, we were never deceived by it.

— GOTTFRIED WILHELM VON LEIBNIZ

Sergeant Tachikoma
First Combat Armor Suit Reconnaissance Company
Afghanistan
Thursday, July 2, 2071

My squad spreads out and starts scanning the ground while I walk to stand beside the Army PACE suit. Then I wait for the pillars to activate. I notice a slight shimmer in the air as it happens, and then there's a different world before me. A snow covered plain stretches out ahead, and in the far distance stand the twin fingers of another set of pillars. Black against the whiteness, beckoning to me.

On my screen the faces of my Marines show their fear. But

strangely I feel the opposite, as if I'm being drawn to walk through. After I step across to the other world, I hear someone in my squad saying, "Where did the sergeant go, man?"

Then the laser-net goes down as I stare across a desolate icy wasteland lit by a setting sun. On the radio Jackson is asking, "Fenris Four, where are you, over?"

I stand in awe, drawn to stare up at the strange constellations in the sky above me. My Dog is running a star pattern recognition package and coming up with a system error—no match found.

"Fenris Bravo, I've walked through the pillars, over."

Behind me in the cavern my squad are talking to each other. Interesting, why is it I'm able to move and they cannot?

As I turn to go back into the cavern, the ice beneath my feet cracks, and my Dog slips and falls to the ground. As I hit the ice, my Dog rolls over, sliding out of control. I sling my arms out to stop my Dog from tumbling and come to a halt at the bottom of the slope.

My radio transmission telltale shows red, shit. The Dog prefers to be shaken not stirred. Still, I can receive, and as soon as I'm in line of sight of my squad the laser-net will kick in. No biggee.

Getting up is a process of being mindful of the Dog's footing on the ice, but there's a crevice, which blocks my route back to the pillars.

So I walk along its length, working my way round the obstacle, heading back to the cavern. My squad members are calling out for me to answer them. Before I can reply, the shimmer between the pillars disappears, and the silence engulfs me as my radio goes silent.

Now I'm all alone surrounded by an icy wasteland and wondering what on Earth made me walk through the pillars. How could I be so stupid?

I guide my Dog across the remaining distance on the ice to

wait beside the pillars I walked through waiting in the freezing Arctic conditions. I check my Dog's mission log to find it's 1830. By my reckoning the pillars shimmer every fifteen minutes, so when they do I can walk through and get back to my squad.

Right on schedule another cavern appears.

It looks like it's my lucky day, and I walk through into the darkness, glad to be back. But I realize that it's not the same cavern. Alarms go off in my cockpit, my screen lighting up with a warning—the air is toxic. My Dog's systems automatically seal the cockpit as my suit starts supplying me air from the canned oxygen.

I consider my options.

Stay here and wait in darkness or go back to the icy wastes. One has oxygen, the other does not. The choice is clear, and I walk back onto the icy world, being careful to not step on the area immediately in front of the pillars.

The outside temperature has now dropped to minus thirty, and the Dog starts pumping out heat to compensate. It means I'm using more power, but at least I don't have to rely on the limited supply of oxygen the suit has, even with the recycling scrubbers. In the deepening twilight the other pair of pillars in the distance light up, but I'm not tempted to travel across the darkening icy plain in case my Dog should stumble and fall into an unseen crevasse.

Had I realized I would end up in these conditions, I could've set it up for Arctic operations. Hindsight is a wonderful thing, but even if I had known, no one would've believed me. What story could I tell that would explain the need to winterize the Dogs for an operation in Afghanistan? None that anyone in my chain of command would believe, for sure.

On the horizon my Dog detects movement about five klicks out. My screen shows lightning flashes in the darkness. I zoom in across the barren waste; there's a black cloud moving across the ice towards my location.

My sensors can't tell me anything more, apart from it's moving.

A couple of minutes pass, and the black cloud is a klick nearer to my position. It now looks like a storm front, one I'd rather not be caught out in the open in. At this rate it will arrive just before the pillars shimmer.

Snowflakes dance all around me, being blown around by a stiffening breeze. The black cloud, however, seems to have a will of its own. I get thousands of low-level radiation readings from it, indicating a distributed power source.

Not a cloud then.

Inexorably it bears down on me as alarms go off. I'm being targeted by hundreds of micro electromagnetic pulses hitting my Dog. The autopilot expert system starts running ECCM polarization protocols.

An electric discharge crackles around my Dog, and I get a red telltale that my ChameleonFlage has crashed.

Without it I can no longer sense where my Dog's limbs are. This forces me to go by what's on my screen and rely on my experience to be able to move and not bump into things. I can hear static pings on the radio from the EMP being aimed at me as further telltales go from green to amber and then red.

My Dog dispenses chaff automatically, and I try to throw off the target lock by taking cover by the pillars. As the chaff disperses the black cloud rises up, and for a moment, the pulses emanating from it no longer illuminate my Dog.

But now it's moving faster towards me.

I kneel on the ground to steady my Dog and light it up, firing 20 mm AP rounds at it to no apparent effect. They're either passing right through or the cloud is absorbing the shots. As my magazine goes empty, I drop it out and change to HEAB, high-explosive air-burst rounds.

I fire again. The warheads are smart rounds that explode on target. I watch in satisfaction as the first of my rounds does exactly that. The cloud reacts to the explosions. A palpable hit upon the unknown darkness, and for a moment I want to cheer.

I lay down a steady stream of fire but realize that the impressive pyrotechnic display seems to have little to no effect upon the speed of the cloud's progress. So I reload my only other HEAB magazine, knowing it will have no effect. But I must do something, anything, and start firing slow and steady.

The cloud is now less than a klick away.

It will reach me before the pillars shimmer, before I can make my escape through them. My radio goes silent. A red telltale appears on my screen that's full of static from the EMP being aimed at me.

Now I'm no longer worried that I've been running my Dog at full combat power for the last thirty minutes, wasting fuel to maintain heat. My focus is on the thing that's approaching.

The black cloud swirls out to either side of the pillars, sweeping around and behind me, and I'm all out of HEAB. Black tendrils reach out to grab my Dog. I fire my grenade launcher's high-velocity canister rounds, which have about as much effect as trying to piss into the wind.

"To hell with you," I scream behind me as the pillars shimmer.

The cloud doesn't so much as stop, but is flung back, rearing up hundreds of feet into the air in front of me. Then the tendrils coalesce, changing shape, mimicking my Dog, only the Dog cloud is hundreds of feet tall. The wind roars outside, and if it wasn't for my suit's plumbing, I would've wet myself in my cockpit.

For a moment I'm frozen on the spot as a chill of fear takes hold of me, and I seize my window of opportunity. The choice to go is mine. That's what I tell myself to rationalize my response to the fear as I step through into darkness.

The alarms go silent.

The air is breathable, and my LIDAR shows I'm standing inside an enormous cavern. In the distance there's the babbling sound of water running over rocks. Behind me the black cloud swirls in the distance, and I keep an eye on it from between the pillars until the shimmer stops. Only then do I relax.

But this cavern is not in Afghanistan, which means I haven't the faintest notion of where I am.

Then I review my system records and realize that the stars in the sky of the arctic world are like nothing one can see from Earth. I struggle for a moment with the thought of what that means. The pillars must go to other worlds, not to other places on Earth, which would explain why I seem lighter, more buoyant here.

The enormity of what has happened is overwhelming.

I've crossed onto a new world, which makes me the first human to step on another planet in over a century, and the first to walk on more than one.

If I ever get back—and I'm allowed to tell my tale—I will be famous. This of course assumes I live to get back and tell the tale, and anyone believes what I tell them. It's too easy to fake images, and I'm sure that my Dog's log will be challenged, because—just because that's the way shit goes down.

I bring up the screen that shows my projected power usage and see that my power consumption has dropped. My current rate of consumption is a line between standard and combat rate, which is far too close to the combat line for comfort.

My Dog starts rerouting around the damage from the alien encounter as systems run diagnostic checks. Without my ChameleonFlage to provide input, I've lost my sense of kinaesthesia, which means driving the Dog from now on is going to be a bitch. It must be my lucky day.

Then I kneel my Dog down, letting it rest back on its heels.

I set up the cameras to record the opening of the pillars, putting my Dog into standby mode, letting the autorepair systems do their thing. A red telltale turns amber. My Dog will run out of power before the predicted end time for the mission, which in this case was meant to be twenty-four hours. By my estimation I'll be lucky to see fourteen at the rate I'm going, less if the batteries have been damaged.

On that cheery note I unplug my suit from the Dog and pop the cockpit open. The first thing I notice is the smell of the air; it's unpleasant, not nausea inducing, but rather something sweet and rotting in the ground. It reminds me of mushrooms.

Taking my KRISS Vector SMG from underneath my seat, I charge it and double-check that my flashlight is working. Then it's time to climb out of my Dog and put boots on ground. The glow from my cockpit screen spreads its wan illumination around the cavern, forming a bubble of light in the darkness.

Given that I've been on the go now for over six hours, I'm guessing I need to come up with a plan on how to survive. Preferably one that means I get back to Earth, as I don't fancy becoming some dishevelled castaway.

On a scale of one to ten, realistically I rate my chances of achieving this as less than one. I'm also starting to get hungry, which is going to be a real problem if I survive, though I'll probably die of thirst first.

Reminding myself to keep a positive mental attitude when facing certain death, I look around the cavern of an alien world that waits to be explored. Another first for the Marine Corps. If I had a flag, I could plant it, but I don't, and there's no one here to photograph my achievement even if I did.

There again I'm not in need of being made into a statue

anytime soon either. Still, I'm a Marine, *I have set foot on another world and the situation is well in hand.* Or perhaps I should say, *One small step for a Marine, a giant leap for mankind.* I find myself starting to laugh at my situation. Here I am all alone in the dark, and unless a miracle happens, I'm never getting back home alive, but damned if I'll give up without trying.

I pan my flashlight around the cavern as I begin my walk. The bright light barely illuminates the walls in the distance, but despite that I can see colors—green and gold glinting in the darkness.

Jones would be right at home here. The cavern is huge, much bigger than the one I left in Afghanistan. I decide to head in the direction of the water, because the walk will give me time to think and my Dog time to complete whatever repairs it can make.

I'm way too underprepared to be settling down here.

Besides I would need to get out into the open to be able to find food and shelter. Of course even if I make it to the surface of this planet, the alien animals may not be edible. Nothing has prepared me for a situation like this.

I walk deeper into the cavern and find the stream I heard. When I find the stream it's too small for me to swim in or try to dive under, and there's no other obvious way out.

Nothing has moved in the time I've been walking, so I stop, as I'm not prepared to lose sight of my Dog to explore the cavern further. If my flashlight dies on me, I'll be completely shit out of luck in the pitch black of the cavern.

But I remember a Marine never gives up.

When Chesty Puller was surrounded at the Chosin Reservoir, he'd said, "All right, they're on our left, they're on our right, they're in front of us, they're behind us…they can't get away this time." I may not be surrounded by Chinese, but whatever happens I can keep going through the pillars until I get home or die trying.

Call me a cheerful optimist if you like, but it's all I've got.

Then I circle back towards my Dog, the light from the cockpit acting as a beacon in the darkness. The pillars have kept up their cycle of opening and closing. I know even when I can't see it happening—because I can feel it, and I'm beginning to be fed up with being here.

Having walked back to where I started, I climb into the cockpit of my Dog. The standard Marine Corps green ChameleonFlage is now a dull gray in the light, as it no longer functions after the encounter with the black cloud.

Storing my KRISS and flashlight, I start my Dog.

My system update now says there's at best six hours of power left, and I'm going to make the most of it. More lights are now green, but the radio is still kaput. Closing the cockpit brings up the main display.

I fast forward through the recordings of the pillars opening and see nothing but darkness. Then the pillars shimmer, and I step forward into darkness, facing my fears and determined to go down fighting.

I enter another cavern; it's small, a lot smaller than the previous one.

With no air here, my Dog seals itself. My suit starts using my precious oxygen supply. I tell myself, *No sweat. Another activation is due in fifteen mikes, so it's all good.*

Time passes slowly before the pillars activate again.

I walk into yet another cavern, which is even smaller than the last one. Bending my Dog at the knees, I avoid hitting its head on the sloping walls. Still no breathable air, and the Dog is on internal power, which saves me fuel but is draining my battery.

I'm sweating, having reduced life support to minimum power, as the next shimmer of the pillars begins. My Dog's screen compensates for the light that blazes from the other side. I walk across and find myself out in the open at last.

Desert sand stretches out in all directions with twin suns glaring in the sky overhead. The air is thin but breathable.

My Dog autostarts the engine, followed by the throb of the pump replenishing my oxygen, and my batteries are now charging. The pillars shimmer again and open into darkness. I decide to take a rain cheque on going through, as I need the oxygen replenished to make it through another fifteen-mike cycle if there's no air.

Around me are sand dunes, and I circle around the pillars to check out the local wildlife. I move cautiously, blind to where the legs of my Dog are going. I override the flashing red danger of impact warnings on my control console. Another red telltale lights up to warn me that my Dog is overheating, and the air-con kicks in hard to compensate.

It appears my choices are: freeze, boil, or die from a lack of air.

I take a sip of water. Like it or not, I realize as a radiation warning comes up on my screen—*oh joy of joys*—that even if there was an oasis, this planet is not suitable for life, at least not my life. I trudge through the sand back to the pillars.

Time is unquestionably not on my side.

I start a counter running on my power consumption with an estimated time of when my Dog will stop. It's not looking good as I walk unsteadily through the pillars and find I'm in another cavern. Not as large as the biggest I've walked into today, but certainly not the smallest either. It's starting to look likely that the pillars are mostly situated in caverns.

When they're not, they open up on to inhospitable worlds not fit for Marine nor beast.

Two more cycles of caverns that would no doubt be fascinating to explore under different circumstances, but these are not those circumstances. Not when I keep hitting my Dog on obstructions each time I walk through the pillars. Also, piloting a

Dog for a living means I'm not drawn to spelunking to get my thrills. Besides I'm getting enough thrills today to last me a lifetime, which at this rate is going to be very short.

I keep on walking as best I can, all the while watching the estimated time to total shutdown grow closer. One cavern turns into another. Some have air, some don't, and while no two caverns are alike, they're all much of a muchness. Once you've seen a few, they start to merge together. Unless caves and rock formations float your boat—in that case, then I guess you'd be in hog heaven.

I'm more worried about disabling my Dog if I crash it.

The pillars shimmer, and the light of a setting sun, full and glowing red, appears on the horizon ahead. I walk through the long shadows cast by the sun into what could be described as a tropical paradise, for *some* descriptions of *paradise*, as in it looked nice, but looks can be deceptive. There's a sandy beach with waves lapping the shore.

Nothing jumps out and tries to eat my Dog or for that matter moves towards the pillars. I wonder if this means the pillars act upon all living things, causing them to be frozen on the spot. I could see how that would discourage most animals from approaching them. Hell it would discourage most people from going near them.

It seems to me that on many worlds they're buried in caverns underground. Where they're on the surface of a planet, they're in places that are not frequented by living things. Perhaps that's why the gates were unknown.

Except for that black cloud. Something about it disturbs me at a visceral level, and a shiver runs down my spine.

My display says it's nearly 0130 and there's thirty minutes of power left. I decide to walk through the pillars one more time, and if it's another bloody boring cavern, walk back to this island. It has to better than dying in a cavern, and I stand some chance of using my survival training skills.

A weight lifts from me as I wait for the next shimmer of the pillars.

Exactly on schedule they open again. I walk through them for one last attempt to get home. In that instant I'm caught by something.

It's like I've shattered into thousands of pieces, pieces made up of the choices I've made. Moments caught frozen in time, or juddering, moving back and forth between two points, ripples of movement from the same actions repeating over and over again. And in the middle of it all are my life's options, and I see myself touching one of the two pillars in a cavern in Afghanistan.

Then everything goes black.

20. BAD NEWS

No one starts a war—or rather, no one in his senses ought to do so—without first being clear in his mind what he intends to achieve by that war and how he intends to conduct it.

— CARL VON CLAUSEWITZ

Captain Johanson
First Combat Armor Suit Reconnaissance Company
Afghanistan
Thursday, July 2, 2071

A chill goes through Johanson as he reads Sergeant Tachikoma's message. He and McCarthy were close and the news of his death would hit both families hard. Updating Sergeant Ramirez on the events, he puts his feelings aside as best he can. They're a distraction he doesn't need to deal with now.

Instead, he focuses his attention on Lance Corporal Gentle, who has taken point. She's advancing cautiously through the dark, undulating tunnel, working her way round rocks that can trip her

Dog up. Private First Class Brownlee follows her. Johanson is next in line. Following him are Sergeant Ramirez and the other two members of the Hellhound Bravo Squad bringing up the rear.

Their progress moving through the tunnels is agonizingly slow.

The map provides a clearer picture showing the branches leading further down into the depths of the mountain. The complexity of the tunnel system begs the question of why the people who'd built this place had gone to such effort. It must've taken an enormous number of them to make this underground fortress.

More worrying is what had caused them to abandon all their hard work, and how did any of that lead to the Chinese becoming involved? Did their presence mean they had built the device that was emitting the energy pulse? Damned if he knew any of the answers.

His thoughts are interrupted as the tunnel widens out into the next cavern, and Gentle signals the squad to halt. Johanson moves up alongside her and makes a hard link with her Dog.

"What you got?"

"Don't know, Captain, but I thought I caught a heat emission ahead of us. Then it just disappeared."

"OK, let's wait and see if it reappears."

"Yes, sir, sounds like a good idea to me."

Johanson messages everyone to take cover and keep scanning the surrounding area. Better to be cautious than dead. They wait for fifteen minutes. Nothing happens. No movement, no sounds, the cave ahead seems empty. He makes a decision.

"Lance Corporal Gentle, go forward and check out what's ahead of us."

Acknowledging his order, she crouches her Dog over to be better able to move forward and enter the cavern ahead. Nothing happens, and she signals the way is clear.

"OK, let's follow her in."

"You heard the captain, move it and stay frosty people," says Sergeant Ramirez as the rest of the squad advances into the cavern, heading towards a ridgeline in front of them.

Gentle's Dog turns and stands up to scan over the ridge. Then the head of her machine is blown off. The sight of this happening is followed by a boom as her fuel ignites and the Dog explodes. The force of the explosion rocks Johanson backwards, and pieces of debris ricochet by him and past the rest of the squad. Her Dog has disintegrated into pieces so small there's nothing worthwhile left to recover.

And the realization hits him she's dead. Shit. Today had turned from bad into one of those very bad days.

Brownlee yells, "Ambush front! Ambush front!"

"Open fire, people!" he shouts over the boom of his autocannon.

The sound of the weapons discharging echoes furiously around the cavern, adding to the confusion of the firefight. He lays down a short burst of suppressive fire. He doesn't expect to hit anything. All he wants is to keep the enemies' heads down, and keep them from returning fire.

In the confines of the tunnel, the boom of the autocannons is overwhelming at a visceral level, flooding his body with adrenaline.

The enemy returns fire, having clearly not gotten the message to cease and desist shooting at his people. So he sends some more 20 mm AP love their way to discourage them from continuing the engagement. But they're keen to carry on irrespective of his hints. And judging by the amount of incoming shots going over his head, they outnumber the squad.

By his estimate they're facing a minimum of sixteen hostiles, which means they outnumber his command nearly three to one. Good odds for the Chinese to continue pressing on with the attack. If they pushed forward now, they could overrun and destroy the squad. It would cost them, but if their situations were reversed, he knows he would do it.

"Anyone got a visual on if they're advancing on us?"

Negatives come back. A comment from Brownlee that there seems to be an awful lot of them firing is an understatement.

"Fall back by sections, left and right, suppressive firing at the sustained rate," he says.

The squad retreats back towards the tunnel as they fire into the darkness behind them. The Dogs are running in full-on ECCM mode, blanketing the enemy's ability to track their progress. Incoming tracer rounds from the Chinese Fatties whiz past him and his people, the strobing from the muzzle flashes makes the cavern look like it's lit by the fires of hell.

The Chinese don't pursue them, and he thanks his lucky stars that their commander isn't aggressive in following up the initial ambush. That failure to press home the attack has turned the engagement into bluster and blunder.

Johanson takes a moment to pause and message Lieutenant Bergeson to meet back at the rally point, regretting his decision to split the platoon. As his Dog moves out of the cavern, he can see the Chinese moving slowly from cover to cover, advancing cautiously because they're not aware of how much they outnumber his command.

The squad has gotten a lucky break.

Letting rip with a short burst of fire from his autocannon to discourage further pursuit, he moves back past Sergeant Ramirez's position. Each of them are taking turns leapfrogging past each other. Brownlee and Ward are doing the same, withdrawing back up the tunnel, firing to cover each other as they move.

The survivors of Alpha Squad's two fire teams lay down a steady stream of suppressive fire at the Chinese, whose advance grinds to a halt.

The return fire slows to a trickle of shots.

Johanson wastes no time pondering the Chinese troops' intentions but takes the lull in firing as an opportunity to signal their withdrawal. They make their way back to the rally point where Lieutenant Bergeson is waiting for them. It's a relief to have survived the attack, but he's dismayed to find they've burned through half of their ammunition during the brief firefight.

With the platoon reformed the odds are much less favourable for the Chinese should they decide to change their minds and continue pursuing the attack. Arguably any advantage the Chinese have in numbers would be negated by the nature of the tunnel complex. But not something he wants to put to the test after losing both Lieutenant McCarthy and Lance Corporal Gentle today.

As far as he's concerned, Sergeant Tachikoma's bad dream was a bit too close to the knuckle. Johanson starts to message her but gets an incoming message from Lance Corporal Kowalski reporting the sergeant is missing, presumed dead. Something about two pillars and disappearing when she walked between them. The report is confused and makes little sense, but he doesn't have the time to try to unravel it now.

It would have to wait until they get out of here. This was only supposed to be a search-and-retrieval mission—find some survivors with only the prospect of facing poorly armed indigenous forces. It was not meant to be a stand-up engagement with Chinese in combat armor.

He messages Perez and Beckford that his platoon is coming back out but gets no confirmation of them receiving his message. The net is down, either by accident or from Chinese interference.

Johanson opens the laser-net conference channel to the platoon.

"I've lost contact with the rest of the company waiting outside. It might be the transceivers being glitchy, but it could mean they're having trouble on the surface. Hellhound Six, have your squad bring up the rear. Keep an eye out for any signs of the Chinese we engaged pursuing us," he says, keeping Bergeson to cover their six.

He pauses for a moment to consider his next move. "Growler, this is Big Dog, take point and lead the way," he says, ordering the more experienced Gunnery Sergeant Locklear to take point.

First Platoon moves out. The Dogs make steady progress back up the tunnels. When they get to the cleft that led them into the mountain, Locklear calls them to a halt.

"Skipper, you've got to come and see this."

Johanson pulls up Locklear's feed and sees destroyed Dogs and Chinese Fatties scattered like litter on the ground. He moves up beside Locklear. His sensors confirm it's the remains of Dogs from both Perez's and McCarthy's platoons mixed in between enemy machines. Johanson takes in the devastation around him and scans back towards the crash site.

He can see more smoke rising in the distance from what had to be Beckford's platoon.

His Dog confirms he has a secure channel to *Hornet*'s CIC. He stands immobile, listening in shock as he's told of what has happened here. It's clear to him that the enemy controls the battlefield.

He switches to the feed from the UAV that's backtracking the shots. Confirmation comes that the Navy has launched missiles to take out the enemy artillery. Until then his company are to remain in cover, in case another artillery barrage is fired at their position. He finishes relaying the mission data back to *Hornet*'s CIC.

So far this day had brought overwhelming misery. Johanson has to bear it and bring the rest of his people back safe.

"OK, Marines, take cover back under the mountain."

As they walk back to the relative safety of the mountain, the ground beneath their feet shakes. This is followed by a sharp cracking noise and the roar of an explosion that deafens him. Rocks fall on his platoon, crushing the Dogs out of existence.

21. THIRD REVOLUTION

This is the best of all possible worlds.

— G<small>OTTFRIED</small> W<small>ILHELM</small> <small>VON</small> L<small>EIBNIZ</small>

Sergeant Tachikoma
First Combat Armor Suit Reconnaissance Company
CSN *Hornet*
Thursday, July 2, 2071

I wake up to find myself whole and in one piece, which is a relief given the experience of seeing my life shatter into myriad pieces, its remains etched into my mind. I'm left with an overwhelming sense of having everything happening at once, waves of fear, excitement, anger, and love sweeping through me. It shakes me to my very core.

Then the feelings fade, and I'm left lying in my rack thinking, *What the heck has happened?* I didn't get blown up this time, but still I find myself back at this point of the day. The bomb must have gone off, but how does that even work when I'm not there?

What's happening must be happening for a reason, but whatever it is, it sure beats the hell out of me.

Instinctively I check my PAD, which confirms it's Thursday again. Everything in the room seems exactly the same. Nothing's changed. People are still snoring softly in their sleep.

It's like I'm reliving *Duffer's Drift*. Seeing the consequences of the decisions I've made and the actions I've taken. I'm calm, which is strange, detached even. But unlike Lieutenant Backsight Forethought, I dread the prospect of having to relive the same day, for a third time. This isn't fun, I don't know what to do, and it scares me.

But doing something is always better than doing nothing.

Therefore I must hold on to what is real. So if it feels real, it must be real. Surely that makes me crazy because only a crazy person would think they're reliving the same day over and over again. My mind goes blank as I try to remember what little philosophy I had in college. Unsurprising really, because philosophy classes used to drive me to tears.

My dad had a saying: "Life is one breath, one action. Eat when hungry, sleep when tired." This thought makes me maudlin from missing him. The loss of him is overwhelming, and a wave of tiredness sweeps over me, as if I've not slept for a couple of days, or perhaps the emotions are draining.

But I cling to the belief I can change the outcome of today. However, the fact that I'm here repeating the day must mean I need to do something different. More importantly, what must I do to stop myself from being killed? Having died twice already is getting to be a bit old.

One thing's for sure, walking through those pillars is something not to be undertaken lightly.

My dad would also say, "Know what you can control, know what you can't, and be happy with that." Perhaps what's happening today is one of those things I can't control. If so, my life sucks, because it sucks having to live the same day every day. What's happening to me must be something to do with the pillars. It's the only thing that makes any kind of sense—for definitions of *sense* that don't make a lot of sense to me.

A chill runs through my body and I shudder.

Now to get through the rest of the day, which means not dying when the bomb blows up the mountain. I check the time. Five minutes have passed with me standing half-naked in the bunkroom. No wonder I'm cold.

So as the Marine Corps likes to say, "The only easy day was yesterday." Since yesterday turned out to be a bit of a bitch, I don't hold out much hope for today's version of yesterday being any easier. Therefore I've got to get my act together. First step—make my way to the head and get washed—ready for the *great* day ahead of me.

OohFuckingRah.

But it strikes me that whatever changes happen, some things in life always remain the same.

Back in the bunkroom getting dressed, I don't bother to check the suit sensors. I figure if they worked yesterday, and today is/was yesterday all over again, I can cut myself some slack. I take them as already checked by the previous me, twice already.

Even I can't be any more thorough than that.

Next I go for breakfast and realize I'm ravenous. Perhaps it's the smell of food, or a combination of smell and not having eaten since breakfast yesterday—how many hours ago is that? I start to add it up, but my train of thought is interrupted by the server.

"What do you want Sergeant?"

"Ham and eggs."

"Anything else Sergeant?"

"No, I'm good here. Thank you."

The service is the same as it ever was. Before I go and sit, I grab a coffee and OJ.

On cue, my platoon says, "Good morning, Sergeant!"

I sit opposite Lieutenant McCarthy, and before he can ask me how I slept, I say, "No I didn't sleep very well, but thank you for asking."

He looks gobsmacked as I start eating my ham and eggs.

He's also hale and hearty, which is no mean feat for someone who has died twice already. And I remember this day is not all bad, just mostly bad. Then a horrible image of him turned into formless red flesh flashes in front of me. My gorge rises, and I force myself to continue swallowing my food.

To distract myself I say, "Hey, Vosloo, did you sleep well last night?"

"Like a babe in the woods, Sergeant. Have I told you the story about the time I was almost eaten by a bear that woke me up in the woods?"

"You mean the time when you outrun your friend who got eaten?"

"Yes, that's the one, Sergeant. Damn I thought I hadn't told that story yet."

Everyone around the table laughs.

"I guess you'll have to wait until we've all forgotten about it and tell it then."

Delgado whispers to Hernandez who is looking confused and says, "Sergeants can read minds."

"No, Lance Corporal, but it's my job to know everything that happens before it does," I say, watching people's reactions to our exchange.

Rodriguez goes into the whole hash browns exchange with Jackson. They high five each other and laugh. It's good to see them all laughing as they eat their breakfasts as fast as humanly possible.

So I join in by saying, "It gladdens this sergeant's heart to see Jones likes eating a traditional Marine Corps breakfast."

"I like SOS, it tastes nice…" says Jones, pausing before taking another mouthful. "It reminds me of home."

"Where's that?" asks Jackson.

"I was born in Wales, I'm Welsh."

"Not anymore you're not, Jones, now you're a Marine. What are we people?" I ask.

A chorus of voices says, "We're Marines, Sergeant!"

"Feeling feisty today, Sergeant?" asks Lieutenant McCarthy.

"Every day in the Corps is like a day in paradise, every formation a parade, every meal a banquet, sir."

"I'll take that as a yes then, shall I?"

Smiling broadly I say, "I would, it's about the best today's going to get, sir."

I finish eating my breakfast and wash back the aftertaste of my food with a glug of the Navy's finest coffee, which strips the lining right off my throat. I guess some things never change.

Again it's 0800 and having experienced what everyone will do and say feels wrong. It's disturbing to watch them repeating themselves. Given that it's the same day, why should I expect them to do anything different? But I want to remember them as they are now, despite what will become of them later.

And I have clarity of mind.

There's the pride and pleasure Gunnery Sergeant Locklear takes from calling out, "Attention, officer on deck."

Then there's the ripple of surprise occasioned by Mr Anderson's presence at the briefing. I must have twitched or something because McCarthy stares at me, and I silently mouth *what* at him, and shrug. Then Captain Johanson starts with his preamble for the mission, and I wonder which bright spark decided to call it Operation Clean Sweep.

So I study Anderson's mannerisms as he talks. Of course I'm familiar with what he'll say. But, by comparing what he says and how he holds himself, I find it obvious he's very controlled. It's clear that he knows more, and he's hiding it from us.

His performance is driven by the fact that the Agency doesn't like to share information. Spooks like keeping secrets. They don't like to, or want to, share information with others, because information is power.

Especially if said *others* are a bunch of Marines who don't have clearance to be told what's happening. I take notes on my PAD for when Johanson gets to the point where he asks for any questions. And I make a list of awkward things to say to Mr Anderson, using my PAD to search for news about what's happening in Afghanistan.

The whole of the Middle East and the neighbouring countries have been a hell hole since the nukes went off back in '51. We wouldn't be here running joint training exercises with the Indian armed forces otherwise. The question is, why would China take an interest in this region? But all I find is the centuries-old border dispute with India.

Then I start a search on geophysical magnetic anomalies, too. These seem to be quite common, but there's nothing about anything closely resembling the stalagmite pillars I saw. The Chinese must know more about them than we do. Otherwise why send forces to prevent us from finding them?

More secrets.

Can the pillars be used as a weapon, and, if so, how would that work? Johanson finishes his part of the briefing and asks if anyone has any questions.

"Sir, I would like to raise a few points and ask some questions."

"Go ahead, Sergeant Tachikoma," says Johanson.

"Mr Anderson says the warlord Yeshua bin Yussuf is active in this area. I found from a quick search he's called the Mahdi by his followers. From my limited understanding this means he's seen as someone who will redeem his people, leading them in the formation of a new Islamic state. I have to wonder whether such a person would take kindly to our presence in his area, sir."

"And your point is, Sergeant?" asks Johanson.

"One has to wonder if he's behind the problems the Army Alpha Detachment has had and therefore responsible for them losing contact with Mr Anderson. Given what has been happening in the region, I think it would be fair to say we would be as welcome as something that was not very welcome at all, sir."

Johanson turns and speaks to Anderson. "What do you say to that?"

"The only movements we've seen are local trucks with men, which our analysis indicates falls within the normal range of historical movements. I would agree we should expect the locals to react negatively when you arrive, but I wouldn't expect them to be able, or willing, to force a confrontation," says Anderson.

"Sir, permission to speak frankly?"

"Go ahead," says Johanson.

"Afghanistan is arguably the most fought over country in the world and has suffered repeated invasions by foreigners throughout history. It's a country where every male goes armed and is happy to kill those who are not of their faith. I can't see how the locals would not react to any presence that offends them."

Then I pause to take a breath, but no one butts in or tries to interrupt me.

"I think the reason Mr Anderson lost contact with his Army

Special Forces team is down to the locals making short work of them, sir. Even if you don't think the locals routinely carry rocket-propelled grenade launchers, then we're still left with explaining the loss of a twelve-man Alpha Detachment by other means."

No one says anything, so I carry on with my monologue.

"To me it suggests that there are outside forces aiding the mujahideen. I don't think this would be the Russian Commonwealth because I gather they're about as well liked as we are. However, the Chinese on the other hand might've found some common ground with a local warlord. My reasoning comes from knowing they're helping the Pakistanis in the Gilgit Baltistan region in return for support of their own claims over the border dispute with India and the Xinjiang province."

Johanson looked at me. "That was some speech, Sergeant. You're remarkably well informed about this area. Better informed than Mr Anderson even."

"Just what I was able to pull from my PAD during the briefing, sir."

"Did you actually manage to listen to the briefing?" he asks.

If only you knew. I'm sure I could recite it back to him verbatim.

"Yes, sir, I paid attention to what you were saying, sir."

"Well, Mr Anderson, it seems one of my senior NCOs has been able to raise some interesting things you might like to comment on."

"Sergeant Tachikoma has made some good points. Some aspects of this mission are classified as top secret, which means I'm unable to comment, and I can neither confirm nor deny such speculations. I'm able to say she's not said anything I would disagree with, but I can only report what we've observed," says Anderson, squirming on the spot as he speaks.

"Sergeant, after that stunning endorsement by the Agency,

have you any other insights into this situation to share with us?" asks Johanson.

The answer to that is, of course, yes, but how to explain what I'm aware will happen without appearing to be some crazy woman?

"Sir, do you recall the book *The Defence of Duffer's Drift*?"

"Yes, I do, and the relevance here is what, Sergeant?"

"It's like I had a dream about a mission into Afghanistan, like in the book, sir, when he makes a plan and it all goes wrong."

"OK, so we're talking a gut feeling here?"

"You could say that, sir."

"When my senior NCOs tell me their gut feeling tells them something's wrong, I tend to listen to them. Go ahead and lay out what your gut tells you we should do."

"Thank you, sir. I think we should expect a hostile reaction from local forces, who are prepared to lull us into a false sense of security by waiting until we are at our most vulnerable before striking. This will be sometime after we've split the company. A good time to strike would be when half the company are under the mountain."

Everyone is now staring at me.

"I would expect the enemy to target both the crash site and the area around the entrance to the mountain with artillery. Therefore we should move the Third Platoon away from the mountainside and place them further back here."

Then I bring up the map to show where I, from what I remember of the day, think we should be.

"I would also liaise with the crew of the Air Force MULE. We can use them to move Fourth Platoon so they can join up with Third Platoon. This would enable us to enfilade any enemy forces that might want to sweep over this ridgeline on the map, here." I pause to draw more lines on the map.

"This would be an ideal point to ambush the company as they

exit the mountain. I would also want the company to move away from the mountain after recovering the Alpha Detachment. So we can avoid any unpleasant surprises that may have been prepared by the enemy."

"I can see you've given some considerable thought to this. I certainly wouldn't want to have to go in and face an enemy force if you were in command of them," says Johanson. "Any comments, Mr Anderson?"

"Are all your senior NCOs flying under the zone?"

"No, but I've had my eye on her for a while. Sergeant, come and see me after the briefing in fifteen mikes."

The next fifteen minutes pass in a flurry of activity as I make sure Corporal Knight covers my absence. I don't even have time to appreciate the moment when Lieutenant McCarthy catches up with me and tells me how impressed he was with what I said at the briefing.

Making my way back to see Captain Johanson, I wonder if this time I'm being called to be praised or ripped a new one.

My doubts now are about being able to pull everything together, given my own abilities and what has happened the last two times. More to the point, if I ever tell anyone how I know what I know, I'll be locked up. But sometimes one has to act, rather than explain.

I enter Johanson's cabin and come to attention.

Mr Anderson is now sitting with him as the captain goes through the same spiel about my performance in the briefing. He then asks me again about accepting a commission to become an officer. I reply in the affirmative. Given how this conversation is going to go, it seems best not to deny the inevitable outcome.

Johanson says, "Good, glad to hear it, Sergeant. I'll write up the recommendation when we get back. However, that's not the only reason I've called you here to see me. Mr Anderson would also like to ask you a few questions. Is that all right with you?"

"Yes, sir, though I'm not sure what I can say that would be of any interest to Mr Anderson."

"Sergeant Tachikoma, what do you know that I don't?" asks Anderson.

"Sorry, sir, but I don't understand the question. What don't you know?"

"Exactly my point, Sergeant. You seem to be more informed about the situation on the ground than I am. How's that possible?"

"I asked myself what I would do if I was the enemy and I suspected more people would be sent to retrieve the first lot I'd killed, sir."

"An interesting answer. Remind me never to get on your bad side then."

"I'll be sure to inform you if that happens, sir."

"One more question though. Who do you think is responsible for creating the magnetic energy pulse we've detected?"

What I want to say is, *Some strange shimmering pillars that let you slip between two different places when you walk through them, which were not made by the Chinese, or the Afghans.*

Avoiding the question, I say instead, "My best guess is that it's something we might be able to exploit to our advantage, and others don't want us to find out about it, sir."

Anderson raises an eyebrow at me and says, "You may well be right, Sergeant Tachikoma."

I'm sure he knows more than he's letting on, but he lets my nonanswer to his question go, perhaps for the reason that spooks don't like giving things away because questions always beg answers. Besides not all things are worth fighting over.

I come to attention as Captain Johanson dismisses me,

relieved not to have made a fool of myself or, worse, looked like a crazy person.

———

Leaving Johanson's office, I make my way forward to the kennels, where the hangar bay is a picture of ordered chaos. Weapon packs, pulled from the armory, are waiting to be loaded on the Dogs. Since everything appears to be running according to plan, the question is, how to not get my ass blown up again?

Dying had sucked big the first time round. It was not getting any less suckitudinous each time it happened.

As I walk along the line of Dogs, I see Lance Corporal Kowalski arguing with Eversmann about a bad leg actuator again, turning the air blue with invectives. We go through the dance with each of them telling me their side of the story.

"OK, I can see we have a difference of opinion here. How long to replace the actuator, Eversmann?"

"About fifteen mikes if I had someone to help me, which I don't, Sergeant."

"So, Kowalski, you prepared to get your hands dirty and help Eversmann replace the actuator?"

"I suppose so, Sergeant."

"Well, what are you waiting for, sweetheart, get working and have Eversmann help you. And afterwards go help Jones. After all, you are meant to be his buddy when we get out in the field."

Kowalski gives me a less than happy look, but at least Eversmann sees the funny side of getting what you ask for, even if I've made more work for the pair of them.

The trouble with Kowalski is, he doesn't push himself hard enough and coasts along in his job. Perhaps I should recommend him for promotion since, if I get back after today's mission, the company is going to need to move people up to fill the inevitable slot left by my departure. Then he'll have to work harder.

These are the kind of weird thoughts I'm having, which only makes sense if you are living the same day of your life all over again. I move along to the next Dog, lost in the weird space that's the inside of my head, and see Rodriguez and Jackson working through the checklists together.

"You both on track?"

"We're good here, Sergeant," says Jackson.

"Everything's goin' by the numbers," says Rodriguez.

"Outstanding work, Marines."

For a moment I see them in front of me repeating the previous versions of the day. Then it's gone, and I shake myself, which gets my head back in the game. Next I walk over to see Private Jones.

"How's it going, Jones?" I ask, remembering the first time I asked him this.

"I'm good, Sergeant, but can I ask something about the mission load-out?"

"You're thinking that carrying a rotary cannon will allow you to carry more rounds, but our platoon needs to travel light for this mission."

"How did you know what I was thinking?"

"It's why I have the stripes, son." As far as I can tell, Jones is a credit to the Corps, as everything he's done is tight and by the numbers. "You've done a good job here." He positively lights up when I say this.

Having finished checking on my squad, I make my way over to talk to Thompson and Washington, who are on the opposite side of the bay from my platoon. Thompson seems ready to start an argument with me and starts laying it on thick as we begin talking.

Before he can go any further, I cut him off at the knees.

"I tell you what, if we return without having to use any of this stuff, I will personally buy everyone in the company a beer when we get into port. How's that sound to you?" I'm pretty confident this is one bet I'm not going to lose.

"Just the one beer?" asks Thompson.

"For you, I'll buy you beers until you fall over."

"I'd take her up on that, Thompson, as it's not an offer an ugly old Marine like you gets," says Washington.

"You should know, Washington, as you're about the ugliest Marine in the Corps," says Thompson. "Well, next time you go and have a feeling, Tachikoma, remember to tell us about the beer first."

"Sure, Thompson, you've got yourself a deal," I say, and I can't help but laugh.

"Anyway, what's up with all this bad feelings shit? You sure drove a truck through the spook's presentation with it," asks Washington.

"You wouldn't believe me if I told you."

"Try me?"

"Let's just say I had a couple of bad dreams and leave it at that."

"Must've been one hell of a bad dream to get you all fired up," says Thompson.

"So what happened in the dream?" asks Washington.

"We all died."

They both have a how-dare-you-say-such-a-thing expression. Like I'll bring down some bad juju on them.

"Well, it's a good thing there's a plan to make sure your dreams don't come true then…"

Then Washington goes lovingly through the details to arm both their platoons with Gauss rifles. The banter flows around me, and I relish the comfort of being part of the team with good-hearted joshing and interruptions.

"Let me guess, you also reserved the right to carry GECAL 50s for yourselves?" I say.

"Damn straight we did. You just took the words right out of my mouth, woman," says Washington.

"It's a dirty job, but someone's got to do it," I say. "Anyway it sounds like a plan to me."

"Yeah, sounds like one to me too, but don't let it go to your head, Tachikoma," says Thompson.

"Good luck, guys," I say before leaving them to walk back and check on how Corporal Knight and the rest of the Marines in my platoon are doing.

"Hey that was some fancy speaking at the briefing, you gunning to become an officer, Tachikoma?" he asks.

"Thanks for insulting me, I work for a living, and both my parents were married," I say, making Knight laugh. "However, it seems no good deed by an NCO goes unrewarded. The skipper is recommending me for officer training."

"You shitting me?"

"No shit, apart from the same old shit we put up with every day. You heard it here first."

"Damn, we will have to call you *ma'am*."

"I think that's the least of it," I say as Lieutenant McCarthy walks over towards us.

"How's the platoon's preparation going?"

"Second Platoon is good to go for vertical insertion, Lieutenant."

"This is the first time I've done a drop for real, Sergeant," says McCarthy, whose face has turned a shade of green.

"I wouldn't worry about the insertion killing you, sir, I'd worry more about being shot," I say, as I climb once more into the cockpit of my Dog, ending the conversation.

I sit in my Dog as the rest of my platoon's cockpits are closed by the hangar crew one by one. These are my friends, also my family. I know each and every member of my company would die for me—had died with me.

And I will do whatever it takes today to prevent that from happening again. None of them might remember what has happened before, but I sure as hell do.

My cockpit lid is closed.

I go through the process of linking into my machine and accessing *Hornet*'s grid. A moment of calm before the fight. I monitor the Thunder Hawk's comms-channel as we sit waiting for the all-clear for launch.

It's the usual chatter from the zoomies welcoming us all aboard for today's flight. Zoomie humour is reminding us all to stay strapped in for the entire flight, as if there's any choice in the matter. Still, I welcome the words, letting them flow over me, evidence that all is well.

Later it will be different.

I switch my feed to *Hornet*'s island camera, which rewards me with a sweeping panorama shot of our Amphibious Readiness Group sailing around us. There's a certain functional beauty about warships that belies their inherent destructive purpose. As for us, we're Marines, the boots on the ground for the Navy when it needs to kick ass ashore.

I hear the sound of chocks being yanked away. The engines begin powering up, bringing my attention back to the flight deck of the *Hornet*. Flight crew in yellow are directing our birds to go, flourishing their arms as they wave us on.

The fans of Johanson's Thunder Hawk scream as they reach full power. The bird wobbles slightly as it starts its run along the deck before taking to the air, where it turns from an ungainly looking chicken into a bird of prey followed by its wingmate. Then it's the turn of second platoons birds to follow.

Our bird begins climbing into the sky.

We swing in an arc around the fleet below, giving time for the following four birds to join us. Our eight Thunder Hawks assume an echelon formation before climbing to an altitude of fifteen thousand feet, and we again fly north towards Afghanistan at three hundred knots.

Below us the green-gray sea is calm, with only a few fluffy white clouds to break the deep blue of the sky. I stare at the screens for a few minutes, appreciating being in the moment, alive. Snapping out of my reverie, I fall back into my set routine of checking on everybody in the platoon.

A part of me knows I will see what I've already seen on the two previous occasions, but that's not the point. Somehow I'm more connected to these men and women than I've ever been before. Having died twice already, my perspective on my life was starting to get a little screwy even to me. I guess death has a way of putting a different perspective on events.

On my screens I see Lieutenant McCarthy is working on his personal PAD. Probably writing a letter to his wife, reminding me I need to record a letter to my mom too. Reviewing what I've said, I think I've done a better job this time because I've managed to tell her how much I love her for being my mom.

I file it on the system in case I die—yet again.

As they say, practice makes perfect, and where one's death is concerned I find it easier to say the truth about how I feel. If I survive today, I'm definitely going to think about seeing a counsellor. Perhaps it would be good to talk about what has happened. There again perhaps not, given how complicated that could get.

It's coming up to that time when Private Jones is going to want to talk to me, so I take the opportunity to preempt him by calling him first.

"Jones, how's it going?"

"Sergeant, I was just about to call you to ask something."

"Well, go on then."

"Why did the Army wait a week before retrieving their team?"

"I think you know the answer to that, so what's the real question, Private?"

"I'm nervous, Sergeant. What if I screw up and get us all killed?"

"Just look out for your buddy and remember your training, Jones. If you do that, you won't have screwed up. Understand?"

"Yes, thank you, Sergeant."

I spend the rest of the flight reading up on stuff. Not realizing how long I've been studying, I find it's time for us to be dropped from the Chickens. The landscape below us, broken up by rocks, is starting to be very familiar. But this time we're dropped closer to the mountain.

I call out for the squad to sound off, then check everyone is fine, reminding the platoon to switch on their ChameleonFlage. We hold still and watch, going through the usual hurry up and wait cycle. Captain Johanson checks his bearings, waiting to hear his lieutenants to confirm they're where they are supposed to be.

In short it goes by the numbers, which is a good thing.

After ten minutes of this, we're on the move, having got the Dogs onto the road and into glide mode. We are veritably speeding across the landscape towards our goal. Of course this means we raise dust, which rather negates the effects of the ChameleonFlage, but no system is perfect.

It doesn't need to be perfect, it just has to be good enough to give you an edge. This time the real edge is me.

22. TRY AGAIN

Proper Planning and Preparation Prevents Piss Poor Performance.

— British Army Adage

Sergeant Tachikoma
First Combat Armor Suit Reconnaissance Company
Afghanistan
Thursday, July 2, 2071

We get to the now-familiar—ever so familiar—cleft in the rock face where we once more enter the mountain's dark interior.

I can see this will give my future therapist the opportunity to comment on the significance of life, death, and rebirth. I don't really need to see a therapist, what I need is someone who can explain what has caused me to keep waking up on the same day. Now *that* would be worth knowing.

Lieutenant McCarthy makes the suggestion of planting transceivers as we go. I let him take credit for his idea, which only seems right. Next I message him I've already dropped some on the way in, so we can maintain a link back to our other two platoons. But to hear him thank me for doing so is weirder than a weird thing.

And he gives me the credit for the idea when he tells the captain. I'd hoped to avoid this happening because it's easy to get it right when you already know the answers. After today, if all goes well, I suspect I won't know the answers in the future.

Our two platoons make their way past the many side rooms cut into the rock. Each time I repeat this part of the journey I remember more. Little things, like abandoned broken chairs, pottery, and other stuff that the people left behind when they stopped living here.

The sense of déjà vu I'm experiencing from hearing people say the same things again is overwhelming, but also strangely comforting. And I know the only events that change are the ones I make change by choosing to do or say something different each time.

Now all I have to do is make sure I *did the right things* differently. Change things enough and have as many of us survive this day as possible. Besides, I really don't want to end up waking in my rack, having to go through it all again, because this day has already gotten old for me.

When we come to the first fork where Captain Johanson stops the formation and splits us into two again, I'm at the rear of the line. However this time I swap with Kowalski to take point. As we get to the next split in the tunnels, I again persuade Lieutenant McCarthy to let me take Bravo Squad along the left-hand tunnel, the one leading towards the ambush. It's a small thing, but it's reassuring to me that small stuff, like changing the order of march, can affect what people do or say. Now I begin to formulate plans in my head of how to make sure McCarthy or Knight don't get shot this time.

We move into the all-too-familiar part of the tunnel where it starts to widen out, and I signal my squad to halt. Then I move up and deploy my sensor mast, looking at what lies ahead of us. Again I wait for my sensors to show the eight Chinese Fatties lying in ambush. They're well hidden, but all it takes is the patience to watch and wait. Eventually the heat and sound they make gives their positions away.

A sense of calm comes over me.

I signal my squad to let them know we're facing an ambush, and wonder why the Chinese don't withdraw now. But I guess their orders say something along the lines of "delay the enemy for as long as possible." It would certainly make sense, given the bomb that will go off later. So the trick is to get in and get out before they can deliver the bomb and set it off. How hard can it be?

Lieutenant McCarthy joins me at the front of the line when his squad arrives at our location. Then I go through the plan with him once more, which for me is starting to get a tiny bit tedious with all the repetition. But because he isn't a mind reader, and I don't want to die again, I get on with it.

Some days you get dealt a good set of cards, others days you get a shitty hand to play the best you can with. Life's like that.

On my mark Bravo Squad enters the cavern first, and the speed of our assault takes the Chinese by surprise. The Dogs lay down a withering storm of fire, their 20 mm autocannons ripping the enemy's light-combat armor to shreds.

The enemy have no chance to mount an effective response. And the cavern reverberates to the sound of our firing. More noise follows with a series of explosions as the enemy's fuel and ordnance ignites.

In my rush to get to the far end of the cavern, I fall again. My Dog slides along the floor as one of the Chinese Fatties tries to escape. But I've got a target lock and take down the Fatty with a shot to the rear.

I call for people to sound off. Everybody except McCarthy and Knight reply. "Who has eyes on the lieutenant?" I ask.

Jones says, "He's been hit, Sergeant."

As I get up and turn, I see the lieutenant's Dog has lost an arm. A sense of relief sweeps over me.

"Corporal Knight is dead," says Delgado.

Shit has happened. "How's the lieutenant?"

"He's unconscious, but alive, Sergeant," says Jones.

I walk over to where Jones's and McCarthy's Dogs are. The lieutenant's machine has taken a bit of a beating and the cockpit is open. Jones has gotten out of his Dog to treat McCarthy and is using the first aid kit's built-in corpsman protocols to guide him through what to do.

"Good job, Jones," I say, taking the situation in. "Vosloo, pull what you can from the PACE suits. Hernandez, see if you can pull any information from the Chinese Fatties we took down. Delgado, you're in charge until I get back, or until the lieutenant regains consciousness."

She replies in the affirmative.

"And, Delgado, see if your squad can strip the arm off Knight's Dog and get the lieutenant's fully operational. I've a feeling we're going to need everybody good to go when it's time to get out of here. Is that clear?"

Delgado gives me a thumbs-up as she starts pulling out her utility tool kit.

After that I message a SITREP to the captain and wait for his reply. It comes back confirming I'm to take command and continue the mission.

Then I ponder the outcome of the firefight and what changes I was able to make, but it seems that either Knight or McCarthy will go down each time we're ambushed. One of them would be killed and the other injured. How did that work? I've no idea, but it does seem to hint that while I could make some changes, the overall picture remains the same.

However, if that's the case, then the bomb will always go off, and everyone will die. What I need is to figure out a way to stop everyone from dying when the bomb goes off. So, no pressure then, huh.

Passing on Johanson's orders to the platoon, I lead Bravo Squad again towards the pillars sitting at the heart of the mountain. As we reach the spot where the tunnel widens out into the cavern, I remind myself I'm the only one who has done this before, and who knows what to expect.

"OK, let's take it nice and easy and fan out when we enter this cavern. Keep your eyes peeled, people." I say the last bit namely to stay in character, as I can't imagine not reminding them to stay alert.

It's my job after all. My job also includes trying to keep them all alive while killing the bad guys.

"Hey, Jones, this remind you of anything?"

"Funny you should say that, Sergeant, but I was just about to say it reminds me of the time I went caving in Wales. You reading my mind?"

"Nah, Jones, that's just her being a sergeant who is on top of everything," says Rodriguez.

"OK, people, let's not start thinking about sharing warm showers together and exchanging spit and all, we have a job to do here," I say, relishing the comfort from doing and saying familiar things.

Heading into the cavern, I pick up the energy pulse from the two pillars standing ahead on my sensors.

"OK, Marines, you can see what I can see. Let's take up positions around those two pillars."

After my squad reports in all clear, I message the captain to tell him we've found the source of the energy pulse. I don't add the word *again*, as, while I might think it is funny, I doubt anyone else apart from me would get the joke. He of course sends back the expected reply to record everything we can.

The remains of four PACE suits lie on the ground. As before, one is sliced in two while the other three are shredded after being shot in combat. Then the space between the two pillars shimmers, the air appearing to ripple, opening up into a small, dark cavern.

I check the time and note we've arrived earlier than on the previous two occasions. Each time the pillars shimmer they open up to a different place. We're here earlier today because of my actions and changing the way the company was deployed. To collect the other half of the PACE suit, I'll have to come back later.

I relax and ask, "I take it you are all frozen where you stand?" and get a chorus of affirmatives from my squad. "Now isn't it interesting that you can all still talk to me?"

"If you say so, Sergeant," says Kowalski as the shimmer between the pillars stops and normality returns to the cavern. Everybody takes one step back from the pillars.

"What just happened here?" asks Jones.

"Don't know, don't care. I'm just glad it stopped. That's some scary-ass shit," says Kowalski.

Jackson and Rodriguez say in unison, "Amen to that."

Now we're back on the clock, and we must get out of here before the mountain blows up.

"Listen up, Marines, the easy bit is over. Rodriguez and Jackson, pack the remains of the PACE suits for transportation out of here. Kowalski and Jones, check out the rest of the cavern just in case. Come on, Marines, move it!"

As we make our way back out of the mountain, my anxiety increases.

I inform Captain Johanson of our progress and the completion of our mission to find the source of the energy pulse under the mountain. I get back a confirmation and an update his squad has taken fire from some Chinese Fatties too. He orders me to retreat back to the surface, which is fine by me because the sooner we can get out of here the better our chances of surviving.

It seems to take forever to reach the original ambush site.

Part of me wishes I'd ordered Delgado to get the lieutenant back to the surface. We get back to where we had left Delgado, Vosloo, and Hernandez with Lieutenant McCarthy, who has now regained consciousness. He'd decided to wait for us to return. So whatever I might have said would have been countermanded by him anyway.

"Good to see you up and about, sir."

"The captain tells me Two Bravo has been grandstanding again, and that you've achieved the mission objectives."

"Just doing my job, Lieutenant."

"So I hear. I understand from the captain we need to get out of here on the double. Lead the way, Sergeant."

"Yes, sir. You heard the lieutenant, let's get a move on," I say, leading the way towards the surface.

But how am I going to tell the captain we need to run for it?

There's daylight ahead of us, then we're out in the open again, and relief pours into me as my screen shows the presence of the other three platoons ahead of us. Now we must get off the mountain and find some cover.

I call the captain over the laser-net. "Sir, we need to pull back off this mountain and find cover, as it is going to blow."

"Say again, Sergeant?" says Johanson.

"This mountain is about to blow up, sir."

"And you know this how, Sergeant?"

"Gut feeling, sir," I say, because what else could I say that wouldn't make me sound crazy or, worse, an idiot?

"Given how your gut has been right so far, I think I would be foolish to ignore it, Sergeant."

Johanson orders everyone to move down the path off the mountain and make our way towards the road. Third and Fourth Platoons had taken up positions on the crest of the ridgeline. Therefore they've got to make their way back down the side of the mountain to get to us, which is going to take time.

They walk down the slope towards us. I watch in horror as the top of the mountain lifts up. Moments later the shock from the explosion hits as the ground shakes beneath us, knocking my Dog off its feet. I scramble to get up. The ground ripples underneath me as a wall of rock sweeps towards the company.

"Run, Marines," I shout out over the laser-net and turn, knowing I'm not going to make it.

My Dog is thrown into the air, and I black out as I smash into the ground.

23. FOURTH REVOLUTION

Machines don't fight wars. People do, and they use their minds.

— COL JOHN R. BOYD, USAF

Sergeant Tachikoma
First Combat Armor Suit Reconnaissance Company
CSN *Hornet*
Thursday, July 2, 2071

For a moment I find myself falling in the blackness of space, and I wake up shouting out, "Run, Marines," before I realize I'm back in my rack aboard *Hornet*.

Someone says, "Keep the noise down."

My chest tightens, and I force myself to relax, breathing out from my diaphragm. I've woken up having to face repeating the same day all over again, and I wonder why I'm not at all surprised. It's remarkable how fast the human mind can adapt to strange new ways of thinking. A part of me is relieved I'm alive. Another part of me is extremely pissed at being killed yet again. Yet another part of me is quietly going *blubber, blubber* slowly in the corner while drooling, having completely lost my mind.

OK, I exaggerate slightly. But it does seem like it's either laugh or cry. And I don't want to start crying, as I don't like how it makes me feel. It would remind me of the time when my father died. Me and Mom cried for days together. I don't want to be reminded of that.

Seeing all my friends in the company dying is just horrible. The grief from the sense of loss is too much to bear. Of all the bad things that can happen, this is what I fear the most.

I lie on my rack, gathering my wits about me, before I pull back the curtains revealing my bunkroom with its floor-to-ceiling racks. The familiar surroundings comfort me. I try to look on the bright side. At least I'm not dead today, not for a few more hours yet, and neither are my friends.

I have another chance to try to change the outcome of the mission.

There must be a way of stopping the atomic bomb from going off. I don't know why the bomb going off makes me come back to the same day, but I'm guessing it's the answer. Otherwise why did I restart the day when I was lost after traveling through the pillars to other worlds. It's the only thing that makes any sort of sense.

This still leaves me wondering why I'm the only one who can remember living the same day over and over again. It has to be something to do with why I don't freeze when the pillars shimmer. Everybody else does, but why not me, what makes me so special?

Mom would of course tell me I *am* special.

I stare at the pictures on the wall of my rack and try not to think about my dad dying. If only he hadn't died…but nothing I can do today will change the past.

I swing out of my rack, getting into my daily routine to get ready.

Some of the women are snoring, asleep, oblivious to my

movements. The lack of change in this little thing is comforting in its normality, which makes me appreciate being alive. Not dying is definitely a *muzu-kashi desu neh* moment in my life, as my Japanese father liked to say, where the definition of *difficult* might be a euphemism for impossible.

Still, it could be worse, I could be dead. And for someone who had already been killed today, I look good. In fact I could say I look drop-dead gorgeous. But it's not much of a comfort, all things considered.

The first test of my day awaits me.

Such as, getting through breakfast without weirding out my platoon in the process. Since I've had the same conversations, or variants thereof, three times in a row now, this is a bit of a challenge for me. As I approach, my platoon greets me with the familiar chorus of, "Good morning, Sergeant!"

Then I sit down with the whole déjà vu feeling amped to the max and go through the morning rituals that mark each day. Rodriguez and Jackson exchange food from their trays, and Kowalski makes a joke about farts.

I just want to stick my fingers in my ears and go *lalalalalala.*

So I watch in silence the replay of today's events unfold before me. Delgado making eyes at Jones as she intervenes on his behalf, followed by the banter of conversation as it goes around the table before cascading into what gyrenes are.

So I sit and eat my ham and eggs, enjoying the taste, being in the moment, the here and now, finding I am hungrier than I remember. I finish eating and wipe my tray clean with a bit of toast before emptying my cup of the Navy's finest Joe. The bitter blackness reminds me I'm alive by brutally assaulting the lining of my mouth and throat.

Then it's the 0800 briefing again. I walk into the room on automatic until Locklear's announcement breaks me out of my reverie, and Captain Johanson starts his spiel about the new mission orders instigated on Mr Anderson's behalf. Followed by Anderson monologuing on what the CIA will admit to knowing, but which he's not at liberty to tell us about.

I'm seeing patterns in how he speaks and moves, which are clearly tells. But whether or not he really knows what's going on under the mountain is another matter. Then Johanson gets to the point of asking if anyone has any questions.

"Sir, if I may make a few suggestions about the mission, sir?"

"Go ahead, Sergeant, say your piece."

"We're relying on limited real-time reconnaissance feeds from a single UAV that exposes the mission to a number of unknown unknowns, sir. Specifically, we've lost contact with the Army Special Forces Alpha Detachment, I think it would be wise to assume they met a hostile force that overwhelmed them."

I'm into my own monologue and have everyone's attention.

"If this is the case, then I would assume any entrenched enemy forces will be able to avoid being seen by our UAV. Easily done as it flies around the area in its automatic holding pattern. Especially since it can only cover a small area at a time. Therefore we could be facing an enemy force in pre-prepared positions, who've already demonstrated they possess the means to attack a force that lands in this area, sir."

"That's a very good point, Sergeant. What do you make of that observation, Mr Anderson?"

"Our satellites haven't spotted any unusual movement in this area, and all we've seen is the regular passage of trucks with men. But I can't argue against the idea. Given the history of Afghanistan, your company should expect a strong negative reaction by the locals when you land."

"Marines are used to negative reactions, Mr Anderson. What do you suggest we do about it, Sergeant?"

"I think equipping Third and Fourth Platoons with direct-action packages would be advisable. This would give us a more flexible set of options to respond with. I've taken the liberty of downloading my suggestions to your system, sir."

"That's quite a comprehensive list of suggestions there, Sergeant. You're not trying to start a land war in Asia by any chance?"

He grins at me when he says that. It's an old joke, one that's grown older every day I repeat this cycle. I grin back.

"No, sir, just trying to keep the company from getting hurt."

"Anything else, Sergeant?"

"I would like the recon UAV tasked to sweep the reverse slopes of the mountains. Everything within eight kilometers north of our landing zone, sir."

"Are you expecting us to come under artillery fire too then, Sergeant?"

"Planning for the worst makes it easier to complete the mission, sir."

"Amen to that, Sergeant. I'll order the UAV be retasked from its present holding pattern. It will be good practice for our new lieutenants to deploy with heavy weapons. Sergeant, please come and see me in my office in fifteen. Meeting dismissed."

Captain Johanson is delivering a lecture to me.

"I've discussed your suggestions with Mr Anderson. He's quite impressed by your insights into the situation on the ground in Afghanistan, as was I for that matter. But it seems to me you're flying under the radar, Sergeant. We need to seriously consider moving you to where you can shine more brightly. The Corps needs people who can shine, and I think you're not in the best place for you to shine your brightest. I remember we've talked before about you accepting a commission to become an officer. As I recall, you said you were happy as an NCO the last time we spoke. The thing is, Sergeant, you're making my junior officers look bad, and that's not good for them, and it's not good for the Corps. So I have written a recommendation for you to be sent to Officer Candidate School. Can I assume you will agree to accept this time?"

"Yes, sir," I say, as there's a fine line between shining brightly in the Corps and getting burned for not playing by the rules and traditions of the service.

Sergeants give advice to young lieutenants, keep them in line, and stop them from doing stupid things. Rewriting their company commander's briefing is probably outside of a sergeant's remit. I was being told I had overstepped the line, in the nicest possible way, of course. Complaining about how I didn't want a commission wouldn't cut me any slack here.

I listen to Johanson's questions and reply automatically, repeating by rote what I'd said before to both of them. Then the captain goes off script and throws me a curveball.

"Excellent, I believe you would like to ask my sergeant a question too, Mr Anderson."

"Yes, thanks, I would. Have you seen anything unusual or out of the ordinary of late, Sergeant Tachikoma?"

"Sorry, sir, what do you mean by 'unusual'?"

"Well, more strange dreams, or feelings of déjà vu perhaps?"

Does he know what's going on, and if so, what can I say that won't make them look at me like I'm a crazy woman? The best answer is usually the simplest.

"Yes, sir, I have."

"Interesting, and what do you make of them, Sergeant Tachikoma?"

"Opportunities to excel, sir."

"Just one more question if I may. What do you think the magnetic energy pulses are?" I see Johanson give Mr Anderson the what-kind-of-question-is-that expression.

"Something the CIA thinks is important enough to go find out what it is, sir."

Anderson is judging my answer and pondering what to say next. If I'm right, and he knows more about what is under the mountain, my answer might put him in a position where he will have to reveal what he knows. He could tell me something that could explain why I'm experiencing the same day over and over again, or *not*, as the case may be.

"You have that right, Sergeant Tachikoma," says Anderson, raising an eyebrow at me.

So, the latter *not*. He tells me nothing because secrecy is everything to the Agency.

I'm dismissed to prepare for the mission. Given that I know what they're all going to do and say, I'm able to relax and take the time to observe our preparations, seeing the little details like Kowalski arguing with his technician again. I'm impressed with his ability to use F-words as adjectives, nouns, and verbs.

"Lance Corporal Kowalski, a word over here with me if you would?" I say in my best get-your-ass-over-here tone.

"Yes, Sergeant," says Kowalski, who acts like he's been caught doing something he shouldn't.

"What's going on here, Kowalski? Do you like making work for yourself and others all the time?"

"No, Sergeant, it's just I like things to be right."

"So, yesterday when you were checking out your Dog, what stopped you from getting your hands dirty and helping Eversmann change the actuator?"

Kowalski looks at me like I've read his mind. "No excuse, Sergeant."

"So un-ass your shit and either replace the part or quit complaining. I don't want to see or hear you do this again. Do I make myself clear, Lance Corporal?"

"Yes, Sergeant, absolutely clear."

"Good, now go and get it done." I take an unwarranted pleasure from having torn a strip off Kowalski, who really needs to push himself more and get with the programme. Of course he has no way of knowing that he can't keep his promise, and part of me regrets putting him in a lose-lose scenario. On the other hand if he only knew what I knew, we wouldn't be having this conversation.

The trouble is, I can't be sure I won't repeat this day again.

It's wearing me down not knowing what parts of what I'm doing and saying make any difference in the way the overall picture turns out. Still, as Dad would say, "You need to know what you can do, what you can control, and be happy with that." I certainly can't control everything that's going to happen today. Better attend to those things I know I *can* control, and be myself, as that's all I can do here and now.

I walk over to where Rodriguez and Jackson are helping prep each other's Dogs. "Good work, you're both a credit to the Marine Corps."

I get back in reply, "Thank you, Sergeant," from the both of them. Turning away I choose to ignore the ChameleonFlage SNAFU by moving on to check on Jones.

"Jones, how's it going?"

"Everything's good here, Sergeant," he says, going off script for reasons I don't understand.

"Any questions?"

"I'm confused as to why they waited a week before sending us to retrieve the Army team."

"What's troubling you about it?"

"I'm worried I will screw something up and let everyone down."

"Trust me, Private, if you just follow your orders and watch out for your buddy, you'll do good. That's all any of us can do. Can you do that?"

"I can do that. Thank you, Sergeant."

I leave Jones with a sense I've said the right thing to him this time.

Or at least a good enough approximation of same because at the end of the day it's all one can do. Nothing is ever perfect; it only needs to be good enough. I then make my way over to the other side of the hangar to talk to my fellow sergeants.

Thompson glances up from checking a connection on his Dog and swears at me. "You come to say sorry for all the extra work you landed on us, Red?"

"Believe it or not, I don't spend my day thinking of ways of making extra work for you, Thompson. So here's the deal, if we get back and you seriously believe it was a waste of time loading the Dogs for bear, then at our next port of call I'll buy you drinks until you fall over. How's that sound to you?"

Washington walks up and interrupts Thompson before he can say anything. "She's got your number, Thompson. It's not every day an ugly old Marine like you gets an offer like that."

"Washington, everyone knows you're the ugliest Marine in the history of the Corps," says Thompson.

"You don't get to be this ugly without knowing a good deal when you see one," says Washington.

"If Tachikoma had told me about the beer first, I wouldn't be ragging on her ass," says Thompson.

"You two slay me. I'll try and mention the beer first next time, but don't hold me to that," I say, listening to them repeat the choices they've made for their platoons. I finish by saying, "I can see that has worked out well then. Got to love those rotary-point defence cannons."

"They're sweet, aren't they though? I just love it when I hear them spin up," says Thompson.

"Works for me too, good luck," I say, leaving them to walk

back over to where Corporal Knight stands as he finishes talking to his squad.

Knight sees me and turns to say again, "Hey, that was some fancy speaking in front of the skipper. You hotdogging to become an officer, Sergeant?"

"Are you trying to tell me I'm a complete bastard?"

"All I'm saying is if the hat fits, Sergeant."

"More like no good deed goes unrewarded in the Corps. The skipper has recommended me for officer training."

"No shit. Damn you should've moved faster, or something. Heck this means I'm going to have to call you *ma'am* at some point."

"Only if you don't move fast enough the next time you see me," I say as Lieutenant McCarthy walks over to talk to us both.

"That was a scarily impressive bit of grandstanding you did in the briefing today, Sergeant."

"Funny you should say that, but Captain Johanson thought much the same thing too, sir."

"That bad huh? What else did he say?"

"He seems to think the best place for grandstanding sergeants is to send them off for officer training to teach them a lesson, Lieutenant."

"And who am I to challenge the wisdom of our company commander? Congratulations, Sergeant, a well deserved recommendation in my opinion," he says. "So how's the preparation going?"

"No worries, Lieutenant, we're all set for vertical insertion." I notice him go a bit green. "Trust me when I say being shot at is much worse than being dropped out the back of one of our birds. Anyway it's time we mounted up, sir." I turn towards my Dog and climb into the cockpit.

As I sit in my cockpit I can't help but worry I've missed something this time around.

That's the trouble with repeating the same day every day, because those things you might remember doing might not be what you've actually done. Whatever I might've forgotten isn't coming to mind. So I sit patiently and wait while the hangar deck crew get on with their job.

Jobs like avoiding any unfortunate mishaps—such as damaging the aircraft on the elevator, or a repeat of an unfortunate incident where a loaded bird got pushed into the water—because those in command tend to have a sense-of-humour failure when stuff like that happens.

But I know if I don't do my part right, today will turn out to be another bad day where everyone dies.

Up on deck our eight Chickens are in a line, noses to tails, each ready to follow each other waiting for the FOD all-clear. The lead Chicken powers up its engines and takes off with a short roll along the flight deck. As soon as it lifts off, the next one goes followed it short order by the third bird, and then our bird follows them with the rest of the company following suit.

I feel a thrill as we climb into the clear blue sky.

Below us CSN *Hornet* and the rest of the ARG grow smaller with each passing moment as they float smoothly on the blue-green sea. I watch until our flotilla disappears into the vastness of the Arabian Sea before beginning to go through the routine SOPs for the mission.

Seeing Lieutenant McCarthy writing reminds me I need to record a letter to my mom again. This is my third attempt to record something to her in case I die. Here, the feeling of uncertainty overwhelms me. I realize I have no way of knowing if she will ever listen to the letter, or whether there are alternate worlds where each had a version of my mom hearing a different version of the letter.

The very thought does my head in. But as far as I'm concerned, there's only the here and now. This letter. Because if I do die and don't wake up again, then it will be this letter Mom will see. So no pressure about recording the right letter then. Just every pressure.

But the reality is this was always true. Especially when you sit and record what might be one's final words to a person you love. It doesn't matter how many times you do this, it doesn't become any easier.

So I keep it simple. Tell her I love her, how she is the best mom in the world, and I died doing what I believed in. It takes a little longer to record what I want to say because I'm feeling the weight of the moment on my heart. Tears start to form in my eyes.

As my mom would say, "It's better to regret the things you've done than regret the things you haven't done." In this moment my biggest regret is not having someone to share my life with and not having started a family of my own.

I've always feared losing the ones I love, and I've made the Marine Corps my family.

Being with my fellow Marines helps me escape facing the truth. Tennyson wrote, "'Tis better to have loved and lost than never to have loved at all." If I survive today, I'm going to do something about changing that. So I sit back in my seat and read more research about space-time, causality, and reality before drifting off to sleep.

The crew chief sounds the ten-mike drop warning, which wakes me up.

I set my screen timer ready for the moment when my Dog will be launched out the rear of the bird. The count drops down towards zero. My harness snatches me back into my seat as my Dog leaves the hold of the Thunder Hawk. The drogue pulls the main chute open, catching me and my Dog before the bottom of the drop sled hammers into the ground. Four tons of Dog and sled grind to a halt.

"Sound off, people, and let's make ourselves not be seen.

Marines, switch your ChameleonFlage on now," I say while checking the tracks for our platoon and company positions.

I realize what I'd forgotten to do, as on my HUD I see we've deployed in our original position. This means our four platoons are arranged around the crash site in a diamond formation. We're concentrated into an area no larger than four hundred meters across—inside the artillery kill zone.

My chest tightens.

My hands are sweating as a wave of dread rises over me. Helpless to change anything, I hear the captain get his bearings and talk to the lieutenants. On my screen the eight Chickens sweep across the valley. They execute a pop-up to see what is on the other side of the mountain. The time before they had turned around and gone back the way they came.

A few moments later the pretargeted artillery barrage arrives. Then all hell opens up around us as shells rain down on our position. The company is destroyed in a fury of fire. I wake in pain, screaming out, surrounded by my dead friends. I fight to survive, but the inevitable happens, and I die again.

24. PIDAN

Judge a man by the reputation of his enemies.

— ARABIAN PROVERB

Shàngwèi Looi
Commander Special Operations Force Falcon
Democratic People's Republic of China
The White Mountain, Afghanistan
Thursday, July 2, 2071

Looi frets, waiting for the bomb to arrive and wondering how many more of his men would die for the mission.

Shàowèi Wang's advance group arrived too late to stop the Americans from entering the mountain. This had forced his platoon to go inside and hunt them down. Their ability to maneuver was restricted by the confines of the tunnels, where the small size of the rooms and tunnels better suited the outnumbered Americans in their power-assisted body armor.

Killing the Americans had cost the lives of two of Wang's men.

The Ministry of State Security has assured him the bomb is coming today. Of course the men from the *Guoanbu* had told him that yesterday, and the day before, and the day before that. In fact, every day since his arrival, he's been promised the bomb would arrive soon.

He hopes that the *Guoanbu* sent the truck with a security detail.

The idea of some local warlord acquiring a nuclear bomb was troubling. To say the least, it would be more than a mere inconvenience. However, he and his shàowèis have made contingency plans for different scenarios, including the late arrival of the bomb.

This means he has to not only conceal the presence of the thing under the mountain, but also hide his company from the Americans.

The challenge will come when the deception is revealed and the inevitable conflict between them and the Americans begins. So they've made plans to deal with all the possible outcomes they can come up with.

Plans that evolved: tested by the assumption that the worst will happen; then contingencies thought through to counter those setbacks; how those contingencies might fail rethought; and the process started all over again.

However, Looi is all too aware he has insufficient forces for a prolonged defence against a determined foe. He's inviting the possibility of defeat in detail; therefore the last element to his plan is to use the warlord's Disciples to divide the American force into smaller units.

Then they can be picked apart one by one.

Two of his men are waiting for the bomb to arrive. The main part of his command are emplaced at choke points under the mountain. He also has a reserve outside to ambush any who might escape from the mountain.

But the plan hinges on the bomb.

He'd been told he must prevent the Americans from discovering the secret within the mountain. At any cost.

He now knows why, and wishes he didn't, because it's a price that would be paid for with the lives of his men. The cost would be borne by their families, who would never know how or why their sons, husbands, and fathers died. He's sure the men from the ministry will think this is an acceptable price for victory that promises access to other worlds.

Looi doubts that preventing the Americans from finding out what the pillars are by destroying the thing under the mountain is worth the price his men must pay for it.

25. FIFTH REVOLUTION

To be somebody or to do something. In life there is often a roll call. That's when you will have to make a decision. To be or to do? Which way will you go?

— COL JOHN R. BOYD, USAF

Sergeant Tachikoma
First Combat Armor Suit Reconnaissance Company
CSN *Hornet*
Thursday, July 2, 2071

I lie on my rack, remembering the pain from every time I've died, and start crying. Then I curl up in a foetal position, knowing I will be flying out to repeat the same mission, and be killed again. The next thing I notice is one of the other women I share the bunkroom with standing at my side in her bathrobe, looking at me.

"Hey, you OK?" she asks.

"I'll be fine," I say, sobbing as tears roll down my cheeks.

"You don't sound like you're fine. How about I take you to see the doctor?"

I've forgotten her name, and her bathrobe is sans name tag. "I'm OK, I don't need a doctor."

"Come on, let me help you out of your rack, where's your bathrobe? Everything will be fine once the doctor sorts you out," she says, and I find myself being helped out of my rack and having my coffin locker under my bed opened for me. Before I really know what's happening, I'm being led off to see the doctor.

I can't stop crying as I walk along the gangways staring at the deck. I'm all too aware that people are staring at me in my bathrobe and flip-flops.

We reach the sickbay, where I'm handed over to the orderly on duty. They log me into the system, processing me for an assessment, while I sit in a chair. After that I'm moved to a small waiting area that has a couple of chairs and an examination table. The orderly tells me someone will come see me soon.

They draw the curtain behind them, leaving me alone.

I wait and flinch from the sound of the curtain swishing open as a doctor comes in and sits next to me, fiddling with his PAD as he reviews my file. He's a small man with glasses and receding hair. And he wears a Naval uniform in a way only a hospital corpsman can get away with, who we in the Marines call a POG, Person Other Than Grunt.

The doctor smiles at me before asking, "What brings you here today, Sergeant Tachikoma?"

"Crying, waking up, and not being able to stop crying."

"Didn't think sergeants could cry. I was told that they had their tear ducts surgically removed by the Corps. That and their sense of humour."

"That's just a rumour we put about to maintain our mystique," I say, and I can't help but smile.

"So I see. I'm Dr Bullock. If you like, you can call me Doc.

So, are you up for me asking you a few questions to find out what ails you?"

"Go for it, Doc," I say and nod at him.

"So what's your story, what brings you here today?"

"Not sure where to start, or even how to begin, because you'll say I'm crazy if I tell you what's been happening to me."

"Sounds like a bad place, Sergeant. I guess you'd rather be under fire than face being told you're crazy?"

"When you say it like that, I guess so, Doc. The thing is though…" I stop, unable to continue speaking.

After a few moments of silence, Doc says, "Huh, huh, go on…"

"Even thinking about what's happened confuses the hell out of me, Doc. I'm sorry, I'm wasting your time. I can't do this."

He peers at me over the top of his glasses and speaks. "It seems like it's hard for you to tell me what the problem is. My guess is it frightens you to even talk about what's troubling you."

"I'm frightened you will tell me I'm insane. I never thought I'd say this, but I'm scared I'm not hard enough and will be seen as a coward."

"Last time I heard, cowards don't get to make sergeant, but you do sure sound like a woman who is frightened. I'd like to help if I may?"

"I'd like that, but I want what's happening to me to stop. But I'm not sure how you can help me."

"Honestly, I don't know yet, but when I do, I promise I'll tell you. So start wherever it's easiest and we'll work from there, shall we?"

Then I take in a deep breath to steel myself. "I keep living the same day over and over again. Every morning I wake up at the same time, and it's the same day all over again."

"That sounds like life aboard a ship to me. Don't the Marines call being at sea Groundhog Day? So what makes this a problem for you?"

"You don't understand. It's not like every day feels the same, every day *is* the same. I know what people are going to say and what's going to happen next, and every day ends up with me dying. Then I wake up on the same morning and do it all over again."

I start sweating; my armpits are sodden and my hands are clammy.

"So what am I going to say next then?"

"Don't know. This is the first time *this* has happened to me. On every other day I've gotten up and just done the best I could to get through it. Trying to change what I do so the day ends differently, but failing each time. The only way I can describe it is, imagine you're dreaming you're awake, only to wake up and find you're dreaming. However, now you're awake you want to get back to dreaming again, because dreaming sure beats the hell out of being awake and dying again."

"I see. What's today's date?"

"It's Thursday, the second of July, and the year is 2071."

"Good, and what time of the year is it?"

"Summertime now. It was winter before we crossed the equator."

"Very good, Sergeant, no flies on you, and where are we now? Start from here and work it out if you can."

"This is the sickbay on board CSN *Hornet*, she's a landing tilt-fan dock ship, part of the Amphibious Ready Group that is transporting the Fighting Thirteenth Marine Expeditionary Unit. We're sailing in the Arabian Sea after transiting from the Indian Ocean yesterday, somewhere off the Indian coast heading towards Pakistan."

"So, tell me, have you heard voices talking to you or telling you what to do?"

"Only over the comms-board, Doc."

"Are these voices of people you know?"

"Of course, who else would they be? They're the Marines in my platoon talking to me."

"OK, uhm...do you think that your mind is being read by other people, or that your thoughts are not your own?"

"No, not all. Why, should I?"

"When people experience a psychotic episode they lose touch with their external reality. Do you think you are losing control of your mind or find your mind racing away out of control?"

"At times it does feel like my mind is racing a bit, but otherwise no, not really, if that makes any sense, Doc."

"OK, do you think you are going to harm yourself, be harmed by others, or harm others?"

"What kind of questions is that, Doc? I'm a Marine, I get paid to harm others. It's what I do. Though I only harm bad people who are trying to harm me, it sort of goes with the territory. As for harming myself, no not really, despite the fact that the same day repeating itself means I might as well be. Apart from that, not planning on harming myself anytime soon."

"Hummh, I see your sense of humour remains intact, but here's the thing, Sergeant—your story doesn't make much sense, does it? So I propose we do a little experiment. In a moment or two I'm going to make a very loud noise, just so you're prepared for the shock. How does that sound?"

"Whatever you say, Doc, I'm used to loud noises—"

I am interrupted by a loud bang as he suddenly slaps his hand against the bulkhead, and I nearly jump out of my chair.

"Thank you, Sergeant, I can safely say you're not insane. But it does appear that you have the signs and symptoms of post-traumatic stress disorder, which can cause psychotic symptoms. The good news is we now have portable TMS, so we can start treatment today. And the sooner we start, the sooner we get you on the road to recovery. Just give me a few moments to prepare."

"Before you go, Doc, what's a TMS-thingy?"

"It's a transcranial magnetic stimulator, which allows me to treat your symptoms," he says before leaving me.

Ten minutes later Doc comes back pushing a trolley with a console sitting on the top. There's an elaborate headband with a cable that could be a prop from some horror movie.

"What will happen now, Doc?"

Next he puts the headset on me and says, "I'm going to run a calibration test first. Please move the fingers of both your hands. You might feel a little odd when they stop moving."

He fiddles with the machine, which emits a low-pitch whistling noise, and I wriggle my fingers as ordered.

The doc studies me as I move my fingers and says, "Do you feel anything happening, Sergeant?"

"No, not really, apart from the need to get up and walk around. Is that what's supposed to happen?"

"That's most peculiar…let me check again." He fiddles with it a bit more before checking his PAD. "How unusual, it's not every day one sees that happen."

"What's up, Doc?"

He switches the machine off and removes the headband. The numbness and depression return.

"Nothing. You should've lost voluntary control over your hands as the magnetic stimulation interfered with the normal function of your brain. It seems you're one of those rare neurologically atypical individuals."

"Is that a good or a bad thing, Doc?"

"Neither. It's unfortunate in this case, because it means I'll need to change your treatment plan. It also means it will take longer for you to recover. Don't worry, we can start you on some oral medication, and I'll schedule daily chats. Then we can work together on a personalised treatment plan. I shall keep you here today for sure, but I think we will be able to clear you for light duties tomorrow or the next day."

"Does this mean I'm not nuts?"

"'Nuts' isn't a very helpful term. There are only situational-appropriate behaviours, like sergeant's never crying for example. We'll get to talk again later today, and I'll try to explain your diagnosis more then. Now I'm going to go and write you up a mild sedative. It will take the edge off, so you won't be jumping every time you hear a sudden noise. Is that OK with you?"

All I can do is nod because I'm too stunned to know what else to say.

A short time later an orderly comes in and offers me a cup of water and two pills. He doesn't say anything, and I'm not particularly interested in talking. So that works out well for both of us. After swallowing the pills I start to go woozy, like I'm floating, and I fall asleep.

Falling asleep in a chair is not hard to do if you are a Marine because you learn to take naps whenever you can. Rules for surviving in the military: don't stand when you can sit, don't sit if you can lie down, and when you are allowed to sleep, then do.

I'm woken by lunch being brought to me on a tray. Now I feel like I'm sick, lame, and lazy. But I tuck into the burger and fries I'm presented like a starving person. However, I leave the fruit bowl; not my thing.

The orderly comes in again and gives me two more pills to take.

I ask him for the time, and he tells me it's 1230 hours. The medication has really knocked me out. It's probably the reason why I'm so groggy, fuzzy headed, and not able to think straight.

By now my company are aboard the Thunder Hawks and on their way to meet their deaths, which should really make me feel bad. However, whatever they're giving me sure takes the edge off feeling anything except sleepy. The chair has proved to be good enough to crash out on. So I get some more rack ops in, nod off to sleep, and start cultivating the Zs.

26. LIMITS OF PERCEPTION

Decisions without actions are pointless. Actions without decisions are reckless.

— Col John R. Boyd, USAF

Captain Johanson
First Combat Armor Suit Reconnaissance Company
Afghanistan
Thursday, July 2, 2071

It seems clear to Johanson that after the complete FUBAR from the bad landing, the surviving members of the Special Forces Alpha Detachment team had left the downed space-plane. It's what he would've done if their situations were reversed and he was in their place. Complete the mission first, and then retrieve the downed personnel at dust-off, but something had prevented them from returning later.

That something was an unknown factor that lay under the mountain ahead.

His company is one down after Sergeant Tachikoma's sick

call, causing Lieutenant McCarthy's platoon to be reorganized. This means Corporal Knight has taken charge of Tachikoma's squad, but it resulted in a deployment SNAFU when they were dropped. All part of the friction in any operation, but Johanson hopes that any further impact on the company's performance will be minimal.

Checking the map, he makes his up his mind about what orders to give. "Wulfgang Six, this is Big Dog."

"Roger, solid copy," says Perez, acknowledging his call.

"Take your platoon and sweep the area for any signs of the Alpha Detachment and then maintain overwatch on Lobo. Once Air Force has gotten the package aboard, Lobo will link up with you and be under your command, out."

Perez repeats back the order and says, "Wilco, out."

Johanson switches channels.

"Fenris Six, this is Big Dog, time for us to move to the mountain ahead, over."

He leads the Dogs of First Platoon forward and hears, "Roger that, Fenris Six Oscar Mike, out," as McCarthy acknowledges the order and they begin marching towards their objective.

Johanson concentrates on leading the company across the formidable terrain while not letting loose rocks that threaten to topple him with every step he takes win out. It would've been better to have split the company, to have half land nearer their objective while the other half could've been dropped closer to the mountain.

He mutters to himself, "Just another day in the Corps."

Ahead of them the undulating hills lead up to towering white-clad mountains that dominate the horizon. They begin the climb, which turns into a long, slow slog. He'd rather be appreciating the stark beauty of Afghanistan from afar—somewhere very far away.

27. GET A MOVE ON

It isn't what we say or think that defines us, but what we do.

— JANE AUSTEN

Second Lieutenant Beckford
Commander Fourth Platoon
First Combat Armor Suit Reconnaissance Company
Afghanistan
Thursday, July 2, 2071

Beckford picks up the Identify Friend or Foe codes from the Air Force MULE as it comes in low over the horizon from the south. The hybrid airship is stealthy through a combination of design and choice of materials. Like the Dogs, it's covered in ChameleonFlage making it harder to see, but underneath that is a multilayer skin with active and passive radar countermeasures designed to reduce the chances of targeting the MULE.

It's kind of spooky to see a hole in the sky rippling as the MULE moves across her field of vision with no LIDAR info to confirm the distance and rate of movement. It's not until the

MULE drops lower, on the final approach, that the noise of the fans can be heard. Even then it's easy to look right through it.

For the aircrew this was dangerously close, entering death's ground.

"Lobo Four, get the platoon on securing the cargo straps to the package," she says over the laser-net.

She hears Washington issuing orders to the platoon. He has them up and running around, securing the straps the MULE has lowered to secure the crashed space-plane. Like most procedures this takes longer to finish than she would like, but goes quicker than she expects. It takes real teamwork to do routine jobs well under field conditions.

Beckford stands at the perimeter of the crash site as the space-plane is winched up into the hold and the crew secures the package.

The roar of the fans increases as the MULE, now burdened with the package, lifts up into the sky, heading north. The MULE climbs to gain altitude before swinging around and heading back the way it came.

"Well done, Marines," she says over the laser-net.

Now it's time to go link up with Perez's platoon. She looks at where the plain ends and the broken ground starts and utters a curse. Why didn't they think to hitch a ride on the MULE? Judging by the terrain they have to cross, she knows it is going to be a hard, slow slog to rendezvous with Third Platoon.

28. SURPRISE

Life is hard; its harder when you're stupid.

— JOHN WAYNE

Second Lieutenant Perez
Commander Third Platoon
First Combat Armor Suit Reconnaissance Company
Afghanistan
Thursday, July 2, 2071

Perez takes up a position at the base of the mountain. From here he can observe both Beckford's platoon and the path leading up to the entrance to the caves. Long shadows cast by the afternoon sun make the boulder-strewn terrain an ideal location to place his platoon.

After a long wait, the MULE arrives and he watches Fourth Platoon as they load the downed space-plane into it. After much running around, Beckford's platoon finally finish their task. Then he tracks the progress of the MULE as it climbs before turning and circling back the way it came.

So far the operation is going by the numbers, apart from the timing of everything, which had gone to pot. All his platoon has to do now is wait for Beckford's platoon to rendezvous with them, which, judging by her progress, was going to take quite some time.

Perez is just about to check on the status of his platoon when the ground next to him bursts apart. Artillery rounds land on top of his position. He mouths, *Oh fuck*, as his Dog is caught in the blast. The artillery rounds tear up the ground, and the shock waves blow his Dog apart, killing him.

29. NOT A GOOD DAY

War is the realm of danger; therefore courage is the soldier's first requirement.

— CARL VON CLAUSEWITZ

Captain Johanson
First Combat Armor Suit Reconnaissance Company
Afghanistan
Thursday, July 2, 2071

Johanson concentrates on maneuvring his Dog through the labyrinth of tunnels as the squad delves further into the heart of the mountain. He takes a moment to check their position on the map. Given their rate of progress so far, it's going to take a lot longer to search these tunnels than he'd thought it would. Up ahead the cavern narrows into another choke point requiring further careful negotiation to get through.

God help them if they come under attack now.

In front of him, Private Gentle slides her Dog through the narrow gap by turning sideways, followed by Brownlee, and then it is his turn. Sergeant Ramirez follows him with Ward trailing behind bringing up the rear. The passageway opens out and curves left, winding downwards and deeper into the darkness. His Dog's feet scrabble as his systems maintain the balance of his machine. In front of him, Brownlee's Dog falls as incoming fire hits the loose rock he had been standing on.

Gentle shouts out over the laser-net, "Contact! Front at eleven o'clock, twenty meters."

Flashes of light from the muzzle blasts light up the cavern, casting dancing shadows that move as if they have lives of their own. Johanson returns fire, selecting targets by tracing their locations from the flashes of their weapons. An enemy moves and is lit up for a moment. He has the satisfaction of seeing a Chinese Fatty go down as the 20 mm round penetrates it.

Johanson shouts, "Lay it on, Marines."

They've found the enemy. The firefight is short and brutal with the roar from the cannons' firing heard through their suits. And then silence as the firing stops as suddenly as it had started. The enemy troops must've realized the disadvantage of fighting up the slope and slipped back behind cover. From the noises, they appear to have exfiltrated the area.

"Sound off," he calls.

"Brownlee here."

"Ramirez here."

"Ward here," comes her reply.

"Gentle, sound off!"

No reply. He sees her Dog's telltales are redlined.

"Anyone have eyes on Gentle?"

Brownlee replies, "Her Dog took a hit to the chest. She's dead, Captain."

Johanson pauses for a moment. "Anyone got eyes on the enemy?"

A chorus of, "All clear," comes in reply from the members of the squad.

"Secure Gentle's Dog, and let's move back out of here by the numbers."

"OK, you heard the Captain, move your sorry selves, we ain't got all day now. Brownlee, that was some sorry shit you did back there, now move it before I say something that will make me sad for the rest of the day," says Sergeant Ramirez.

As they withdraw, Johanson receives a report from Lance Corporal Delgado that Second Platoon is no longer combat effective. Fenris Alpha Squad had been ambushed by Chinese bán, with McCarthy and Hernandez dying in the initial exchange of shots. Delgado and Vosloo had held out until Corporal Knight arrived, but he and Kowalski died when assaulting the Chinese position, which meant they were down to five effectives. McCarthy's death hits Johanson hard. Knowing he'll have to break the news to McCarthy's wife and children causes him a moment's pause.

The company had incurred a grievous blow, the cost of retrieving the PACE suits they'd found too high. He orders Delgado to withdraw and meet back at the rendezvous point.

Not coming to Afghanistan was always a good idea. The British Empire had tried it three times and failed. After them the old Soviet Union had sent in forces to prop up a favoured government last century, which also failed. Then the former United States with British and other allies had occupied Afghanistan sixty years ago after terrorists used the country as a base for their operations.

Every nation that had sent troops in ended up leaving.

Afghanistan was not amenable to outsiders coming in and trying to change things. The culture was singularly resistant, due to a combination of historical choices and the unforgiving nature of the country. It grew a people who were the libertarian ideal of a reduced state, albeit ideals built on a bed of tribalism, Muslim sensibilities on rights, and what was considered moral.

Personally he'd call it downright inbred xenophobia.

What on Earth made the Chinese think that coming here and setting up shop was a good idea? They clearly have ambitions in this area, judging by the way they're aggressively throwing their weight around. They obviously hadn't gotten the memo about not starting a land war in Asia.

Johanson sends a message ordering Lieutenant Bergeson to meet back at the rendezvous point so they can regroup and reform. Once outside they can send *Hornet* a SITREP on their current position.

Failure to report on what happened here would only exacerbate the failure of the mission to find the source emitting the energy pulse. He can't afford to lose any more people in ambushes today, otherwise his command faces the possibility of being defeated in detail, and he'll end up having his command destroyed.

An outcome he cannot allow to happen.

Johanson pushes everyone to move faster. He knows that every time they slow down to negotiate the narrow passageways, it increases their chances of being caught by the enemy. His only consolation is knowing their line of retreat is secure. Perez's and hopefully by now Beckford's platoons should be outside covering the entrance to the mountain. If he can regroup, any Chinese pursuing them will be in for a big shock.

He'd be able to force them to retreat, then he'd take the initiative. Pay them back for what happened earlier and avenge the loss of Gentle, McCarthy, Knight, Kowalski, and Hernandez.

He'd like to teach the Chinese a lesson that payback is a bitch, but not at the risk of losing more people.

Johanson sees Bergeson's squad waiting at the rendezvous point where the tunnels split. Opening the laser-net, he speaks. "Bergeson, move your squad to our six, and watch out for any Chinese who might be trailing us."

The map shows him that Delgado's squad is still far behind them. He messages her to rendezvous outside and remain alert to the possibility of meeting more Chinese hostiles. She acknowledges his message.

Time to call for reinforcements because searching the mountain will require more boots on the ground. That means Corps MARPACE suits. The smaller power armor will be able to maneuver more readily in the confines of the tunnels. Far better than the larger Dogs ever can. The price paid for the INTEL they'd gained was already way too high. He will have to have some serious words with Mr Anderson when he gets back.

Sergeant Ramirez speaks. "Big Dog, this is Hellhound Four, I'm out in the open and I can't see either Wulfgang or Lobo, over."

"Copy that, out," he replies. What's happened?

Johanson tries bringing up Perez's platoon on his tactical screen but gets nothing; furthermore, he isn't getting anything from Beckford either.

It's at that moment Johanson realizes his mistake. He's assumed all the Chinese are inside the mountain in force. Doing so has made an ass out of him and his people. The first incoming round flies past him and hits Private Ward's Dog, blowing the leg off.

Ramirez shouts, "Incoming, contact line of march fifty meters!"

They're in death's ground, caught in crossfire from another Chinese bán. The eight Fatties are tearing his Dogs to pieces, and if they try to withdraw now, the platoon will be cut to ribbons. Now the only option is to fight their way through the ambush.

He shouts over the radio, "Follow me, Marines. Charge!"

Incoming missiles from two sides rip up the ground around their position. Lance Corporal Langford's Dog is blown off its feet. Firing as she falls forward, she manages to destroy a Fatty in the process. Then another missile hits her in the back. It hammers her Dog into the ground, killing her.

Johanson lays down fire, emptying his autocannon with two long bursts. He hits one of the Fatties, causing it to explode as the fuel and ammunition ignite. He reloads while moving forward, pointing at Bergeson and the rest of the platoon to follow him.

"Come on move it, people," he shouts as Locklear's Dog goes down on one knee and starts firing at the enemy to the right of them. A Fatty blows up as it's hit by multiple shots from Locklear's autocannon, which rips open the enemy machine's armor.

Spader's and Lopez's Dogs, from Bergeson's squad, are then both caught in the enemy crossfire. They fall to the ground like broken puppets.

"Give them hell!" says Sergeant Ramirez. "You heard the captain, move it, Marines."

Johanson sees Brownlee's Dog dive to the ground as a Fatty fires its missile pack. Brownlee fires back, his shot hitting the front of the enemy machine, destroying it with a loud *whumph*! Missiles land behind Brownlee, and now Locklear is taking fire.

Johanson moves through the middle of a swirling circle of confusion, his people trying desperately to get through the ambush. Fighting to survive.

He watches Brownlee's Dog roll as it hits the ground, coming up on its feet and firing past Johanson. He turns and sees a Fatty preparing to shoot at them both. It blows up. But now they're mixed in with the Chinese. His platoon has grabbed the enemy by the belt buckle.

The fire from the other half of the enemy formation ceases.

Johanson fires again, catching one of the Fatties in the leg, causing it to topple over as it's about to fire a missile. The enemy machine hits the ground and sets off a chain reaction as its missile pack explodes.

Around him the remainder of his platoon continues to lay down fire. The thunderous roar of the autocannons drowns out all other sounds as they take out the remaining two Fatties on their right-hand side.

"Keep moving, people," he says, leading the survivors out of the ambush to where they can regroup. He looks around him and asks, "Where's Locklear?"

"Gunny's gone, Captain," says Brownlee.

"Squad, circle the wagons. Roger up, Marines." He orders the squad to form an all-round defence and sound off.

Only four of them have made it through the ambushers' line: him, Bergeson, Ramirez, and Brownlee.

Before they can move, they're hit by fire from a second enemy bán. It has been placed as a backstop to support the ambush in case they managed to break through. The leg flies off Johanson's Dog as it takes a hit. As he falls he sees the rest of his Marines being cut apart before another shot kills him.

30. CRIMSON RAIN

Be polite, be professional, but have a plan to kill everybody you meet.

— GEN JAMES "MAD DOG" MATTIS, USMC

Second Lieutenant Beckford
Commander Fourth Platoon
First Combat Armor Suit Reconnaissance Company
Afghanistan
Thursday, July 2, 2071

Beckford awakens in darkness and starts to shake in fear.

What's happened?

Then she remembers the explosions of the enemy artillery falling around her platoon. Beckford is hanging from her seat straps and realizes that her Dog must be lying facedown on the ground. Struggling with the controls, she manages to roll it over. Now lying on her back the cockpit's virtual screen goes from dark to light. Her eyes adjust to the brightness, which shows the sky with wispy white clouds floating high above.

As she sits her Dog up, red telltale warning lights appear across the board. Some wink back to green, others flicker between red and amber. Her Dog's systems show intermittent faults, either from the damage caused by the explosions or from glitches in the sensor readings.

Scanning around she finds she has been thrown into a gully. None of the other Dogs in her platoon show any activity status. This could mean they're all dead, or it's her systems malfunctioning—Beckford hopes it's not the former and wishes for the latter, but as she stands she sees the remains of her platoon.

She's overwhelmed, stunned by the sight of the carnage strewn around her. Tears begin rolling down her face. She starts to sob. Beckford makes herself stop crying. It isn't helping her with what she has to do next.

She switches on her comms-channel and barks out, "Status, people?" but gets no reply.

She walks towards the closest Dog and can see where the blasts ripped through the rear of the machine. The next Dog is broken into pieces. Each Dog she checks is the same. All of them have been broken apart by the force of the artillery explosions. Everyone is dead.

But, by some miracle, the gully had shielded her from the direct force of the artillery barrage.

Beckford takes stock of her Dog's damage log. It shows that her backpack and auxiliary motor have been ripped off, but her rear armor held. Her Dog is running on battery power, and time is against her. Apparently it's her lucky day, but right now she would trade her own life for those of the men and women of her platoon.

She looks towards the mountain as she calls up Perez. He must've seen her platoon being hit and think her dead. She gets no reply.

Her worse fear is being alone out here with no support.

Starting to hyperventilate, she slows her breathing to calm herself. Beckford tries to open a link to *Hornet*, but again no reply. But it seems unlikely *Hornet* has been destroyed, so it must mean her transceiver is damaged.

As Beckford runs a diagnostic again the green telltale turns red.

That could mean Perez is watching her now and wondering why she doesn't answer his transmission. She turns to face the mountain and starts the long walk across the plain, hoping the battery is fully charged because, even so, it will be barely enough power to make the trip.

In the distance Beckford sees Johanson's platoon exit the side of mountain. Soon Perez will make contact with the captain and bring him up to speed about what has happened out here. By her estimate she's still at least fifteen minutes away from the rendezvous point, if the batteries hold out.

Then she sees the flash of guns firing. Johanson's platoon is being ambushed. This can only mean that Perez's platoon providing security have also been taken out. Nothing else makes any sense. She follows the fight in the distance, seeing the platoon charge through the enemy ambush line.

Beckford silently cheers them on, *Go, Marines, go, retreat hell!*

She tries to move faster, but the broken terrain makes it impossible for her to get there sooner. Her battery charge indicator moves into the red zone. Trying to shoot at this range, she'd likely as not hit one of her own.

The four remaining Dogs of Johanson's platoon take up an all-round defence. Horrified, she sees them fall one by one as a second group of Chinese All Terrain Suits take out the remaining survivors. But she knows there's nothing she could've done to have changed the outcome of the battle.

She catches herself in that moment. Not nothing, she can take a few more of them out. Now the line of fire is clear. With a little bit of luck she can make the Chinese pay, all of them, pay for what they've done.

Beckford lowers her Dog to the ground, checking again that her main weapon telltales remain green. Settling into place, she takes one last look at the photo of her partner, Alice, *I love you so much*, and remembers all the good times they've had together. Her one regret is she will not be able to tell Alice now how much she loved her. Tears start to well in her eyes; she forces herself back into the task at hand.

She pulls two spare magazines out to allow her to quickly reload. Lying prone, she shifts the Dog's position so it's mostly hidden, nestled down on a back slope in the ground. Now that she's no longer walking, the battery briefly flickers to amber. She uses her fire control system to designate her priority targets.

One of the Fatties is acting like the leader. It's only a guess, but even a guess can be right. Worst case, she has a one-in-seven chance. A boom reverberates through her Dog as she fires the autocannon. Her effort is rewarded by the sight of the target falling over.

Beckford lets the Dog's autotracker do its job. As the confirmation of a target lock comes up, she fires again. The sound of the boom reverberates through her. Her second shot hits another of their compatriots.

But the enemy aren't fools. They've turned to face her position and see the muzzle blast of her autocannon. The remaining five Fatties take off as they kick in their flight packs.

Shots fall around her, kicking up dirt.

They have the direction, but not her exact location, her Dog's adaptive ChameleonFlage blending her into the ground. Under the circumstances she has no good reason to move nor the power to spare should she want to. Whatever happens next she is stuffed. Besides, the remaining Chinese seem more than keen to come find her.

Boom! Firing again, she takes some satisfaction from seeing another Fatty explode. It collides into the one flying next to it, and they both career into the ground. She sees metal crushed and ripped apart by the impact, followed by a loud explosion and a fireball rising into the sky. With three Fatties to go, she tracks her next target.

A missile explodes off to her left, which cause her next shot to miss.

Beckford fires a long burst that empties her magazine to keep the Fatties too busy to take advantage of now knowing her position. They fly wild to evade her fire, giving her a moment's respite to change the magazine. She fires again and misses. The Fatties might waddle when walking, by comparison making Marine Corps Dogs look like graceful hounds gliding over the ground, but when in the air they're very fast.

The remaining three Fatties are closing in on her position. She's going to need more than luck to survive. Given how well the day had gone so far, she isn't counting on any more luck coming her way. She's sure she's used it all up when she survived the artillery barrage.

Beckford rolls the Dog over onto its side and catches another Fatty as it crests the ridgeline ahead of her. The other two Fatties sweep in from opposite sides. Shit, she can only get one. She fires at the Fatty on her left as it fires on her, resulting in a mutual kill shot.

Beckford doesn't get the satisfaction of seeing the surviving Fatty crash as her Dog explodes.

31. GLORY & DEFEATED

Opportunities multiply as they are seized.

— Sun Tzu

Shàowèi Zhan
Platoon Leader Special Operations Force Falcon
Democratic People's Republic of China
The White Mountain, Afghanistan
Thursday, July 2, 2071

Zhan stands in the tunnel with Zhongzhi Chén beside him. They're waiting in the shadows in their combat armor, hidden by the overhanging rock at the entrance to the tunnel complex so as to not alert the Americans to their presence by being spotted by the UAV flying overhead. Zhan touches Zhongzhi Chén's suit and connects with him over a secure link.

"A moment to share our thoughts together?"

"I'm OK, Shàowèi, it's the waiting that's hard."

"It's hard for me too, Zhongzhi. I wish the Americans would hurry up and head back to the surface."

"If wishes are being granted, then I wish we had planted this bomb long before the Americans had arrived here, sir."

"If we're going that far, then I wish another unit had been chosen for the honour of being here today under the mountain waiting for the Americans. We could be at home with our families while refitting the lián and restoring our unit's strength."

"That would've been good, sir."

His zhongzhi seems to him to be the right man to stand beside him under the mountain. Finally, the truck pulls up in front of them. The truck's driver and guards give him the bomb and the arming device. It requires him to plug it into his combat armor suit. As he does so, a window comes up on his screen notifying him that his suit is being calibrated, and the bomb is now armed.

Zhan reads the scrolling message on the screen.

It informs him that if any of his suit's systems fail, the bomb will detonate. If the system detects his death, then it will detonate. Removing the arming device from the suit will also cause it to detonate. The device can be set to detonate the bomb at any time.

He's advised that the minimum safe distance when detonating the nuclear bomb is four kilometers. It lists in pedantic detail the necessary conditions for detonation: his suit must not be in direct line of sight of the bomb blast, or, with a further explanation added as a subclause, under hard cover, defined as occupying an entrenched position or inside a pillbox. All things he doesn't have access too.

To add to his misery, he's now a walking detonator for a bomb big enough to vaporize him in an instant. This mission has reached a point he never would've imagined finding himself in. The thought of being victorious has suddenly become more frightening than the thought of losing.

"Come, Zhongzhi Chén, time for us to plant this device. Then we can leave this place."

They carry the bomb together into the darkness to a fortress built under the mountain. The Afghans had dug in to hide and then found something that frightened them even more than the threats of the outside world. Something so fearful that it had made them welcome their enemies into their home. It tells him everything he needs to know about the locals' resolve to defend themselves against outsiders; whatever it was had shaken them to their very core.

When they'd set out on the mission, it had seemed straightforward enough. But the mission had unfolded in ways he never imagined. As they walk past empty rooms, Zhan senses a palpable presence threatening them. Finally, they reach the cavern. As they enter, the *kongjù de zhizhù* shimmers, dispelling the darkness and stopping them where they stand. Zhan watches the scene of another place, which delays them, but he reassures himself it will last only a few minutes. Relief at being able to move again comes as the shimmer stops.

"Have you experienced this before, Zhongzhi Chén?"

"No, sir, this is my first time here, but I heard the other men speak of being frozen, and hadn't believed how frightening it feels until now."

"I wondered at the reports I heard too, Zhongzhi, but now we both know the truth. It will hopefully make it easier for us to explain to our superiors when we get back."

They carry the bomb and place it next to the pillars; their moves are being recorded. Their must be no doubt in his commander's eyes that he has properly fulfilled his duty here. They move out of the cavern before they can be frozen again and trapped here when the bomb goes off.

The tunnel is welcoming, in spite of the fact that it's too small to allow them to fly along it. Still, Zhan feels good to be walking because moving gives him the illusion he's in control. Zhongzhi Chén follows him as they walk towards the light outside, which promises escape. As they reach the surface they move apart and take to the air. Accelerating quickly, they fly across the valley towards safety.

Zhan notes they've nearly reached the minimum safe distance when the bomb detonates. He watches in fear as the mountain collapses in on itself, and a wave of rock and debris chases after them at a frightening speed. They both turn into a small canyon that opens on their left and land. As they touch down, the blast wave seeps over their suits and knocks them to the ground, but they will live to fight another day.

32. ALLAHU AHKBAR

Every day of your life is a page of your history.

— ARABIAN PROVERB

Warlord Yeshua bin Yussuf
The White Mountain, Afghanistan
Thursday, July 2, 2071

Yeshua bin Yussuf, with Abdi at his side, stops to glance back below where his Disciples sit; twelve great guns. His followers are busy disassembling the former Russian artillery pieces, getting them ready to be moved somewhere safe because that which is not destroyed can be used again.

"I need to stop and get my breath back," he says.

Abdi nods as they come to a halt on the path where it widens out into a flat area. He waits for his leftenants to catch up to where he sits, and he can hear them mumbling about the Chinese.

"I don't understand why the Chinese demanded we fire all our ammunition when attacking the American shayateen. The first barrage was more than enough to destroy all of the enemy," says

Abdul-Baser as he draws closer. The man liked to complain about everything.

"How dare you say that. Have you no respect for your elders?" asks Abdi.

Yeshua bin Yussuf speaks. "It's not about respect. I too was reluctant to agree to use all the shells we've carefully hoarded over the years, but seeing the destruction of our enemies gladdens my heart." To him the Americans and Chinese are exactly the same. They are infidels. Infidels who would bring about the demise of the world. "The American shayateen will not tolerate what we've done to them this day. Their retribution will be swift and brutal. And death will strike from the sky at all those they can find."

His two leftenants nod in agreement.

"The infidels shame us with their anger," says Churagh-Ali.

The Chinese had been angry at his followers' performance, calling them incompetent for firing too late and allowing the airship to escape with its cargo.

"They're infidels," says Abdi. "One cannot expect anything else from infidels."

He speaks again. "The Chinese commander has promised us three shells for each one we fire…"

"Which only proves that the servants of Shaytan know how to tempt a man!" replies Abdul-Baser.

"True, but we will turn temptation into opportunity. Three trucks are on their way here. Our people say, Allah willing, they should arrive in a few days," he says, pausing to acknowledge his leftenant's presence before continuing. "I am not concerned by words, but with the Americans taking possession of something that can only bring a great evil into this world. The Chinese are shayateen too, the only difference is that they consider the Americans their enemy."

He hears murmurs of agreement.

"The enemy of my enemy is my friend," says Abdi.

But it's not true. When he had studied in the West, he had learnt many things. One was that the enemy of one's enemy is still one's enemy, but sometimes you can get your enemies to kill each other. That, he believed, was true.

"Today is the day our enemies kill each other. We may not have seen with our own eyes the destruction the Disciples have wrought on the American shayateen, but for me it is enough to know we did."

"Allahu Ahkbar," says Abdi.

"Today marks the first blow marking the beginning of the times that will lead to the Yawm ad-Din, the day of judgement. We must pray to Allah for guidance on how to prepare for the Yawm al-Qiyāmah, the day of resurrection."

"Allahu Ahkbar," says Abdi.

"My grandfather had a dream. He dreamed of a place of safety for us, under the White Mountain. Today we will see our life's work, our homes, destroyed. A sacrifice we make for the greater good of Islam. In the heart of the mountain lies the cursed Afrite. It will be destroyed by the followers of Shaytan, and we will have prevented a great evil from being unleashed on the world. I promise you all we shall start anew."

"Allahu Ahkbar," say his three leftenants, beginning a chant.

They had started work on building a new home beneath another mountain. A place where they could retreat to. For one day the time would come when the faithful would need to hide from the cruelty of the shayateen. A time when the faithful would have to face and kill the Masih ad-Dajjal, the false messiah.

"Allahu Ahkbar," he says, silencing his followers. "Allah has a plan for us. Our duty is clear, we must prepare to bring justice to this world. A world that has become full of cruelty, injustice, and tyranny. To do this, we need a safe base to work from. Our consolation is knowing it will be a place where our families, our friends can live. Where it will be possible for honest men to work hard and prosper by following the laws of the Qur'an." He pauses for a moment.

Today confirmed something he had learnt as a young man. Some situations are win-win; in his mind today was one of those days. Now the Chinese advisors had left to report to their commander; his followers would soon forget their rudeness.

"I stood with you when we fired the great guns. The Chinese helped us to aim the guns. And it pleased me to stand with you as the artillery fired. Every round I heard fired cheered my heart for the death and destruction brought upon heads of the Americans."

"Allahu Ahkbar," shout his followers.

"Let us continue onwards," he says, getting up.

When they reach the top of the slope, he lies down on the ground, peering at the White Mountain through his binoculars.

His father had carried on his grandfather's works, and in turn had passed the task to him, his son. He'd failed, not because he hadn't tried, but because of the evil hidden beneath the White Mountain. So he waits for a sign that the Chinese have destroyed the evil the mountain contained.

In spite of what he'd said this still felt like a bitter victory.

His grandfather had started working on the fortress when the Americans left after trying to defeat the Taliban, who fled into the mountains to hide. All that had been achieved was to disperse the faithful like seeds throughout the land to bring forth a future Islamic state and cultivate another generation of mujahideen.

When the ammunition for the guns arrives, they can be used in the jihad against the shayateen.

He feels before he hears a rumble as the stillness of the mountain is broken in a whirlwind of the destruction, as evil is destroyed by evil. What he sees makes his heart rejoice. It is the destruction of the evil that has lain hidden from the eyes of man for so long, but his heart also weeps. It weeps for the loss of the home his family had dedicated their lives to building.

Moments later the shock wave of the explosion reaches him. With the roar he sees the ground around the mountain rippling like water. A great cloud of dust and rubble spews forth, rushing across the valley below, turning the ground black. The force of the wind blows debris over them both.

Death is in the air. And in that moment he realizes that victory can be a bittersweet thing indeed. The land is poisoned, but the will of Allah guides them. He hopes he has done a holy thing today because then it will be reward enough for the price the land has paid. Time passes as he contemplates what has been wrought upon the land.

Abdi-al-Hazred asks, "Mahdi, are you all right? We must go now, the American shayateen will be angry and will strike back with their infernally accurate missiles."

"You are right, it is time we must go, but please do not call me the Mahdi. What I've done does not make me worthy of that title, and the end days are not yet here," he says, but he knows whatever happens from now on, he has earned his place in Jannah —paradise.

It's now time to make their way back to their new home.

In the distance the sound of American missiles reverberates around the valley as they skim low overhead and descend behind them. The American shayateen are seeking out the Disciples, but they only manage to hit the decoys his followers had planted. He gets up and looks back down into the valley where the Americans have vented their fury on nothing of any great importance.

33. AGENCY

Real knowledge is to know the extent of one's ignorance.

— CONFUCIUS

Mr Anderson
CIA Analyst
CSN *Hornet*
Thursday, July 2, 2071

Anderson listens to Colonel Philmore talking to the officers in the CIC. They're watching the screen with the feeds from both the satellite and the drone, stacked one on top of each other, tracking the mission's progress. To Anderson the feeds are like the games he played as a child.

He hears, "Incoming fire detected aimed at Alpha-Bent crash site."

Two red lines appear on the screen showing the trajectory of the enemy fire heading towards the crash site where the Marines had landed. The naval officer behind speaks again, updating the status of the mission as the attack unfolds. The first rounds from the enemy's guns landed, and the CIC are tracking the second salvo to find where it came from. Reports from the two platoons' lieutenants come in updating their situation and their status.

Anderson watches in horror as sixteen hostile combat armor suits are tagged on the board. What the hell just happened?

"It looks to me like the Chinese have some new way to spoof our sensors, Mr Anderson. So much for this being a simple retrieval operation because we may yet start a land war in Asia."

"It wasn't the Agency's intention, Colonel."

Colonel Philmore turns to the fire control officer, ignoring Anderson while he issues more orders. By the time the drone arrives on sight, all of Johanson's platoon are confirmed dead. Then two of the enemy combat suits are taken down in quick succession by a lone Dog.

"Who's that?" asks Colonel Philmore.

"Unknown, no IFF, but it has to be a survivor from Cerberus Four Papa," comes the reply. It had been Lieutenant Beckford's platoon.

The enemy flies towards the lone Marine, who shoots them one at a time. In the end fate intervenes as an enemy machine crashes into the Marine, and they both burn on the plain in front of the mountain. He has to marvel at the bravery it took to face certain death.

Whoever it was deserved a medal. No doubt the Marines would say they were doing their job. He didn't know much about Marine culture, but he can see that duty and honour drive them to complete their mission.

The UAV circles overhead, showing the rising smoke from the fighting. A simple retrieval and reconnaissance has turned into a full-on battle. Now the remaining Marines must fight for their survival.

"Target solution now set, first missile away in three, two, one, launch!"

Confirmation comes from the fleet fire control officer as the first of twelve missiles launch from the fleet's escort destroyer, CSN *Forrest Sherman*, leaving a trail of flame and smoke in their wake.

"The enemy is about to find out that payback is a bitch once the Navy missiles say hello," says Colonel Philmore.

Anderson feels like he's trapped in treacle as he watches the progress of the counterstrike.

About twenty minutes pass before he sees an incoming message flash up on the screen. He hears Colonel Philmore update Lance Corporal Delgado, who was the highest ranking person still alive on what has happened to the rest of the company. The screen shows the platoon retreating back inside the mountain, taking cover from any other enemy attacks, and to avoid being hit by incoming friendly fire.

He counts the minutes to when the missile will strike. Before they can arrive, the UAV shows the top of the mountain lift up into the air.

Everyone in the CIC is stunned for a moment, then he hears general quarters being called. The ground around the mountain shudders under the force of the explosion, and then it collapses in on itself as rocks sweep into the valley below, delivering a wave of destruction.

Oh my god. A nuclear device has been detonated.

34. PRICE PAID

You have to believe in yourself.

— SUN TZU

Shàngwèi Looi
Commander Special Operations Force Falcon
Democratic People's Republic of China
The White Mountain, Afghanistan
Thursday, July 2, 2071

Looi leads the remains of his lián down the reverse slope of the mountain. He doesn't understand how expending his command on this mission makes any sense. He'd started with forty-eight men and five of them had been lost in the first day's fighting against the Americans. This had been a bad blow.

Today the Americans sent combat armor to retrieve their comrades. Machines far tougher than his own. Even out in the open where his kuijia could maneuver, his company were ill-suited for this mission. Beneath the mountain the Americans used this to their advantage because slowness did not hamper their movements enough to make a difference. During today's fighting he'd lost a further twenty-four men to keep secret what was under the mountain.

Under his breath he curses the person who made the decision to give them a bomb with a fixed time to detonate once armed. It was an insane thing to do.

But he knew that destroying the *kongjù de zhizhù* was the right answer because of how it affected him and his men. Even if he couldn't understand the explanation the scientists gave for why it did this, he understood the need to keep the thing from falling into the hands of the Americans.

It was the price he and his men paid with their lives that troubled him.

35. SAME DAY DIFFERENT SHIT

What is is what must be.

— GOTTFRIED WILHELM VON LEIBNIZ

Sergeant Tachikoma
First Combat Armor Suit Reconnaissance Company
CSN *Hornet*
Thursday, July 2, 2071

This day is taking a very different course from all the others. It's certainly a whole bunch easier in some ways, but it leaves me feeling lost and useless. Strangely this is a lot harder to deal with than getting on and doing something practical, like shooting back at people shooting at me.

I stare at the wall and think about stuff. Stuff like what the heck I am going to do if I'm still in the sickbay tomorrow. That would certainly rain on my career. It's torturing me knowing my company is out there dying without me. How crazy is that?

So it's a relief to see Dr Bullock return to check in on me and ask, "How's it going, Sergeant?"

"OK, I guess. Those pills sure zonked me out though."

"Good, you looked like you could do with a good night's sleep. So are you ready for another little chat to finish off your assessment?"

"Sure, Doc, why not, I haven't got anything else better to do."

"Let me see," he says, using his PAD. "Where were we? Ah, OK, let me start then by asking you—how do you understand your problem?"

"Well, Doc, the crazy answer is I believe I'm living the same day over and over again, so I don't really know how I understand that."

"Let's assume you're right, and you really are reliving the same day each day, what's so bad about that?"

What to say? "Apart from the whole dying and waking up each time?"

"Yeah, it sounds like a stupid question, but what does it mean to you?"

"That's easy, it means I'm stupid and a failure because only a totally stupid person would allow themselves to get killed again and again if they know how they're going to be killed."

"I get that, but what's so bad about being stupid?"

"Who'd want to be stupid? Like duh!"

"I get that, but it's not what I've asked you. What's bad about you seeing yourself as stupid?"

"I'll be responsible for getting people killed. It's all my fault they died."

"OK, so if I'm stupid, then I'm a failure, and failures are people that get others killed. Then if I get other people killed, people will avoid me. And what would be so bad about that, Sergeant?"

"I'll have no one, I'll be all alone, and when the time comes I'll die alone, all by myself with no one there for me."

I embrace myself with my arms. There's a chill in the air.

"That sounds like a bad place, Sergeant. So what do you do to stop yourself from being seen as stupid?"

"Gosh that's a hard question, Doc. Be the best I can be. Improvise, adapt, and overcome. Never give up, never surrender."

"And I'm sure your drill instructor would love to know you are a true Marine, but try digging a bit deeper. What can you do to show others you are not stupid?"

I shrug. "Listen to what others say, I suppose."

"Listening is good. So do you listen to people, Sergeant?"

"I suppose so. How would I prove it though?"

"A good question, Sergeant." The doc has tilted his head sideways with a quizzical expression on his face.

It clicks. "I guess I could repeat back what they've told me and ask if I've heard them correctly."

"Yep, that would work. Lot of sergeants get the men and women under their command to repeat back their orders, asking them what's been said to make sure they've heard and understood the order."

"Certainly done it in my time, usually with a side order of verbal chewing out to make sure they don't repeat the same mistake."

"OK. So what's changed then?"

"Not sure that's the problem. It's more like I can't tell people what I know, because they'll think I'm acting above my pay grade."

"Humh…it says in your file you turned down becoming a commissioned officer. Why's that?"

"I believe officers give orders that get Marines killed. I don't want to be the idiot who gets all her Marines killed by giving stupid orders they've got to follow."

"OK, Sergeant, I'll buy that for a dollar, but here's the thing. If you were an officer, wouldn't you have a senior NCO to rely on?

Don't officers and NCOs work together, supporting each other to get the mission done?"

"I guess so. It's what my job is all about. Keeping the new lieutenants from getting the platoon killed," I say, pausing. "But surely it can't be so simple?"

"I doubt it is, Sergeant, but it's a start to understanding yourself, isn't it? Let me put it this way. Bad stuff has happened that you feel you're responsible for. And here's the thing, you can't change what's happened, but you can change what you decide to do from now on. So my last question, Sergeant, is what's the one thing that has to change for you to not do something stupid?"

"Not to get me and my company killed by the enemy."

"Good answer, but how? Think about what you must do to not get your company killed, and do that. OK, good, that's all I've got time for. Anyway we'll send you back to your bunkroom tonight so you can sleep in your own rack. Meanwhile, I need to fill in the forms on the system, and we'll keep you under observation in case you suffer from adverse side effects."

"Like what, Doc?"

"Disorientation, fainting, nausea. I'm pretty sure if you were going to have an adverse reaction, we would've seen it by now. I imagine after a good night's sleep you will start to begin to feel your normal self again."

I thank him as he leaves, and I start wondering what normal is. If I wake up tomorrow, and it's Friday, then it will mean I'm not normal. If I wake up, and it's Thursday all over again, it will still mean I'm not normal, because what's happening is abnormal.

Anyway I sit and doze off again in the chair; rule number one: remember.

In my dream I'm reliving my death.

My body crushed in an avalanche of rocks as the mountain above me explodes. The sound of general quarters being called wakes me up with a start. The sound reminds me of my screaming in pain.

But I realize I'm still dreaming. My dream shifts back to the mountain collapsing in upon itself. Everyone dies again as the rock sweeps over them. Then I wake up to find myself in the sickbay.

My life feels like a dream as I drift off back to sleep.

I wake to see the spook from the CIA. He has a cut on his head that is bleeding. A corpsman comes in to attend to him. "I guess you hit your head on a hatch, Mr Anderson?"

"I did, and how did you know?"

"You don't look like you belong on board *Hornet*. Everybody bangs their shins and knocks their heads on the hatches for the first few days aboard a ship."

"Yeah, I get that bit, but I meant how did you know my name? Who are you?"

I realize we haven't met today, at least not in this version of today. It leaves me in a bit of a quandary over what to say next.

"I'm Sergeant Tachikoma, you were briefing my company earlier for a retrieval mission."

"OK, don't remember seeing you there, and I'm pretty sure I would recognize you from the red hair, if nothing else."

"Well, you might, but usually it's all tidied back and squared away in Marine Corps fashion. Not my best look, but there again, being caught in sickbay in my bathrobe isn't great for making good first impressions either."

"If you say so, but I think you underestimate yourself. So what brings one of the Marine Corps' finest here?"

"If you would like to sit and take the time to talk to me, I'll tell you."

"How can I resist an offer like that?"

"I like a man who knows when not to resist."

A flicker of a smile crosses Anderson's face.

"Let me tell you a story about what brought me here today. I was flying out on a mission to Afghanistan and search under a mountain to find out what was generating a strange energy pulse. You had sent some men from the Army to go and have a look-see, but then they disappeared and needed to be rescued by some Marines."

"How can you possibly know that?"

"Be patient, Mr Anderson, just sit, listen, and all will be revealed. That's what the doctor told me to do. Listen to what people are saying and not do something stupid like allowing my company to get killed."

"You're shitting me, right?"

"No, but that's not really important right now. What's important is the mountain is going be blown up by a nuclear bomb. When I went under the mountain, I found two pillars. Then the air shimmered and I could see through the space between them, and it led somewhere else. Does that make any sense to you, Mr Anderson?"

"OK, I'm not saying anything, but I'll go with you on this."

"I decided to walk through the pillars and found myself outside. Not in Afghanistan, as there were two moons in the sky, and the last time I checked our sky only has one moon. As I walked back to my squad, they were unable to move, frozen on the spots where they stood."

He's hanging on every word I say.

"Then I did something very stupid. I got out of my cockpit and tried to walk back through, but I brushed against the pillars and was thrown backwards. I was told I lost consciousness for a moment or two. But to me it was like I saw everything in the universe, all at once. Do you like my story?"

"So how are you here and not there lying dead in Afghanistan with the rest of your company?"

"A good question, Mr Anderson, and one I was hoping you could answer for me. You see I did die, then I woke up in my rack, and it was the same day all over again. I remember what happened to me, and the day just repeats all over again."

Anderson stares at me kind of strangely.

"So are you saying all this has happened to you before?"

"Yep, and will likely happen again. This is the fifth time I've woken up to find it's the same day. This time the day is different because the last time we were killed on landing. So I never got to go under the mountain and find the pillars. You know what, I've just had a thought about why it made today different."

"Yes go on, tell me why the company getting killed on landing made a difference."

"Well, I just remembered something the doctor said to me. It was about his treatment plan involving magnetic fields to fix my problem. The pillars emit a strong magnetic pulse. So when I walked through the pillars, they affected my brain in some way."

"But how does that explain what's been happening to you?"

"It doesn't explain how I keep repeating the same day, but it does explain why I was so affected by dying the last time, but not on the previous occasions I died."

"Let me check if I've got this right. You're saying you've been to the mountain on five occasions and died every time?"

"No, I've relived the same day five times. I didn't go out today and die, so I've only died on four occasions. I realize that must sound totally crazy to you, but you're listening to me, so I guess I'm not bonkers."

"Hey, don't cry. Is there anything I can do for you? Do you need me to call the doctor for some medication?"

"What I need is for you to tell me the truth, Mr Anderson. Tell me what the pillars are doing under the mountain."

"Truth is, I can't tell you, as you don't have the clearances. However, I've just come from the CIC where I saw your company die, it seems you know more than I, so I'll take a chance on you. Let's just say you've made a good first impression."

I remembered hearing general quarters being sounded in my dream. It's happened all over again without me there to stop it from happening.

"It's not often men say that to me. I'm told I can be a bit scary."

"You're rather formidable, which is why I guess you've survived what's happened to you. I imagine most people would be driven crazy by the experience."

"I'm not so sure about the crazy part. The doctors say I'm suffering from something called hyperstartle response due to post-traumatic stress disorder."

"Be that as it may. I'd like you to tell me your story again from the beginning if you don't mind."

"No, I don't mind, I've nowhere else to go and nothing better to do."

And I proceed to tell him, and by the time I get to the end of my story I relax for the first time in days. The relief is palpable. Sitting and having someone listen to me and believe what I tell them makes a difference.

"OK, I got all that. This is a big breakthrough for me. Thank you for what you've done."

"No, I need to thank you for listening, but as the doctor said to me: here's the thing; if what I've told you is true, then tomorrow I'll wake up in my rack and remember all of this, but you'll not have met me. I'll be right back where I started from. That's going to be a problem."

"Damn, I hadn't thought of that."

"It sucks, trust me. It sucks even more to be me though."

"I guess it does suck to be you, but I have an idea. Call me crazy if you like, but if I tell you something, you will remember it if you wake up tomorrow—assuming it is the same day all over again, right?"

"Yes, but how does that help anything?" I ask.

"It doesn't, not directly, but from the way you tell it you've got a pretty good handle on how to save your company from being blown up. So, afterwards, when you get back from your successful mission, my guess is you will need to write a report, which I will get to read. You with me so far?"

"Yes, but I don't understand how that helps me."

"Well, I want you to write the phrase RED SLIPPERS in your report three times: once in the introduction, once during the report, and once in your summary. I will pick up on the phrase and call you in to explain yourself. Then you can tell me this story all over again."

"That sounds like a pretty stupid idea. What if you don't believe me?"

"Trust me, I'll believe you. Plus I have good reasons to want to talk to you again."

"You do? So going over the top of my head here."

"Trust me when I say I like talking to redheads and let's leave it at that. Besides, it's really doing my head in thinking that there's a good chance tomorrow never comes."

Anderson gets up and leaves. He turns and waves at me from the hatch before disappearing from my sight. Unfortunately, he's right, he won't remember having this conversation with me, which is rather sad because I rarely meet men I find attractive. When I do, the circumstances tend to conspire to prevent any relationship from going anywhere. Those circumstances usually arise once they find out I'm a Marine Corps NCO, so today sucks in more ways than one.

36. NOW WHAT?

Thus, what is of supreme importance in war is to attack the enemy's strategy.

— SUN TZU

Sergeant Tachikoma
First Combat Armor Suit Reconnaissance Company
CSN *Hornet*
Thursday, July 2, 2071

After Mr Anderson leaves, I get to sit and wait a bit more before another meal is delivered to me. Later on I get taken back to my bunkroom, where an orderly gives me some more medication, once I'm lying in my rack. To say that the operational tempo of being sick is glacial would be an unfair comparison to glaciers, as I'm sure they move faster.

Still, it gives me time to fish out my PAD and try to read, but my head is still a bit fuzzy. Mostly I surf stupid stuff on the Net. This passes the time, in the strange way that happens when one is absorbed when you've done nothing useful at all.

I fall asleep again and wake up a bit later. My display tells me it's 0129 on Friday, the third of July. I blink and I'm amazed to see it's changed to 0530 on Thursday, the second of July, 2071. It's happened again despite not being blown up, but I've woken up refreshed, like a new person even. Beats me. Checking the display again, a minute has passed me by, my life slipping inexorably towards the past.

Time to get my act together. I feel the need to go give the Chinese a good kicking. Hearing the familiar sounds of snoring is comforting, so I swing out of my rack and resolve myself to get with the programme. The walk along the gangway is familiar, yet somehow new, like I'm seeing everything for the first time, but I mean *really* seeing it.

How crazy is that?

All the little paint chips and blemishes on the bulkheads, and how the handles on the hatches hang at different angles; the same, but slightly different, and it strikes me that perhaps I'm not traveling back in time. Perhaps something else is happening. Otherwise surely I would feel the same each time and not be hungry, etc. Whatever is happening, this must be what it's like to be *mindful.*

I revel in the freshness of the normality of life aboard *Hornet.* I hear the thrum of the engines and feel rooted in the now. It's a bit weird sitting on the head and being able to tell what the person ate from the smell they left behind. A bit of an odd thing to notice when you think about it.

The POD schedule is chock-a-block full with lot of stuff to juggle to make sure everything goes according to plan. In this case, my plan. The one where we don't all die, which involves me making the most of the wait cycles punctuating the day ahead. The one where I figure out what the fuck is going on.

I'm greeted by the same sight of the chow line. As I enter the mess hall, I'm drawn by the aroma of the food. My sense of smell is heightened and I'm salivating. I load my tray with my favorite ham and eggs. But before going to sit with my platoon, I add some hash browns and beans to my plate.

The other good thing about having to replay the same day all over again is seeing all my Marines alive. Even the ones who are total pains in the ass. I'm greeted in the usual manner as I take my seat opposite Lieutenant McCarthy.

"Good morning, Marines, what a glorious day to be in the Corps." And then I say, "Good morning, Lieutenant. I hope you slept well, sir?"

He smiles. "Good morning to you too, Sergeant. I guess you slept well?"

"Yes, I did. Good to hear you're ready for the day and the drop ahead of us," I say, a micro twitch on his face betraying his nervousness over his first combat jump. "Consider it a present from the Corps to you, sir. A chance to prove you are more than just the five-jump qualifier, sir."

"Thank you. I now know it's true sergeants can read minds and always know the right thing to say," he says, and I laugh with him.

I see Lance Corporal Delgado talking to Private First Class Hernandez. "You OK, Delgado?"

She replies in the affirmative and seems genuinely happy I asked how she is. I guess asking questions and listening to people, like Dr Bullock says, really works. Private Vosloo is well into his tale by this time.

When he gets to the end of his story, I say, "Vosloo, if I ever go camping in the woods with you, remind me to go armed for bear, every bear."

"Sure thing. I'll remember to give you the heads-up, Sergeant," he replies, and his infectious laughter makes me smile. Everyone laughs.

"Rodriguez, Jackson, I have some spare hash browns and beans. Do either of you growing Marines need some more?"

"Yes, Sergeant, but how did you know we wanted more?" they say in unison.

"It goes with the stripes. Besides how are you going to live up to your moniker of 'fart dispenser,' Jackson?" Jackson laughs. I continue. "So Jones, you enjoying your traditional Marine Corps breakfast?"

"Yes, I am, Sergeant."

"Best meal of the day. If I can, I always try to eat my favorite food before going on a mission. Reminds me of home and what's important to me in life. Do you know what's important, Jones?"

He stutters, "I don't know, Sergeant."

"Remember your training and follow your orders. Do that and you'll have done good, Marine."

"Thank you, Sergeant."

"You follow the sergeant's advice, and she will make you into a true gyrene, Jones," says Kowalski.

"What's a gyrene?" asks Jones.

I cut in before Kowalski can reply. "It's what a lance corporal thinks happens when you cross a grunt with a Marine, but they only think that because they're not yet sergeants." I turn towards Kowalski. "So how's the leg actuator on your Dog?"

"I'm trying to persuade Eversmann to change it out."

"Well, it might help if you volunteer to help Eversmann change it. I shall be keeping my eye on you, Kowalski, understood?"

"Aye, aye, I hear you clear as a bell, Sergeant."

I get back to my breakfast, finishing off my meal by drinking the Navy's finest antidote against sleep. It also removes the greasiness of the breakfast like paint stripper strips paint off a wall. Contrary to the rumours, this is about the only thing Navy Joe doesn't actually do.

As 0800 rolls around I'm studying Lieutenant Perez as he talks to Sergeant Thompson. They're discussing what he wants to do with the platoon on today's mission. From Thompson's neutral expression, which one might generously describe as benign boredom, I gather the lieutenant has been telling Thompson how to suck eggs.

I sit and watch, and wait, while working on what to say this time around. Time passes as I use my PAD, searching for stuff I need to pull together for today's mission, letting the routine of the briefing flow over me.

My cue to speak comes. "Permission to speak frankly, sir?"

"Go ahead, Sergeant."

"We're missing the big picture here. I believe we risk losing the whole company because we're relying on limited real-time reconnaissance feeds from a single UAV. This exposes the mission to a number of unknown unknowns, sir."

"Those are pretty strong words, Sergeant, do you have anything to back them up?"

"I do, sir. I'd like to explain my thoughts and reasons for them, with my suggestions, if I may?"

"Go ahead, I assume it's going to be good."

"Mr Anderson talked about the situation in Afghanistan and the involvement of three local warlords led by Yeshua bin Yussuf, whose followers call him the Mahdi. They believe he's the one who will save all Muslims and lead the founding of a new Islamic state. This doesn't sound like someone who will take kindly to an American Special Forces team landing in his backyard."

I pause to gather my thoughts.

"My best guess is that his forces attacked and destroyed the Army Alpha Detachment while they were searching inside the mountain. Otherwise, if the team were alive, they would've done something to draw attention to themselves. They haven't, therefore I think it is safe to assume they're dead…"

"Slow down, Sergeant, how do you know the Army team got into the mountain?" says Johanson.

"If they'd been involved in a firefight while outside the mountain, they would've been in communication via the satellite tasked by the CIA."

"I can see how that might be a reasonable assumption, carry on."

"Therefore, the locals must be armed with enough weaponry to take out a power-armored Special Forces team. This means at a minimum heavy machine guns and rocket-propelled grenade launchers. I know we tend to think of RPGs as obsolete weapons because of their crudity, but they're still capable of taking out tanks, and, more importantly, destroying our combat armor suits. I'd rather not be inside my Dog when an RPG round hits it."

"Good points, Sergeant. Do you have anything to say, Mr Anderson?"

"Well, our satellites and UAV haven't spotted any movement of military forces other than the usual trucks with men one might expect. However, given the history of Afghanistan, I would expect the locals to react negatively to the presence of your Marines."

"Marines are used to negative receptions, Mr Anderson. Anything else to add, Sergeant?"

"Just to go back to Mr Anderson's comments on the locals reacting negatively to us, sir. Afghanistan is arguably the most fought-over country in the history of the world. They've been invaded time and time again over the centuries. As a result every male goes armed and is happy to kill those who are not of his faith."

By now I'm into the flow and on a roll.

"I decided to put myself into the shoes of the local forces and ask what I would do if I suspected an attempt to retrieve the Army Special Forces team would be made. What I've come up with I suspect you won't like, but I believe they'll be prepared to destroy us. The best way to infiltrate the area would be to use local truck movement to hide the build up of forces."

I mark up the map to show what the enemy might do.

"Therefore we could be facing an enemy force in pre-prepared positions. An enemy who has already demonstrated they've the means to attack a force that lands in this area. If I were in their shoes, I would want to place my artillery somewhere to the north of the crash site. The battery could be preregistered to fire on the crash site and the entrance to the mountain."

"That's a big leap you've made there, Sergeant, to go from local forces with RPGs to having artillery emplaced," says Johanson.

"Given a week to prepare, it seems a reasonable supposition. Admittedly it's based on a sparse set of data I pulled up about past conflicts in this region."

"She could be right. The mujahideen have a history of being able to field considerable forces. The only thing that lets them down is their logistics chain. They're hampered by the fact that they find it difficult to resupply themselves effectively, but this might not hold them back from initiating a confrontation."

"So, Mr Anderson, given that the CIA lost a whole Army Special Forces PACE suit Alpha twelve-man Detachment I think my sergeant has made a rather acute point. I'm looking forward to her suggestions on how to deal with what is admittedly a hypothetical adversary, but still not one I would want to meet unprepared. Carry on, Sergeant."

"Thank you, sir. We also need to consider if the mujahideen are receiving any help from outside forces hostile to our best interests in this area. But it's highly unlikely either the Turkic Alliance or the Russian Commonwealth are involved here."

It's only fair that being blown up by the Chinese means I can name them as our adversaries. It's the least I can do. Later I will take great pleasure in killing them all before they can kill me and mine.

"This leaves the Islamic Republic of Pakistan, the Republic of India, or the Democratic People's Republic of China as the main players in the region. Currently Pakistan and India are working together to resolve the disputes in the Gilgit Baltistan region, as they both see the real threat being from their borders with the Chinese Xinjiang province."

"Sergeant, you seem remarkably well informed about this area."

"Just what I was able to pull up on my PAD during the briefing, sir."

"It seems one of my senior NCOs has been able to raise some interesting observations you might like to comment on, Mr Anderson?"

Mr Anderson turns and says, "There's no denying her observations. Unfortunately, there are certain aspects of this mission that are classified, which means I've nothing further to add. I can say there's nothing I would disagree with in terms of the assumptions made about the hostility of the locals."

"That, Sergeant, is about the closest thing I've ever heard to an endorsement by the Agency, in my career. So what else does your gut tell you we should be doing, Sergeant?"

"My gut feeling is the mujahideen will try to lull us into a false sense of security by waiting until we're at our most vulnerable before striking. Their main problem is giving their presence away to us. Either taking obvious positions or by open communication, which would be vulnerable to easy detection. So for our deployment I suggest we split the company with one platoon dropped to secure the crash site while the rest are deployed here..." I bring a pointer up on the map. "Where there's a road that we can take to get us up to the mountain side here," I say, highlighting the drop points with icons.

"I can see you've given this some considerable thought, Sergeant. I certainly wouldn't want to face an enemy force if you were in command."

"Thank you, sir. Once we drop, if we deploy the Third Platoon away from the mountainside and place them further back, then they can act both as a reserve and a rearguard for the First and Second Platoons while we are searching the mountain interior…"

"One moment while I interrupt, Sergeant. What's your opinion, Lieutenant Perez?"

"Sir, it seems like we are adding a lot of extra grunt work to achieve the mission goals."

"Fair point, but let's see this as an opportunity to train hard so we can fight easy," says Johanson, nodding at me to continue.

"I would also liaise with the crew of the Air Force MULE and get them to move Fourth Platoon closer to the mountain after the space-plane has been loaded. This can be achieved by the simple expedient of hanging the combat armor off the MULE and fast-roping to the ground to disembark. This will put the Third and Fourth Platoons in a good position to enfilade any enemy forces that might try to sweep over this ridgeline here…" I mark the line of advance on the map. "And ambush anyone who tries to attack the other half of the company when we exit the mountain."

"Lieutenant Beckford, any thoughts?"

"Works for me, sir."

"Works for me too. Sergeant, anything else you want to add?"

"Yes, sir. If we go for a mixed load-out for the deployment, we can arm First and Second Platoons for speed. This then gives us the option of having Third and Fourth Platoons carry a mix of indirect fire support and heavier anti-armor ordnance. It will give us a more flexible force with which to respond to any increase in local force concentration. I've downloaded my suggested weapons mix to the system, sir."

"Anyone like to add any suggestions?"

"One last thing, sir," I say. "It would be useful to task the UAV with circling north of its present holding pattern." Pointing on the map, I show them where I guess the enemy artillery will fire from. "So we can check out the reverse slopes of these mountains here."

"I'm so glad the enemy doesn't have you on their side, Sergeant, because you have evil thoughts."

"Are all your senior NCOs flying under the zone?" asks Anderson.

"No, but I've had my eye on Sergeant Tachikoma for a while. Upload the adjusted plan, and get your Dogs prepped for this mission. Sergeant, will you please come and see me after the briefing in my office in fifteen?"

Captain Johanson tears a strip off me.

"That was quite the performance you put on during the briefing, Sergeant. But it's in the best interest of the Corps to put you somewhere where you won't make my junior officers look bad in my sight. It's not good for them to be grandstanded by a sergeant."

"Yes, sir, I can see it might not be good for the Corps."

"Glad you agree, Sergeant. So here's the thing I want to ask, why now?"

"It was a gut feeling, sir."

"That was some gut feeling to make you step up to the plate like that. Anyway, Mr Anderson here wants to ask you some questions."

Anderson asks, "Sergeant Tachikoma, have you ever considered a career in intelligence?"

"I must admit I haven't given it much thought, sir. I tend to see myself as a hands-on kind of person who goes where she's told and kicks ass, sir."

"You may be underrating your abilities, Sergeant."

"Thank you, sir," I say, but I'm not really underrating myself, because I only appeared to be sharp from the fact that I've been blown to bits four times by a nuke. This is, to put it mildly, a bit of a harsh learning curve even by Marine Corps standards.

"I've reviewed your last performance report again, Sergeant. And I see we've already had a discussion about you becoming a commissioned officer, given your past. So I'll ask you again: What do you see as your future career options, Sergeant? Have you reconsidered your position on this matter since last time?"

"Sir, in light of what you've said, I accept I need to take the opportunity you offered me before to become the potential officer you see in me."

"Excellent, Sergeant. I would've been disappointed to make it an order. One other thing, I get the whole gut-feeling thing, but you do appear to have given today's mission considerable thought. I wonder what's behind your thinking?"

"I was channelling the *Marine Corps Counterinsurgency Field Manual* and *Warfighting* doctrine. It seemed to me we needed to get inside the enemy's OODA loop. It came to me a bit like the story of the dreams of Lieutenant Backsight Forethought as he played through in his mind the outcomes of his plans, sir."

"That's an interesting answer, Sergeant. Good to see you were thinking about the 'observe, orient, decide, and then act' process. What particular parts of the COIN manual were you channelling?"

"Well, in particular, sir, the bits about the Iraqis having lots of preset firing positions and using decoys to pull American forces into kill zones."

"Very good, Sergeant. I shall write up the recommendation for officer training when we get back. Do you want to ask my sergeant any other questions, Mr Anderson?"

"Thank you, I do. Have you experienced anything unusual of late, Sergeant?"

"What do you mean by 'unusual,' sir?"

"Feelings of déjà vu or very vivid dreams."

"Yes, sir, I have."

"What do you make of them, Sergeant?"

"Opportunities to excel, sir."

Anderson asks, "Sorry, let me rephrase my question. What have these feelings taught you?"

"That we better be prepared to expect the worst, because it's always foolish to underestimate the enemy and not expect them to want to ambush us when we try retrieve our lost team, sir."

"One more question if I may. What do you think the magnetic energy pulses are?"

"It's something the CIA thinks America might be able to exploit to our advantage, which our government doesn't want us to know about, sir."

"You may well be right about that too, Sergeant. I've no further questions," says Anderson.

I guess his questions were his way of trying to figure out the curveball he'd been thrown by me stomping all over his search-and-retrieval operation.

"Dismissed, Sergeant," says Johanson.

I come to attention, turn, and exit in an orderly military fashion. I go back to the kennels and figure, since I've already checked everything repeatedly, I can probably tick off the checklist without worrying about it too much. Let my hair down, go wild, and take a chance.

After that I go check how my Marines are doing because people aren't like machines. And the one thing I've learnt is I can make a difference, even if it's only little things. Even the difficult things, like knowing that there will be a lot of letters sent to families, sits better with me.

Especially since my mom will receive one of those letters.

It's bad enough to die once. Getting killed repeatedly is worse. Having to go through the whole mission again and not get myself killed, knowing that everybody in the company will die if I fail, is worse still. For the first time I truly understand what Private Jones meant when he says things are totally bone.

This is my life stripped down to the bare essentials.

As my father used to say, "You have one day, and it is today. Yesterday is in the past, and tomorrow hasn't happened." Except now I've the chance to take yesterday and make it different. To make this one day really matter.

I leave the tech crew to finish charging my Dog for the mission. This time round Kowalski is working with Eversmann and Jones on the leg actuator of his Dog.

"How's it going?"

"We may not look it, Sergeant, but we're ahead of schedule here. As soon as we're done here, I'm helping Jones with his checklist. It's a good opportunity for him to stand in on an actuator change."

"Kowalski, well done on setting a good example for everyone in the company. You learning anything new, Jones?"

"No, I mean yes, Sergeant. It's really good getting a chance to give a hand with this. Lance Corporal Kowalski has been explaining the ins and outs of preventative maintenance."

"Good job, Jones. Just keep with your buddy and you'll do all right today."

"I can do that. Thank you, Sergeant."

I leave Kowalski, Eversmann, and Jones to go check on Rodriguez and Jackson, who are checking each other's preparations.

"You two good to go?"

"Nearly, Sergeant. We're finishing off by running down some minor glitches in my Dog's ChameleonFlage system. Nothing to worry about," says Rodriguez.

"We're tight, Sergeant," says Jackson.

"Everyone knows you two are tight."

"Everyone's jealous is all, Sergeant," says Rodriguez.

"I shall pretend I didn't hear that. I would hate to split you two into different platoons. You understand me?"

"Aye, aye, loud and clear," says Jackson.

"Clear as a bell, Sergeant," says Rodriguez.

"Good. Now carry on and stop making everyone else envious."

I leave Rodriguez and Jackson to get on with finishing going through the list together. Next I walk over to the other side of the hangar bay; it's time to shoot the breeze again with my fellow sergeants, who greet me with friendly abuse.

I let myself go with the flow and realize if I survive the day and go off to officer training, I'm going to miss all this.

We go through the whole thing of me giving them more work to do. At the end of the conversation, I say, "You guys slay me. You two ever thought about doing stand-up comedy together?"

"You hear that, Washington? She offers me beer and then insults us by telling us we are a pair of comedians."

"At least you got offered beer, Thompson."

"You're breaking my heart here with your sob story, Washington."

"I'm working like a dog to get my platoons ready for the get-go here and you think it's a sob story," says Thompson.

"Spare me the dog jokes," I reply.

"See, she no longer thinks you're funny, Thompson."

"Yeah, but you are still ugly."

"Be that as it may, we also added indirect-fire missile packs to our two Dogs. In my book that makes up for a lot of things in life, like being old and ugly with no sense of humour when it comes to being shot at," says Washington.

"You can say that again," says Thompson.

"Please don't. It's a sure thing that if you mess with the best, you die like the rest, is what I say," I say.

"Ain't that the truth," says Thompson.

"If we've finished sharing the love here, we've work to do," says Washington.

"Still got to get both the lieutenants' Dogs fitted out with the antitank missile launcher as you suggested, Tachikoma," says Thompson.

"Should keep them out of trouble though?"

"Keeping the lieutenants out of trouble is our job after all," says Washington.

"Scuttlebutt has it we will be keeping you out of trouble soon, Tachikoma," says Thompson.

"I'd like to say you shouldn't listen to scuttlebutt, but yes, Captain Johanson has recommended me for officer training."

"Well deserved in my opinion," says Washington.

"Did you just imply Tachikoma is a bastard?"

"We are all Cousin Sam's misbegotten children in the Corps, Thompson. You know that."

I leave them to it and go back over to check on what Corporal Knight and Lieutenant McCarthy are talking about.

"Hey, that was some fancy speaking in front of the briefing, you gunning to become an officer, Tachikoma? I only ask because it's going to be weird to call you *ma'am*," says Knight.

"Scuttlebutt sure travels fast around here, doesn't it?"

"Corporal Knight was agreeing with me. It was a scarily impressive bit of grandstanding you did in the briefing today, Sergeant," says McCarthy.

"The captain thought much the same thing too, sir. Fortunately for me he has a solution."

"That bad huh? What did he say?"

"The captain says the best place for grandstanding sergeants is for them to be sent off for officer training to become a lieutenant."

"So the scuttlebutt is right. Such is the wisdom of our company commander to cultivate the potential hidden inside us all, Sergeant."

"So I was told. So how's the prep going?"

"I was telling the lieutenant all our Dogs are on their sleds and Alpha Squad is good to go, Sergeant."

"I can confirm Bravo is all set to go too. All we've got to do now is make sure we don't get our asses blown off when we get there."

"Always the cheery optimist, Sergeant."

"Prior planning prevents piss-poor performance, sir."

"I think we all heard the message loud and clear at the briefing, Sergeant. Anyway it's time to get it on."

"Aye, aye, sir," I say as we all turn to go and get into the cockpits of our respective Dogs.

I look around the hangar deck one more time before buttoning down my Dog. In the glow of the cockpit's red light, I put her systems into flight mode for the trip out in the Thunder Hawks.

Rapid preparation and deployment is what I'd call a relative term for our operational tempo today. But it only has real meaning when it's compared to the time it takes to get armies into battle. Reality limits how fast things can happen because not everybody can be combat ready 100 percent of the time.

And patience really is a virtue when it comes to getting ready for any operation, as it is always hurry up and wait, but the wait cycle gives me time to think. And the only thing that comes to mind is kill them, kill them all before they can kill me.

The simplest plan seems to be to wait in the cavern and shoot whoever enters it carrying the bomb. The best plans are usually simple. Complicated plans will trip you up when something stupid happens. And stupid stuff always happens. Once the shooting begins the plan is no longer something written in stone. It's, at best, a guideline. At worse, no longer relevant.

The zoomies go through the welcome-aboard spiel. "Thank you for choosing to fly Thunder Chicken Airlines today." All part of the typical banter to allay the boredom from the routine before the shit hits the fan. As the engines power up, I take the time to appreciate the functional beauty of the ship. Something I haven't really thought about before. *Hornet* sure does feel like home as our birds climb into the sky leaving her behind.

The fleet gradually disappears into the gray-green-blue sea and sky receding into the distance with every passing moment. I take my attention away from the serene blue sky and check the feeds. It's good to see McCarthy using his PAD again. And it reminds me I need to record a letter to my mom, which is easier this time, because I know what I want to say.

Now I can record it without feeling bad about my choice to join the Marine Corps. Not out of a sense of patriotic duty of serving my country, but because it was the right thing for me to do. Putting my life in danger to protect my friends made sense to me. I grew up in a country where I've the freedom to choose, and freedom is worth fighting for.

"Dear Mom," I say, then take a moment to gather my thoughts and stare at the screen.

"I hope you never have to see this, but if you do, then you know what I'm about to say—I love you. Just going out to do my job, but the thing is that today has gotten a bit weird. I'm not sure you'll even believe me when I say I'm living the same day over and over again. If you're listening to this, then I'm no longer trapped and repeating the same day, but I am dead."

Then I have to pause the recording and blink back the tears in my eyes.

"I've had a lot of time to think about what's been happening to me, and I can tell you it's nothing like the stories you've seen or heard. Each day I face knowing I and the people I know will die from an unstoppable force that cannot be reasoned or bargained with. It's like I'm being ground down by the inevitability of the consequences of things I've no control over."

Before continuing, I stop and wipe my eyes.

"And the death of the people in my company is just the result of a series of small events that relentlessly pile one on top of each other. I try to nudge events in a different direction, but inevitably I face an avalanche that comes down on top of me. So far I've failed, and the irony is that, if I succeed today but still get killed, my reward is knowing you get to listen to this."

Then I look away from the camera for a moment before turning back to speak again.

"Sorry, Mom. I'm doing my best so that you don't have to hear this, I'm sorry I've failed. I love you so much, bye."

Switching off the recording, I sit back in my seat to distract myself from the overwhelming grief that consumes me. I try to make myself comfortable and start reading about alternate realities and the multiverse. Anything to not think about what happens next.

Our bird begins doing its shake, rattle, and roll as it drops from altitude to go the rest of the flight flying NOE. The rocking motion is enough to send me to sleep for the rest of the journey. I've always found clear-air turbulence rather lulling, but some people take it as a sign they're about to fall out of the sky—if we do this time round, then there's sure as hell nothing I can do to stop it from happening.

The sound of the ten-mike drop warning from the Chicken's

crew chief wakes me up, and my Dog is readied to be thrown out the rear of our bird.

The zoomies say farewell and, "Remember to collect your frequent flyer air mile points when you leave the craft, and thank you all for choosing to fly Navy today." I smile as the screen shows the countdown to zero.

The force of my Dog leaving the bird snatches my harness tight as I fly through the air with all the grace of a brick falling off the back of a truck. The drogue does its job of pulling the main chute open. But the bottom of the drop sled still hits the ground like a sledgehammer hitting an anvil.

My Dog slides across the ground, protected as the drop sled sheds pieces, and we come to a halt surrounded by a cloud of dust. I fire the release bolts to allow my Dog to stand and move away from what some might describe as a controlled crash.

But as pilots are wont to say, any landing you can walk away from is a good one. Works for me too.

The chute dissolves into small pieces of chaff that blow away in the afternoon breeze. The drop sled has been turned from a support structure into a small pile of stuff that no longer serves any useful purpose.

"Sound off, people," I say over the laser-net, confirming everyone's down and five by five. Next I scan the area around me for any signs of movement and see none. "OK, switch ChameleonFlage on. Let's make ourselves not be seen."

From the outside the Dogs would appear to dissolve into apparitions. Blending into the background, all I see inside my virtual environment are the Dogs' status icons change. We then wait in place, not being seen.

Over the company command channel, the lieutenants confirm that their platoons are in position to Captain Johanson. My HUD displays the positions of the other three platoons in relation to ours. Beckford's Fourth Platoon has taken up position around the crashed space-plane. Perez's Third Platoon is to the rear of us.

We sit and wait, listening to the exchanges on the radio.

"Lobo Four, take your squad in and search the plane, over," says Beckford to Staff Sergeant Washington.

"Roger, taking Lobo Bravo Sierra in to search the plane, out," comes his reply.

"Let's move, we've got a job to do, out," says Johanson, signalling the rest of Cerberus Company to start moving.

Our Dogs have landed nearer to the road, allowing us to pick up the pace and make better time to our objective.

As we reach the ridge leading up to the mountain, the captain says, "Wulfgang Six, go and form a line on the back slope here, over."

"Aye, aye, out," says Perez as his platoon peels off to our left to guard our rear, leaving a wake of dust to settle behind them.

Then I take the opportunity to speak privately to McCarthy on the platoon command channel.

"Sir, don't forget to suggest to the captain about using the IFF transponders as receivers for transmitting messages when we're under the mountain."

McCarthy asks, "I won't, Sergeant, but how did you know I was thinking that?"

Before I can reply, Beckford reports in over the company net, "Big Dog, we've found two dead in the cockpit, no other signs of Alpha Detachment, over."

"Good work, Lobo Six. Secure the crash site and wait for the MULE to come in and pick it up. Once the package is secured, hitch a ride back to support Wulfgang, over," says Johanson.

"Aye, aye, out," Beckford replies.

"I like it when a plan comes together," I say to McCarthy.

We traverse the road as it begins to narrow into the path that takes us up the mountain. Sergeant Ramirez of Hellhounds Alpha

Squad finds the first cave entrance, but we move on until we get to the cleft, the order of events having changed the course of the day.

So, once more forward into the darkness to face the changing outcomes of different choices.

37. OK AGAIN

Marines don't know how to spell the word defeat.

— GEN JAMES "MAD DOG" MATTIS, USMC

Sergeant Tachikoma
First Combat Armor Suit Reconnaissance Company
Afghanistan
Thursday, July 2, 2071

As our two platoons move into the cleft, I take point for my squad, which is, strictly speaking, not where sergeants are supposed to go. However, given my prior reconnaissance from dying on each mission, I think it wise. It will minimize the opportunity for Murphy's Law to come and bite us on the ass.

Forewarned is, as they say, forearmed.

Besides it's not every day you wake up knowing what's going to happen before it does. Well, except for today of course, which is real peachy, for definitions of *peachy* that include today being a total pain in my ass.

The plan is unfolding with all the pieces falling into place as we move slowly through the tunnel, making our way forward with Jones behind me. Kowalski is bringing up the rear, tasked to plant transponders to get our net up. Ahead of me the tunnel starts to widen out into a cavern.

I call my squad to a halt through the low-band link and move slowly up to the point where I can pop up my sensor mast. Then I passively scan the cavern ahead because, even though I know there are Fatties ahead of us, my Dog doesn't share with me my special privilege of knowing what happens next. So it takes time, but it's time well spent, as I get confirmation on the enemies' positions waiting to spring their ambush.

I've no doubt they know I'm here.

But they don't know I know they're waiting for us. They think they're golden. So they'll sit and wait for us to make the first move. The six Army PACE suits are lying on the floor, an invitation for us come in and check them out, which we would, but not in the way they expect us too. Walking into their ambush all happy, unsuspecting like. Acting stupid.

Then I draw back from the entrance to the cavern. Turnaround is going to be a bitch of a lesson for them. I'll show them who's going to look stupid when we storm in all guns blazing. I've tagged all the Fatties and predesignated the order they're to be taken down in and dump a SITREP to the platoon. Now we wait and I use this opportunity to review information to pass the time. Soon enough McCarthy comes alongside, and I link with his Dog to speak.

"Lieutenant, my squad is stacked up and ready to go in and take the Fatties down. I've got Kowalski and Jones going left, with Jackson and Rodriguez following them going right, and I'll take center."

"Where do you want Alpha Squad, Sergeant?" asks McCarthy.

"If you count five and follow us in, it will maximize our chance of enfilading the Fatties, who will be focussing on Bravo Squad. All the targets are designated on the HUD."

"Sounds like a plan to me, Sergeant, let's do this."

Then I signal my squad—*go*.

Kowalski and Jones speed past on my left slipping into the cavern using their 20 mm autocannons to light up the Chinese Fatties. One of the enemy suits blows up, bursting into flames as its fuel ignites from the explosion. The flare bathes the interior with a warm red-and-orange glow.

Jackson and Rodriguez move in going right as a Fatty fires at them but misses, with the shots going between them. Their predesignated return fire catches the offending Fatty dead center. It goes down as a 20 mm round eviscerates the machine, instantly killing the enemy pilot.

Next I follow my squad in, and go straight through the middle, laying down suppressing fire as I move. My Dog drops off a two-meter ridge, throwing me off target, but this is all up-close-and-personal stuff. There's no need to deal with windage and leading the target; I'm in death's ground. And the only thing to do is fight.

I hear the lieutenant order his squad to *go*!

The boom of the autocannons firing fills the cavern with a reverberating roar that I can feel in my bones. The flashes from muzzle fire act like a strobe, freezing the headlong motion of the moment. My Dog slips, sliding along the cavern floor.

Bang! A shot from one of the Fatties flies over my head.

I double-tap it back. The first shot glances off the arm, flies off, and hits the wall of the cavern. My second shot misses completely, blasting into the rock behind the Fatty, sending splinters flying everywhere.

My opponent pops smoke, but I've got a lock now.

Boom, boom! I double-tap the Fatty hitting it dead center this time. It collapses to the floor like so much dead weight. Smoke billows around me, but it doesn't hide the one last Fatty trying to bug out. I catch it as it turns to run to the tunnel at the other end of the cavern.

It seems like everyone fires at once.

One shot must've hit the ordnance and fuel, and the Fatty blows up with a *whoomph!* The enemy combat armor disintegrates in front of me as I'm trying to get on my feet. The back blast throws me back into the middle of the cavern, and I go crashing back down onto the floor as a thousand pieces rain down around me.

The explosion makes me grateful for being inside the coolness of my air-conditioned Dog. As I lay on my back winded from the fall I think, *That went well, all things considered.* I call, "Sound off, people."

"Jones clear."

"Kowalski all clear here too."

"Jackson clear, all enemy down."

"Rodriguez all clear."

I call, "Cerberus Two Alpha sound off."

"We're clear, but the lieutenant is down, and my Dog is not going anywhere else anytime real soon," says Knight.

Knight's Dog is standing on one leg propped up against the wall of the cavern. The lieutenant's Dog has been turned into a colander from the number of armor-piercing-round hits it has taken. Shit, McCarthy is dead. Proving that no matter how well executed a plan is, there will always be some casualties. Damn, I'd done my best, but the lieutenant still died.

"Delgado, get Hernandez to help you fix up Knight's Dog. Strip parts off the lieutenant's machine."

"Aye, aye, Sergeant," says Delgado.

"Vosloo, see what you can pull from the PACE suits here, then bag them for transport."

"Aye, aye, Sergeant."

"How you doing, Knight?"

"A bit banged up. I think I was knocked unconscious when I was hit."

"OK, that's not good. Pop the lid and let Delgado run the corpsman first aid kit on you. Delgado, Knight thinks he was knocked unconscious during the fight. Check to see if he's showing signs of concussion, and you're in charge if he's not fit to take command. Am I understood?"

"Copy that, Sergeant, I'm on it."

"Hernandez, while Delgado's patching up Knight, I want you to check the Fatties and see if you can pull any info off their machines."

"Roger that, Sergeant."

"OK, Bravo Squad follow me," I say, leading them towards the next goal of the day.

I update Captain Johanson with a SITREP and change the empty magazine on my autocannon. Confirmation comes back for me to take command, which is logged for the record, as we start our walk through the tunnel towards the pillars. It's time for me to take action to stop this day from repeating again.

As the tunnel widens ahead of us, there's a flicker of light and I order my squad to peel off in pairs to go left and right as we enter. We go in by the numbers and light up the area with IR. An unnecessary caution, but not one I am willing to give up.

It always sucks to die from being sloppy, because dying always sucks.

"OK, people, let's fan out and make like we have a purpose. The Corps is not paying us by the hour here, let's move like we mean business."

The replies from my squad come back as we slowly traverse

the ridges that break the floor up into a patchwork of uneven surfaces. We fall into a rough arrowhead formation as we go forward. On my screen the magnetic field is glowing around the pillars.

"Looks like we've found what Mr Anderson sent us here to find. Let's check it out," I say, hearing aye, ayes in reply.

The size of the two pillars becomes more apparent as we get closer and is brought into scale by the PACE suits lying on the ground in front of them.

"Form an all-round three-sixty defensive position and sound off."

Kowalski says, "Set and clear, Sergeant."

"Clear here too," says Rodriguez.

"I've got nothing, Sergeant," says Jackson.

Jones speaks. "All clear, Sergeant."

After confirming we're all clear, I send a message back to Captain Johanson and get the expected "Record the site and gather as much useful intelligence as you can" back in reply.

"OK, the captain says to scan the area for anything the Army Snake Eaters might have dropped around here. So start searching," I say as the pillars shimmer and everyone but me freezes on the spot.

My squad starts swearing, turning the air blue with mouthing off. So I soothe their anxiety by barking at them to shut the fuck up as I move around to where I can look through the pillars. There I see yet another dark cavern.

When the pillars stop shimmering, Jones says, "That was weirdly upsetting."

"I'm damn glad it's stopped. It scared the shit out of me," says Kowalski.

Rodriguez asks, "Sergeant, why could you move and we couldn't?"

"Dunno, but we need to get a move on, people. Listen up,

Marines, the easy bit is over. Kowalski and Jones, check out the rest of the cavern. Rodriguez and Jackson, get these damaged PACE suits bagged for transport," I say, thinking about what to do next.

Do I wait here for the Chinese to arrive, or take a chance and risk meeting them coming in through the other tunnel, which must lead to here from outside? There's really no way of knowing the right answer. On balance, if we wait here, we can ambush them and therefore reduce the risk of taking more casualties.

After that I message Captain Johanson about finding the source of the energy pulse. I get a message back that his squad is under fire from more Chinese forces. This seems like a good reason to wait where we control the ground, rather than run into more trouble.

I check in on Delgado over the net. She reports they're still working on Knight's Dog, he'll need stitches for a head wound, and he's complaining his vision is blurry. So not good.

"Listen up, the captain reports First Platoon is currently engaged with more enemy where they are. So we're going to settle our Dogs in here and wait in case any Chinese come our way. Let's see how they like walking into an ambush for once."

I receive a mix of "OoRahs" and shouts of "Time for payback!" from my squad.

We hunker down, taking cover in the cavern, and wait. Waiting is always difficult because everyone has to sit where they are and suck it up as the adrenaline builds in anticipation of the moment. I pick up movement at the opening to the tunnel.

Then the moment comes. There's a palpable rise of excitement that washes over me as two Fatties walk into the cavern carrying what must be the bomb between them. We're all behind cover, monitoring the area around us through our sensors, which hides our presence from the enemy. I track their movements, which are overlaid on a composite image showing the arcs of fire of each of Two Bravo's Dogs.

As the Chinese Fatties walk into center of the kill zone, I give the signal. We all open up and fire in unison.

38. AGAIN & AGAIN

Why is there anything at all rather than nothing whatsoever?

— Gottfried Wilhelm von Leibniz

Sergeant Tachikoma
First Combat Armor Suit Reconnaissance Company
CSN *Hornet*
Thursday, July 2, 2071

I get the sense of a flash of white light. Blackness envelopes me, and I feel as if I've been caught in a trap. I fall with events unfolding in front of me, then the moment is gone. As I wake up in my rack, I realize we must've detonated the bomb when we fired at the Chinese. This makes no sense at all. Nuclear bombs are usually made to be single-point safe, but clearly this bomb isn't.

I turn in my rack and confirm it's 0530 on Thursday, the second of July, 2071 again. So I have to get through breakfast, our briefing, and prepping the Dog for the mission without forgetting to say and do the right things again. Honestly,

I'm too confused to know what the right things to do or say are anymore.

Apart from maybe the obvious ones like trying to not get me and everyone else killed. Though the latter point is rather moot, as I'm the only person who remembers what happens today.

Time is a terrible thing that has shattered my world. This *today* has seen Corporal Knight die in the assault on the cavern full of Fatties, and Lieutenant McCarthy has been knocked unconscious. All my tomorrows are like some sort of pattern unfolding in time. A sort of cosmic *either-or* flip of the switch, to reach a solution where all the solutions seem to lead to death.

On the flight in, I used my PAD to check up on stuff.

I've downloaded a ton of information about alternate realities and multiverses. This is all based on some understanding of quantum mechanics and such like. With photons being waves, or particles, and uncertain cats in boxes. What catches my attention is some old dead guy who was writing back when dinosaurs ruled the Earth.

I don't mean literally, but way back when everybody was dirty and nobody washed because they didn't have things like showers.

Anyway, this guy talked about this world being the best possible one. Not because of what happens, but because it's where no person's existence contradicts the existence of another. He called this "compossibility," and I wonder whether this is what's happening to me.

Perhaps the pillars are causing me to live through all the different possible outcomes, forcing me to repeat this day until I find one where we can both exist. In the process the pillars have become the most impressive memento mori the world has ever known.

So I'm hunkered down again in cover, waiting in the cavern for the Chinese carrying the bomb to appear. I've given orders to everybody to hold fire until they put the bomb on the ground. I told my squad that I don't want us to set it off accidentally when we shoot the Chinese. Not adding "like last time." There again, I didn't need to because people take on board real quick the concept of blowing yourself up as a bad thing.

Marines have a reputation of being dumb, but we're not stupid. However, we like to take advantage of the fact that our enemies think we are, because it's always good to be underestimated by an opponent.

The two Fatties walk into the cavern, carrying the bomb. I track them on my pop-up sensor as they walk towards the pillars and place the bomb on the ground in front of it. As they turn to leave, the pillars shimmer, and everyone freezes in that moment, except for me.

Then I stand up and take aim. I fire two rounds into the first Fatty, then fire another two rounds into the other.

Then everything goes white, and I wake in my rack to find it's again 0530 hours on Thursday, the second of July, 2071. There is a lingering sense of the after-flash. And I realize the Chinese must have the bomb rigged to explode. Some sort of failsafe linked to the one of the Fatties, which makes no sense at all.

So it's another day, another breakfast, followed by another briefing. Then back to prepping the Dogs to repeat the same mission. I'm starting to want to shout out it's not fair, but when has life ever been fair? We've lots of mottos in the Marine Corps, but this is the most appropriate: "The only easy day was yesterday."

If we're taking it easy, it means we're alive, getting ready for the next task. But it's a lie—there are no easy days in the Corps, because we are not paid to take it easy. *OoFuckingRah*, I love the Corps.

Can I hold it together for another repeat of the same day? Honestly, I don't know. Part of me doesn't care anymore, the other part of me wants to kill everyone who is trying to kill me. Once I've killed them all, I want to stomp on their remains, just to make sure they're really dead.

It's a bit like when you shout at actors when they forget to cut off the monster's head in a movie. You know they don't know the monster will come back to life, but you do. That's how I feel.

So here I am back inside the mountain. I can't sit it out, been there, done that, it doesn't work. Unfortunately, today has not come with an instruction manual telling me what to do. So it's definitely one of those days that can be defined as having a bit of a difficult learning curve. As in: find out what the right thing to do *is* and do that.

Lieutenant McCarthy died in the assault and Corporal Knight is unconscious. So far we've been unable to revive him this time. I'm trapped in a cosmic game where the outcome of the firefight collapses possibilities, leading to my death and everyone with me.

One thing about sitting around during the wait cycles is I've read more about Schrödinger's cat, which has given me a headache. It seems whether I look or don't look into the box, the cat assumes one state or another: dead or alive. But it's not cats that are dying out here with me, it's the people I know and like.

But I don't have the luxury of people being in a state of superposition. I see them die. One way or another they all end up dead. The outcome of each day as the explosion collapses the uncertainty down into one where the pillars and I exist.

My life has become all kinds of crazy; it's driving me nuts!

So I'm hunkering behind the same bit of cover waiting for the Chinese to enter the cavern with the bomb. I've outlined a different plan to my Marines this time. We'll allow them to come and go before trying to disarm the bomb.

I'm not sure they were entirely on board with the plan, but the whole dying-if-the-bomb-has-a-failsafe idea sold them. If only because my order makes some sort of sense. Otherwise they're trained to question orders that are contrary to the mission objectives.

Fortunately for me, this is a retrieve-and-recon mission.

This means we keep fighting to a minimum. We're not here to chew gum while we get to kick ass. That would just get us all killed again.

The two Fatties walk into the cavern, place the bomb on the ground, then freeze in place for nearly five minutes while the pillars shimmer. Once they're gone I signal to move up and check out the bomb. It's an old Soviet Union MIRV warhead with a refurbished plutonium core. It has been fitted with a collar with Chinese kanji on it. I can read enough to understand these are safety instructions of sorts.

Where instead of the normal "beware," safety means "this will explode if tampered with."

"Judging by the labels, I don't think we will be able to disarm the bomb."

"I agree with you, Sergeant, my translation software says this thing is set all the different ways to hell to explode if tampered with," says Kowalski.

"Good thing we...no fire...at the Chinese...when they carry this bomb in here, Sergeant," says Rodriguez.

"What are we going to do, Sergeant?" asks Jones.

"OK, here's the plan, we drag it between the pillars, and when they shimmer again, it will cut the bomb in half, disarming it. Jackson give me a hand here."

"Are you sure that will work Sergeant?"

"Best idea I've got." He's got to be wondering how the hell do I know what to do.

"Aye, aye, Sergeant," says Jackson.

Next I walk through the pillars and position the bomb so it

will be cut in half. Then we all back well away from it. No one wants to be standing close to the pillars when they activate.

Though if this doesn't work, it won't matter where we're standing, but the fear from being frozen by the pillars affects everyone except for me. I'm not frightened by the thought of being frozen on the spot, I'm afraid I will die and have to face going through this day all over again for the rest of eternity.

The pillars shimmer, and the heat hits me as a flash of white light sweeps over me. And I'm dead.

I wake and turn to see it's 0530 on Thursday, the second of July, 2071. Only someone who is effin' bat-shit crazy insane would rig an atomic bomb to go off regardless. I fear just looking at the bomb the wrong way will set it off.

So it's rinse and repeat the day again.

But this time instead of placing the bomb between the pillars I place it by the pillars and wait for the shimmer, then pull it through and leave it on the other side. That's gotta work, right?

This time we hear what sounds like a herd of elephants leaving the mountains after the two Chinese leave. Everything seems to go according to plan as the shimmer stops and nothing happens. Afterwards we go outside, and I'm told that Third and Fourth Platoons had seen the Chinese fleeing the mountain.

We haven't a snowflake in hell's chance of catching them, but I bet they were sure as hell surprised when their precious bomb failed to go off.

Johanson orders the company to dig in and defend the entrances to the mountain, but the expected counterattack never comes. I guess the Chinese decided to cut their losses. Can't blame them for that; they'd faced Marines, and we'd kicked their asses. The remains of destroyed Fatties are testament to that.

We sit around and wait for orders to come down the chain of command.

Delgado is gutted by Gentle's death. Everybody is angry and

upset by our losses, even those not close to Perez. My recordings go back to *Hornet*, and we are told to stay put till morning when the birds will come in and pick us up.

We're informed that the Air Force will be delivering a package to seal the mountains, which sounds all well and dandy, but after I go to sleep that night I wake up back in my rack. When I open my eyes I see doubles of everything, sort of. Like seeing double only not. It is like I'm seeing stuff happening in two worlds at the same time. Then my head starts throbbing with the worst headache you can imagine.

It is so bad I go see the doc in the med-bay. So I spend the rest of the day sleeping or chatting with him. It doesn't take much persuading to get him to treat me with the transcranial magnetic stimulator, which helps a lot. The medication also makes the headache go away.

Also I get the jump on Anderson and blow his mind when I tell him I know about RED SLIPPERS. And it is so totally worth the look I get from him when I say it. For a moment I think he is going to have me arrested, but after he calms down I go the through the story with him again. After that I pump him for information, for anything that might help me. What I learn amounts to diddly-squat.

So I take advantage of the enforced idleness to read a bunch more about multiverses and theories about the space-time continuum, revising my theory about how the pillars are screwing with my day. My best guess is I have become entangled with them, and whatever happens to them happens to me. But there is nothing to help me deal with the problem.

Still, it makes a change to my routine of being blown up.

I went to sleep last night in my own rack and wake refreshed. But

I'm fed up of eating ham and eggs and go for SOS instead as a change, which draws comments from everyone in the platoon who knows how much I like ham and eggs. What's worse is I put sugar in my coffee to hide the bitterness. Which in my book is a sin against the Navy.

The effort it takes to not snark my way through the mission briefing is worth my next Good Conduct Medal, and while I love my Dog I feel the need to get out more. Did I mention I'm starting to want to kill people too?

That's everybody, by the way.

I'm really pissed off by being made to look stupid every time the bomb goes off and I die. I figure all I've got to do is make sure the bomb doesn't go off, and I'll be home and dry. Hell, if I die, and don't get to wake up again today, it will be a result.

Compossibility my ass.

So we're back inside the mountain. The cosmic switch has flipped, resulting in Lieutenant McCarthy living through the assault today. This leaves Corporal Knight's body an unsightly mess, the result of being blown apart by Chinese 12.7 mm rounds, their equivalent of our fifty cal, ripping his Dog apart.

But we're here earlier than we've ever been before, and I've made my mind up to do something different. Now I'm inside the enemy's OODA loop, and I swear today I will collapse the uncertainty surrounding the survival of the pillars into a compossible world. One where I live and they exist. I order Rodriguez and Jackson to bag the remains of the PACE suits and carry them out with us.

Then I message Captain Johanson and tell him I found another way out of the mountain. He replies that he's under fire from Chinese Fatties in another part of the mountain, and I need to take command. It's the answer I expected, my opportunity to take the fight to the enemy.

We may be recon, but today we kick butt.

"OK, squad, Fenris Alpha has encountered enemy, and I've told the captain we're going to take another way out of here. Let's see if we can secure the other entry into the mountain. Jones, take point. Kowalski, take rear. Let's move it, we don't have all day."

With their usual laconic brevity, my Marines reply with a chorus of "OoRahs!" Jones leads the way as we go along the tunnel, which again appears to have been shaped to act as a main thoroughfare into the mountain. So it doesn't take long to start seeing light from outside ahead of us.

Jones's Dog moves up to the entrance, and he swings out his sensor pod to check on what awaits us outside. Then I move up beside his Dog and hard link to him. Looking through his feed on my screen, I see two Fatties standing in cover outside the entrance.

"Looks like they're waiting for something to arrive, Sergeant," says Jones.

"Sure does, Private. There's a truck approaching now."

"What are we going to do?"

"We're going to do what we do best, kill them. You take the one on the left, and I'll take the one on the right, on my mark of three." I send a message to the rest of Fenris Bravo to follow us. "One, two, three, mark! Go, go, go!"

We rush out and shoot the Fatties where they stand before they get the chance to react. I fire twice and then once more, just to make sure. The satisfaction when both Fatties explode as their ordnance cooks off in a violent cacophony of heat and thunder is its own reward.

Then I turn and kneel, lining up to take the next shot at the truck coming down the road. It's at an angle to the right of us. One shot to the engine compartment. *Boom!* My round goes right through it and out the other side because it was, after all, only a soft-skin vehicle that had been hit by a 20 mm armor-piercing round. Sliced and diced.

So no big Hollywood explosion, no tumbling of the truck from the special effects unit. Just a hole through the hood with the truck carrying on moving along the road, gradually slowing to a halt. The truck rolls to a stop fifty meters ahead of us. The rest of Two Bravo has joined up with me and Jones.

Shrapnel has shredded the occupants, turning the interior of the truck red.

"Kowalski and Jones, go check out the back of the truck and tell me what it's carrying." I turn and look around at the other side of the mountain. "Rodriguez, Jackson, did either of you two lovebirds remember to plant transponders on the way here?"

"I did, Sergeant," says Jackson.

"Good, glad to hear it. I want both of you up on the slope there," I point to some big rocks, "and form a defensive line."

"Aye, aye, Sergeant," they say together.

"What you got for me, Kowalski?"

"Looks like an atomic warhead to me, Sergeant, which has been disassembled for transport. These guys meant to do some serious business here."

"OK, grab the bomb and move it over there." I transmit the location marked on my map to him. "I want to enfilade any other Chinese who might decide to come our way when they leave the mountain."

There's a glint of sunlight from the mountain on the other side of the valley across from us. I can only hope we don't get hit by artillery fire.

Next thing I do is send a SITREP to Captain Johanson informing him of our capture of the bomb. After that I try to contact Third and Fourth Platoons but get nothing, as the satellite has dropped off over the horizon. I check when the next satellite is due to come overhead. We've lucked out with only two minutes' wait until another comes up. We now stand a chance of being able to link back to *Hornet*.

Then I move up next to Jones and Kowalski, and I fold my Dog into the ground, waiting for the Chinese inside the mountain to appear. We couldn't outrun Fatties on a good day, and today is not a good day, as it's never a good day to die; no matter what some gung-ho idiots might tell you.

Better to make the enemy die for their country instead.

I take a moment to message Delgado for an update on the lieutenant's condition. She reports he is now conscious. They've also been able to fix the leg on his Dog, which is good news. Then I dump back a SITREP to *Hornet* on Fenris Bravo's current position, and after that order Delgado to bring Alpha squad to us, reminding her to watch out for Chinese Fatties.

It will take Delgado's squad a while to get here, but even if they arrive late to the party, it might make all the difference.

39. VICTORY

There is only one decisive victory: the last. Blood is the price of victory.

— CARL VON CLAUSEWITZ

Captain Johanson
First Combat Armor Suit Reconnaissance Company
Afghanistan
Thursday, July 2, 2071

Johanson moves along the tunnel and switches to the feed from Private First Class Lopez's Dog, who is on point.

The transponder map is building up a picture of the tunnels under the mountain. The picture reminds Johanson of a story he read a long time ago as a child that had involved dragons and dwarves. However, if they met anything here, it would be unlikely to be something as fanciful as a dragon guarding its hoard of gold.

His platoon is traversing a series of tunnels connecting together small caverns that are like misshaped pearls threaded together on a string. Their journey is one of slow down and stop, speed up for a bit, and then slow down and stop again to traverse the obstacles in their path. At the end of the cave, he sees from Lopez's feed two exits to choose from.

"Bergeson, I want you to take One Bravo along the right-hand tunnel."

Johanson doesn't like splitting the platoon, but given the time it took to get here, he has little choice if he wants the mission to stay on schedule. He only hopes he isn't setting his force up to be defeated in detail.

Bergeson replies, "Roger that, Captain. Lopez, you're on point, Gunny, please take the rear."

Johanson watches Bergeson's squad disappearing into the right-hand tunnel before speaking. "Private Gentle, take point and move out."

"Roger that, Oscar Mike," she replies.

"Sergeant Ramirez, bring up the rear. I'll be the middle of the line."

At least this way he has a chance of moving either way to assess anything that might come up. The cavern they enter slopes down. The surface is slick, making progress more than a little bit tricky. Johanson has to agree with Private First Class Lopez's earlier assessment of the situation: it would be a whole lot easier to traverse these tunnels in MARPACE suits.

Then he tenses when the contact alert light flashes in his HUD. It's from Lieutenant McCarthy's platoon; they've engaged the enemy. This is the kind of news he could do without because there's no way for him to provide any kind of support.

Then he waits for several minutes for a SITREP. It's bad news.

Sergeant Tachikoma reports Corporal Knight has been killed and Lieutenant McCarthy wounded in the firefight with eight enemy Fatties. This can only mean that the rest of the Chinese platoon is somewhere else. The only good news is that six Army PACE suits have been retrieved.

The Chinese must also be here for Anderson's mysterious energy pulse. A Chinese platoon is smaller than a CSMC company, which should mean the odds are in his favour—of course this assumes the Chinese only sent in one platoon to recon the mountain.

But he wouldn't bet on his assumption turning out to be true.

40. CURSING

*War is the father of us all, king of all. Some it makes gods, some
it makes men, some it makes slaves, some free.*

— HERACLITUS

Second Lieutenant Perez
Commander Third Platoon
First Combat Armor Suit Reconnaissance Company
Afghanistan
Thursday, July 2, 2071

Perez sits in the cockpit of his Dog and swears at Sergeant
Tachikoma's deployment plan. A plan she managed to persuade
Captain Johanson to sign off on. Who the hell does she think she
is to get them all loaded up and then get them to march over some
of the roughest terrain he has ever had to maneuver a Dog across?

It's like some damn recruit training exercise made to push
them to the limit. Hell, he doesn't need any more *Moto* shit to do
his job. As far as he's concerned, this whole mission is a way to

rag on the new lieutenants by making it harder to do their jobs properly.

He checks the map and the platoon's position relative to the marker set by the captain and realizes that they won't be able to achieve their objective in the allotted time. That won't look good in the After Action Report. Perez knows if you don't look good on your reports, then it reflects on your next assignment.

"We need to pick up the pace, Sergeant."

"Aye, aye," says Staff Sergeant Thompson. "Green blurs Marines, we're not being paid by the hour. Let's get a move on, we haven't got all day. Jackman, get your thumb out of your ass. You too, Schwartz. Move it, the pair of you."

Perez scans the terrain as Thompson chivvies the platoon to move faster. If he'd been in charge, he would've dropped his platoon on the target. He would've had Beckford's platoon do the sweep after the Air Force MULE had picked up the crashed space-plane. That way it would've saved time, and his platoon wouldn't be trudging around in the open for no good reason.

When he makes captain, he'll make sure every job is done in an orderly fashion to minimize the hurry up and wait endemic within the Marine Corps. New blood is what's needed. People like him with fresh ideas, who will use modern technology to drag the Corps into the twenty-first century ready for the challenges of the twenty-second.

Back at the crash site, Beckford's platoon is fucking around under her leadership. Busy getting nothing done. Mind you, he's grateful his platoon wasn't assigned that job, as sitting around with his thumb up his backside waiting on the Air Force pilots to arrive in their big-ass MULE would definitely suck.

Long shadows fall across the ground ahead of them as the sun passes behind the mountain range. He estimates his platoon will hit the mark on the map in fifteen mikes. A signal from Beckford informs him the Air Force MULE is inbound towards the crash site.

Whoopee fucking do.

Third Platoon reaches the line on the mountain that has been designated for their deployment. They arrive as the shimmering shape of the MULE descends in the distance, and Perez takes a moment to enjoy the view.

Beckford's platoon swarms around the MULE. At least she has to do some work now, instead of just standing and waiting around while his platoon hauls ass. Now he can catch a moment and assess the situation here on the ground. He'll show Sergeant Tachikoma that boots on the ground beats a bad gut feeling every day of the week.

Perez watches Beckford's platoon being carried across the plain by the MULE. As the MULE climbs higher, he hears the sound of incoming artillery and shouts, "Incoming, incoming!"

He dives into the ground, hugging it for cover as the barrage lands about four hundred meters in front of his position. This is danger close by any definition when it comes to artillery. Luckily nothing hits him. He hates to admit it, but that bitch of a sergeant had guessed right about artillery. Still, it don't mean nothing. It's only a lucky guess, after all.

He orders the platoon to sound off. Confirmation comes in across the board that everybody is OK. No one managed to do anything stupid when taking cover.

Then he checks on Beckford's platoon, which has hunkered down after being dropped by the MULE. He gets a message from her about the crash site being the target of an artillery barrage. Like he gives a shit, as she wasn't standing in the danger-close zone where he is.

The shells stop falling, so he gives the all-clear. Then he sees the first of the Chinese Fatties fly over the ridgeline. They're sweeping down on where his platoon would've been had they deployed where originally intended.

The day has started to get interesting because now he can show everyone how his platoon kicks ass. He orders his platoon to mark their targets and fire when they've got a target lock. The sound of his autocannon rocks his world, as he sees the first of the Chinese combat armor suits blown apart into a thousand pieces.

"Give them hell, Marines!"

"They're behind us, sir," shouts Jackman.

He feels his Dog being pushed aside by Schwartz, but it's too late. A moment later they're both dead as the enemy missiles hit them.

41. PAYBACK

Our best successes often come after our greatest disappointments.

— HENRY WARD BEECHER

Second Lieutenant Beckford
Commander Fourth Platoon
First Combat Armor Suit Reconnaissance Company
Afghanistan
Thursday, July 2, 2071

Beckford listens to the background chit-chat from her platoon as she scans around the crash site. In the distance she can see Perez's platoon making its way up the mountain. His orders are to deploy on the ridgeline.

On the way, his platoon has been searching for any signs of the Army Alpha Detachment being caught in the open by local forces. They have found zilch. Not at all surprising as the CIA had eyes on what happened here. The Agency only lost contact with the Special Forces team after they'd entered the mountain.

The trouble is, she's sure the Agency isn't telling them the whole story.

Beckford gets a message from the Air Force MULE. They say they're about an hour out. Strong headwinds are slowing their progress, which is always a thing with hybrid lifting body airships. As long as nothing untoward comes from the delay, then she can live with it. Beckford gives her platoon the heads-up on the ETA of the MULE.

Talking to Staff Sergeant Washington confirms her sense that everyone is bored but otherwise fine, which is good to know. She takes a moment to stretch back in her seat. Then she scans the feeds on her screen to pass the time.

Finally, the airship comes in low over the horizon to the south of her platoon's position. But it's hard to get a good visual on the ghostly shape flying towards them. Even the noise from the fans is muted, making the craft hard to hear until it's nearly right on top of them. Now it's time for Fourth Platoon to do its job and get the space-plane secured. She takes pleasure in seeing the men and women in her platoon getting the job done in a timely manner.

But she's glad the captain had OK'd Sergeant Tachikoma's suggestion to have her platoon get a lift from the MULE. It had been prescient of the sergeant to think of it. Otherwise the next part of the mission would've been a hard slog.

Once the space-plane's secured, the MULE drops ten lifting cables, and she orders the Dogs to hook up for the trip. The MULE revs its fans to full power, and the noise penetrates her Dog as the airship takes flight. It doesn't climb very high for the short hop, as they're only going three klicks to their drop point. Soon they arrive at their destination. To Beckford it feels like virtually no time has passed at all.

Beckford makes sure to thank the pilots and crew chiefs for the lift. The MULE climbs away from them using the draft of the mountainside to assist its flight to gain altitude. After it clears the crest of the mountain, she hears the sound of shells whistling overhead from an incoming artillery barrage. The area around the crash site erupts with explosions. They'd gotten a lucky break.

Then the enemy sweeps over the crest of the mountain, coming in behind Perez's platoon, chewing his command to ribbons. It's time for her platoon to earn their pay. She orders her people to start laying down fire on the enemy. Mess with the best, die like the rest.

42. END RUN

They're on our right, they're on our left, they're in front of us, they're behind us; they can't get away from us this time.

— LtGen Lewis Burwell "Chesty" Puller, USMC

Sergeant Tachikoma
First Combat Armor Suit Reconnaissance Company
Afghanistan
Thursday, July 2, 2071

As we wait for the Chinese to appear, the company command net icon flashes on my screen. At last I'm able to link up with Third and Fourth Platoons. We exchange info dumps, and I find out that Third Platoon beat off an attack, which is a bit of good news.

The bad is that it has come at a price in lives.

Beckford is holding position with Fourth Platoon, and I advise her on the chance of Fatties arriving later to rain on Fenris Bravo's parade. I get a confirmation back she's on her way. It's all I can do, but at least the bloody bomb hasn't gone off this time.

In the entrance to the mountain, I catch sight of movement.

Not enough to get a target lock, but I fire a shot to discourage them. Call me generous if you want, or foolish for giving away our position, but I'm under no illusion about the Chinese inside the mountain. They will soon lock on to us when they leave their tunnel.

Any delay will buy us time, and time is what we need. So I fire again to keep their heads down.

"OK, any minute now they will figure out how few of us are out here and come storming out to ream us a new one," I say, wondering: If I die now, will the day repeat for me now that we've moved the bomb?

"I need reaming about as much as I need another hole in my head," says Jones.

"Keep focused, Jones." I take a moment to think. "The captain reckons we could be facing a platoon-sized formation, so no heroics, as help is on its way."

"Got that, Sergeant," says Kowalski as he fires a single shot to keep on discouraging our Chinese friends.

At that moment the first Fatty leaves cover. It flies out into the open and is shot up by Jackson, who shouts out in his Texan drawl, "Yeehaw!"

And then the rest follow. I count fifteen.

We can't hit them all as they rush forward, swinging out and around for their assault on us. We are at less than three hundred meters range. In death's ground. Their speed at this distance means it's easy to miss, even with computer tracking, as the Fatties jinx around, dodging our fire.

Still they lose two, but Kowalski's Dog has its gun arm blown off, and we are down to four effectives. It has become a numbers game. Fifteen to five is three to one, which means the odds are in their favour. Now it's thirteen of them and four of us, which is still good for them and bad for us.

The sort of odds that will lead to all our deaths.

They're going to overrun us and kill every last member of my squad. Then they will get possession of the bomb again. I can't allow that to happen.

"Lay it on, Marines, make them pay."

"I've got some," shouts Jackson as he double taps an enemy machine and changes target. "You want some too," he says, as his Dog comes under a fusillade of shots ripping it into pieces. His machine falls to the ground.

"No!" screams Rodriguez, who goes full on releasing a stream of 20 mm on autofire.

"Controlled bursts, Marines, lay down some grenades and pop smoke—pop all your smoke now!"

I'm hoping the combination of the grenades exploding and the smoke will cause the Chinese to waver in their advance, buying us some more time. *Come on, Beckford, where are you?*

"Controlled bursts, Sergeant, I'm on it, sir!" shouts Jones, in his excitement.

"Jones don't call me 'sir,' I still work for a living."

The Chinese formation bursts apart. It separates into two groups to attack us from both sides, using speed to move their line of attack and envelope us. As they move we take out another of theirs, but Rodriguez is hit in the leg and goes offline.

Twelve to two is not good because it means game over for us. All I can do is watch in grim fascination as the assault comes rushing towards our position. Two Fatties disintegrate right in front of my eyes. The sonic boom from a Gauss round sweeps over me. On my screen I see Beckford's platoon has deployed on the ridgeline behind us.

"Fenris Bravo, we've got your back, Cerberus Four Six over."

"Good of you to join us, Cerberus Four Six, over," I reply.

"Ripple, I say again, ripple incoming, out."

Beckford gives us due warning of incoming fire from the Fourth Platoon Dogs' missiles before they land between us and the enemy. It's satisfying when three Fatties blow up, one cartwheeling as it crashes in the ensuing explosions. They don't know it yet, but they're all about to die.

"Lay it on, Jones, give them all you've got."

The area in front of our position turns into a killing field as more missiles are launched by Fourth Platoon. A salvo of rounds from an M21-A8 Gauss rifle flies across our front, leaving visible trails in the air. Our two functioning Dogs now face six fleeing Fatties, then reduced to five as one is caught in our crossfire as it turns to try to get away.

I call, "Cease fire. I say again, cease fire!"

Killing is one thing, butchering retreating people another.

The smoke starts to clear, and we wait to see what will happen next. But it appears the remaining Chinese have lost the will to fight and keep going, which is fine by me.

McCarthy turns up with Fenris Alpha, carrying Knight's remains in their cocoon on the back of his Dog. I give him the full update on what's happened. Then Captain Johanson comes on the company net and tells us we've been tasked to guard the mountain until tomorrow.

Kowalski survived despite his Dog being hit and losing an arm. He gets to live and fight again, but the butcher's bill for today's victory is high. The company is down six good Marines: Jackson and Knight from my platoon, Gentle from First, and Perez, Jackman, and Schwartz from Third.

Casualties of war, for definitions of *war* that include actions that will never be reported as such. Delgado is shocked by Gentle's death. Everyone is dealing with the stress of the day as best they can—some quietly, others letting off steam. Whatever works for them.

Captain Johanson reorganizes the company, moving Lieutenant Bergeson from First to take over Perez's Third Platoon. He's keeping people busy, getting them to focus on doing stuff. He orders us to set up a defensive position with Fourth Platoon on this side of the mountain. The captain then takes the First and Third Platoons back to cover the other side.

I check the time and ask the captain for permission to go back and sweep the cavern to search for the other half of the PACE suit that we found. When he asks me why I think I'll find it, I tell him it's a gut feeling. He nods in acknowledgement and gives me permission to proceed.

I take Jones, Delgado, and Vosloo with me for the pleasure of being frozen in place while I walk through the pillars. We get back to the pillars at 2120 and wait ten mikes for them to shimmer. The first opening leads to another cosmic cavern with nothing much to see. So I order my squad to sweep the cavern while I wait for the next activation.

They grumble at the busy work but do as they're ordered. The next shimmer still reveals nothing, and the grumbles continue. No one, it seems, likes being frozen in place.

We wait for the next cycle, and luckily for me this time there're two moons hanging low in the sky, and the other half of the PACE suit lies on the ground. When I walk between the pillars, a thrill of excitement rushes over me as I stand again on the alien world.

I pan to record everything and walk in a circle around the pillars. The realization hits me that this man must've been like me, able to walk through the pillars. He couldn't have been sliced in half otherwise. It means I'm not the only one. There are others like me.

Far in the distance the bird-bat-like creatures fly up from the canopy of the jungle, and I catch the faint sound of something roaring in the distance. Definitely not Kansas.

Checking the time, I turn around and grab the PACE suit and drag it back with me to where my squad are squawking over the radio about me disappearing from sight. After hearing me bark reassuring orders, they collect themselves, not believing what they've seen but witnessed all the same. Their Dogs have recorded my movements through the pillars, which will be useful when I submit my report.

But for now we need to wrap the PACE suit up to take back. He may have been an Army puke, but I have the satisfaction of not leaving a fallen compatriot behind. I send the captain a message over the net reporting our success as we trudge back out into the open, where night has come.

Given that this is Afghanistan, it gets really dark. I take a moment to pop the lid on my Dog and look up at the night sky; it's full of familiar stars. They're beautiful to behold. It strikes me that one of the stars above me might actually be one I stood under the sunlight of. Awesome.

I take first watch. At midnight I'm relieved by Kowalski. As soon as I snuggle down into the seat of my Dog, I fall asleep.

I'm falling again into infinite space. Stars are all around me, but I realize the stars are not suns, but fragments of my life, the choices I've made and the consequences thereof. But then I realize that I'm dreaming and have an epiphany.

These are not fragments of my life, but different lives, different me's, in different universes. All of my lives are happening at once. This isn't one day repeating itself, but my mind coping with trying to understand that I'm living all the days of my life simultaneously.

My falling stops, and it feels like I've stretched and snapped into one place. Now I'm standing in front of two pillars in the middle of a plain of shifting darkness under an alien sky. As I stare at them I'm sucked back up into space, and a whirl of colors twists and turns around me, branching every which way. Spiralling out through time and space, a multidimensional fractal pattern that's pulsing all around me.

Then my shadow and the shadows of my platoon members

move around me. Suddenly I'm awake with a crick in my neck from sleeping in the seat of my cockpit and it's 0530.

I try to hang on to my dream. But it fades into a memory and is lost in time and space. I become aware that I'm cold and hungry and I check the date; it's Friday, the third of July. Tears start running down my face as I realize I've made it.

Getting out of my Dog, I go through the whole using-baby-wipes-to-wash-myself thing. We may be out in the field, but personal hygiene still matters. Now I need to wash the tears off my face because Sergeants can't be seen crying, it's not situation-appropriate behaviour. Besides I wouldn't want to destroy the myth that our tear ducts are surgically removed when we're promoted.

Stories and myths are important in helping us understand what life throws at us. After cleaning myself up, I find a less than yummy rat-pack for breakfast. Still, it makes a change from ham and eggs. As I finish eating I hear the sound of the Thunder Hawks in the distance. This signals it will soon be time for dust-off and a return to *Hornet*.

They arrive in a cloud of dust, which settles to the ground as they spool down their fans. We drag the damaged Dogs aboard the birds, then take the disassembled Chinese nuke with us so we can dispose of it safely when we get back aboard *Hornet*. With the Dogs loaded we lift off in a furious cloud of dust, and the mountain starts to recede in the distance.

The word from *Hornet* arrives to tell us that the Air Force is sending a package to seal the entrances to the caves. They're as good as their word. A series of massive conventional explosions strike each side of the mountain. This ends the mission. Now it's time to sit and be bored, chew the breeze, and generally unwind.

It's all the reward I expect, which is good, because it's the only reward worth a damn. That, and being alive.

43. DEFEAT

There are only two kinds of people that understand Marines: Marines and the enemy. Everyone else has a second-hand opinion.

— Gen William Thornson, USAR

Shàngwèi Looi
Commander Special Operations Force Falcon
Democratic People's Republic of China
The White Mountain, Afghanistan
Thursday, July 2, 2071

Looi sits in the cockpit of his *yíng huo chóng*, firefly. The armored suit sits in the darkness of the mountain waiting for the Americans to arrive. His orders are simple: delay the Americans and prevent them from securing the mountain.

His lián had set up where they'd ambushed the first American team. It seems likely that the American rescue party will use the same route into the mountain because of the ease of access.

Looi wonders what he might do if he was in their position.

His screen shows Shàowèi Zhan and Zhongzhi Chén standing outside the mountain. They're waiting for the truck to arrive. An update from Shàowèi Xiang's pái informs him they're ready to attack the Americans when they come out of the mountain.

All the elements of the plan have come together.

Shàowèi Li's bán reports they'd been engaged.

Somehow the enemy has made quicker time in the narrower tunnels than anticipated. Status icons turn red on his screen each time one of Li's men is killed in the firefight. Then they're all dead.

Xiashi, corporal, Chou signals he has picked up a contact ahead. The Americans' arrival has threatened the success of the plan. Looi orders everyone to fire. The yíng huo chóng kuijia next to him blows up, and he realizes he doesn't want to die today. Not here under this mountain.

But the Americans retreat. So Looi orders his pái to withdraw. They've delayed the Americans, killing one of them. That's enough.

It's difficult to maneuver their kuijia inside the cramped confines of the maze of tunnels that link all the natural caverns together. This slows their progress back to the entrance of the mountain. The status icons for Shàowèi Zhan and Zhongzhi Chén turn red.

In that moment Looi fears the mission has failed.

His pái are now close to the opening that leads out of the mountain. Looi launches a disposable UAV, and his screen shows Zhan and Chén's yíng huo chóng suits burning. The truck abandoned, hit by enemy fire.

One of his men flies out of the cave's entrance and is destroyed.

Looi knows he's facing death. Whatever decision he makes he has to advance into death's ground. This makes giving the order easier, as there is no right answer. No right plan of action. There is only do nothing and be killed, or do something and be killed. Doing nothing and being killed is by far the worst option. So he orders his people out of the mountain.

Looi breathes a sigh of relief as they fly into the light to find they're only facing five enemy combat armor suits.

He leads a sweep around the enemy in an advance by bán to assault the enemy through fire and maneuver. He might win this fight. If he does, he might still be able to complete the mission.

One of the enemy combat armor suits loses an arm, but accurate shots from the Americans' deadly autocannons kill two of his men before they can destroy another enemy suit. The melee is a swirl of confusion that fills his heart with fear and elation. Another enemy combat armor suit falls to the ground helpless as one of its legs flies off.

Now he knows he has gained fire superiority. But the enemy launches smoke to cause confusion. His men respond by using their yíng huo chóng's superior speed to avoid the kill zone the enemy are trying to funnel them into. His remaining kuijia surge forward.

The moment is theirs, but then two of his yíng huo chóng break apart, hit by fire from the mountain above them. The supersonic rounds leave trails in the air leading back up to the ridgeline. Then missiles start landing all around him. In a matter of seconds he's lost half of his remaining men.

Looi orders the retreat and sees another of his men die. Only himself, Zhongzhi Wú, Xiashi Chou, Lie Bing Ch'eng and Huáng escape. All he has achieved this day is to snatch defeat from the jaws of victory.

44. AFTERMATH

Never was anything great achieved without danger.

— NICCOLO MACHIAVELLI

Mr Anderson
CIA Analyst
CSN *Hornet*
Thursday, July 2, 2071

Anderson observes the action slowly unfold on the screens of *Hornet*'s CIC. Inserting the company and the pickup of the Aries space-plane goes by the numbers. The artillery strike on the area around the crash site not so much. The attack confirms that Sergeant Tachikoma had nailed the situation on the ground and, as a result, saved the mission from utter disaster.

Having lost the Alpha Detachment was bad, to lose the 1st CASR Hound Dogs Company sent in to retrieve them would've been worse still. Perhaps even a career-ending event, given the likelihood that he would've taken the fall for whatever happened.

The area around the space-plane is like pictures he'd seen of the trenches in World War One. The features around the crash site obliterated, changed into a morass of churned-up ground. Fortunately, no one had died in the attack, but it showed that the enemy was playing hardball.

Another attack by Chinese combat armor is repulsed by the company rearguard, but with the loss of Marines. Anderson can't recall the last time American troops died in combat. Loss of material, yes, but people dying in combat, no, not in twenty years. A brutal firefight ensues with the surviving Chinese forces fleeing, signalling that the Marines had gained control of the mountain and destroyed the enemy's will to resist.

Anderson ignores cheering around him as he scans the mission footage from the Marines' suits. He bites his lip waiting for the files to finish downloading. Sergeant Tachikoma's squad's files are tagged "magnetic anomaly." He opens the video showing the first contact with the pillars and knows he has hit pay dirt.

Pulling on a headset, Anderson opens a secure comms-link to Langley and attaches the files with his abbreviated interim report. He sees Moss, Wayland, and Scott appear in front of him.

"You should be receiving the video data feed from the Marines I sent in to rescue the Army Alpha Detachment. Unfortunately, there were no survivors, though their bodies have been retrieved. My feeling is that we should withdraw from the site and seal the entrances as discussed earlier."

"Well done, Glen, a good job," says Moss as she scans the attached files.

"This will give us plenty to think about, Mr Anderson," says Dr Scott.

General Wayland stops perusing the files to speak. "All I can say is that I hope the cost in lives paid for this information was worth the men and women we lost gaining it."

Anderson has to agree with the general on this point. His own feelings on the matter are mixed. It would take time to know whether the price in lives lost for the information gained was too high.

"Well, Dr Scott, it seems your team was right about the magnetic anomaly, and the Agency's concerns over Chinese involvement proved to be well founded. Are we all in agreement about the next step?" says General Wayland.

"It's a pity we can't keep the access to this site open for further research. What we could discover there would be of great benefit to furthering our knowledge if we could compare our pillars with these," says Dr Scott.

"We need to know the limits of our remit and accept that we can't gain control over the pillars in Afghanistan without starting a major war, which we're in no position to prosecute. Our best option is to stick to the plan and seal the site," says Anderson.

"I agree with the Agency's position on this matter. The Air Force has been authorized to deliver a package. It's the only way to be sure we've denied the Chinese access to this site," says General Wayland.

Anderson sees the order for Echo Papa One being sent to seal the entrances to the mountain and knows he can relax now that his mission is complete.

45. JANNAH

When what you want doesn't happen, learn to want what does.

— ARABIAN PROVERB

Warlord Yeshua bin Yussuf
The White Mountain, Afghanistan
Thursday, July 2, 2071

Yeshua bin Yussuf stares through his old binoculars across the plain that separates the two mountains. He remembers the boom of the artillery when they were fired and their failure to destroy the American shayateen. Now he sees two Chinese waiting for the bomb suddenly fall to the ground. American shayateen emerge from the mountainside, and he's helpless to do anything while they take hold of the bomb. He curses the fact that all their shells are gone. He wishes he had kept some in reserve.

Abdi-al-Hazred comes and lies on the ground beside him. "What has happened?"

"The American shayateen have beaten the Chinese and now control the Afrite in the pillar."

"What shall we do, Mahdi?"

"Abdi, I keep telling you I am not the Mahdi."

"Sorry, I mean Guided One."

"I am the one in need of guidance now, Abdi."

"What shall we do to get guidance?"

"I will lie here and see what happens."

Abdi leaves to go and get blankets and tea for the night vigil. The hours of darkness pass slowly, and the cold bites into his old bones, but the blankets help to keep him from freezing. Above him the stars twinkle in the night sky, and eventually the sun rises in the east.

The American shayateen are camped out guarding the entrance to the mountain but seem to be doing nothing else. More time passes.

Then he hears the sound of engines in the distance as two aircraft come and land and take the enemy inside them. They take off and rise into the blue sky. The next thing he hears is the sound of distant thunder as explosions rock the mountainside. The American shayateen have dropped bombs to block the entrances to the Afrite.

"Who would've thought, Abdi, that the American shayateen would blow up the mountain entrances?"

"Not I, Guided One."

"Sometimes Allah works in mysterious ways."

"So he does, Guided One."

"I think though we have not won, we have not lost today. If this is not a sign, then I don't know what is."

"Allahu Ahkbar," says Abdi as he helps him get up off the ground.

They walk down the mountain and back to the new caves to plan for the future. The Afrite has been buried under the mountain. He and his followers will make sure it remains buried, with the help of the other warlords if necessary. Together they will harass and destroy any who come to try to dig the Afrite out of the ground.

45. A NEW DAY

Some people spend an entire lifetime wondering if they made a difference in the world. But, the Marines don't have that problem.

— RONALD REAGAN, 40TH PRESIDENT OF THE UNITED STATES

Sergeant Tachikoma
First Combat Armor Suit Reconnaissance Company
Afghanistan
Friday, July 3, 2071

There's a lot less banter on the way back. The deaths of Knight and Jackson have hit everyone in Second Platoon hard. So no one jokes as we fly back to *Hornet*.

The Chickens leave NOE as we cross into Pakistani airspace. Then the birds climb rapidly up until we reach an altitude of fifteen thousand feet before levelling off at a steady three hundred knots.

I switch my screen to the feeds from the nose of our bird to watch the clouds on our way home. The world looks so small below us.

This time I can't sleep, so I stare at my screen lost in my thoughts. In the distance is the fleet. The ships appear to be floating in the sky ahead of us as the sea and sky blend into one. Their wakes are like contrails, furthering the illusion of the fleet below flying along with us.

Then our Chickens start their descent towards our ARG. For the first time I see *Hornet* as the sailors must feel about her; she's such a beautiful ship. *Hornet*'s deck becomes larger as our zoomies bring their birds down nice and steady.

Coming into land is when the pilots make the most of the Chickens' ability to do short take-offs and landings. This is another reason why the bird is ideal for carrier operations. The captain's bird lands first. It halts alongside *Hornet*'s island on the starboard side of the ship. Then our bird lands next, pulling up to the left of it on the port side. Our other birds mirror us, and we're arranged in a neat oblong formation on deck ready for the next stage.

The aircraft are swarmed by the deck crews in their colorful jerseys. Movement officers, dressed in yellow, direct where the aircraft handlers, dressed in their blue jerseys, should move us. They take our birds across the deck and put them onto the elevators.

As our bird shifts I can see *Tortuga* trailing astern of *Hornet* and, in the distance, the *Forrest Sherman*.

Getting the birds into the hangar bay is a repeat of the precision ballet it took to send us off. Except our ballerinas are sixty tons of fully loaded tilt fans that can crush someone if control of their movements is lost. Fortunately, today is a fine day to be at sea with little chop on the waves, and the transfer from deck to hangar goes without a hitch. The hangar crews secure the birds for unloading. Now it's time to let the Dogs out.

As the rear ramps on the Chicken drop, our safety people are waiting: medical crew in white to deal with our casualties, and ordnance personnel in red waiting to make safe our unexpended ammunition, which will be unloaded and returned to the ship's magazines.

They already know we are coming in with an extra egg. The nuke will be disposed of in due course. And I'm grateful it's not my problem.

Rank has its privileges, so I'm second out the back of the bird and to get my cockpit open. Once my Dog is stacked in the kennel, I unstrap and climb down onto the floor of the hangar deck.

We're told the debrief will begin in an hour.

Time to head to the changing room for a shower and then go grab something to eat from the chow hall. They've got ham and eggs, but I decide to take a rain cheque on them today. So instead I grab pancakes, bacon, and maple syrup.

It feels good to get back home to *Hornet*.

Making my way to the briefing room I catch up with Lieutenant McCarthy on the way in. Lieutenant Beckford and Staff Sergeant Washington are already there, and a few minutes later Sergeant Thompson joins us looking gray. Gunnery Sergeant Locklear comes in next with Sergeant Ramirez and Lieutenant Bergeson behind him.

This constitutes a full house of the remaining senior NCOs and officers of the Confederated States Marine Corps Hound Dogs 1st CSAR Cerberus Company.

Captain Johanson walks into the room accompanied by both Mr Anderson and Colonel Philmore. Gunnery Sergeant Locklear calls out, "Officers on deck!"

We come to attention as the colonel says, "At ease people." He pauses, to look at us. "First off I want to say well done. I know you're all dealing with the deaths of your fellow Marines on this mission, and there are no words I can say that will make this easier for you. But I do know you would've died for them, and I ask you remember they died for you while serving their country."

It could've been so much worse, was worse, so I can't really complain at how bad it has been.

"Captain Johanson will you start by giving us your account of the mission," says Colonel Philmore.

"Thank you, Colonel."

I let Johanson's words flow over me as he describes the progress of the mission once it hit the ground in Afghanistan. At various points the downloaded data from the Dogs is played to illustrate or clarify points. My name is mentioned in passing, and so of course are the outcomes of the various engagements, including the battle at the end.

"Sergeant Tachikoma, would you like to add a few comments about finding the magnetic anomaly under the mountain?" asks Johanson.

"Thank you, sir. I would start by drawing your attention to the footage here of the source of the magnetic anomaly. I've taken to thinking of them as 'shimmer pillars,' because when they cycle they cause the air to shimmer between them."

I pause to allow those who haven't yet seen the footage or weren't present to assimilate what they've been told.

"As you can see I walked my Dog through the pillars to retrieve the Army Alpha Detachment PACE suit. The suit appears to have been cut in half when the person was moving through the pillars."

"What happened when you walked between the pillars, Sergeant?" asks Colonel Philmore.

"Well, sir, I don't know how, but I stood somewhere else, outside the cavern. I found myself in the open."

Next I bring up the recordings from my Dog. These show the mountain and the jungle in the distance as I turned to walk back through the pillars. "I would like to draw attention to the sky here."

Their pause between seeing and realizing what they are seeing seems to last forever, but as I breathe out I can hear the bubble of voices fill the room.

"Quiet people," says Gunnery Sergeant Locklear.

Mr Anderson asks, "Where do you think you were, Sergeant Tachikoma?"

"I think I went through to another world, Mr Anderson."

"That's impossible," says Thompson.

"Not impossible, at least not according to the readings from the sergeant's Dog," says Mr Anderson, which brings the hubbub to a close.

"Sergeant Tachikoma, I would like a full written report in one hour. I then want to see you in my office for a debriefing with Captain Johanson and Mr Anderson," says Colonel Philmore.

"Yes, sir."

"Captain, is there anything else to discuss to do with the mission?" asks Colonel Philmore.

"No, sir."

"If I may be permitted to speak, Colonel?" asks Mr Anderson.

"Go ahead, Mr Anderson."

"This is to inform everyone present in this room that this mission has been classified above top secret, and no details of this mission are to be discussed outside of this room. Furthermore, this mission's existence will be sealed under national security authority. Thank you."

After we're dismissed I go and find somewhere to sit and write my AAR. After Action Reports have a standard format. It starts with the mission name, then the date, the name of the person who is writing the report, followed by Confederated States Marine Corps. In case it wasn't clear enough.

I start with the easy bit first. Our time out and the time we returned. That's taken from the official lift-off time from the first Thunder Hawk take-off to touch-down time of the last bird on deck. All nice and formal, and easy to follow.

I then give a brief outline of the mission.

Stated simply, it was to go to a mountain in Afghanistan and retrieve an Army Alpha Detachment of PACE suits. I cut and paste bits from Captain Johanson's official briefing orders for this. This is followed by the situation, which I take from Mr Anderson's official briefing.

The rest of my report is only a matter of slotting stuff into the standard format to cover execution of the mission, what were service and support requirements, and the chain of command. The meat of the writing is in the main body of the report and summary.

I start my AAR by saying the objective was to retrieve the missing Army personnel and locate the source of the magnetic energy pulse, which I call RED SLIPPERS, written out in caps to make sure whoever reads this knows it's a code name.

I follow this with a brief outline of our casualties. The death of Corporal Knight and the head injury sustained by Lieutenant McCarthy when his Dog was damaged in the assault to retrieve the three PACE suits. I follow this by confirming I had received orders to continue with the mission.

This leads to Two Bravo's descent into the mountain, and the cavern with the shimmering pillars, and I mention again RED SLIPPERS, as Mr Anderson had suggested when I talked to him in the med-bay, which seems like a lifetime ago. I briefly describe going through the other tunnel to get out of the mountain, which could be seen as a loose interpretation of my orders.

The firefight and resulting retreating enemy finishes off the report, as well as describing Jackson's death, then how Rodriguez and Kowalski both were wounded during the firefight.

I then add my summary because no one has time to read everything written in the reports. So here I add another mention of RED SLIPPERS. Job done, I send it off, and then go for my interview with Colonel Philmore, whose office is only slightly larger than Johanson's. This means it's going to be an intimate occasion with the four of us in the room.

I arrive and announce my presence at the ordered time, and hear, "Please wait."

Time passes slowly as I wait outside to hear my name being called. "Please come in, Sergeant Tachikoma," says Colonel Philmore.

"Yes, sir." I enter and come to attention.

"At ease, Sergeant. Thank you for your report, most interesting, as I think Mr Anderson will attest."

"If you need me to rewrite any of it, sir…"

"No, that's not necessary. This is more of a debrief about your actions that led to you walking through the pillars, which you've used the code name RED SLIPPERS for. Why did you choose to name the pillars that?" asks Colonel Philmore.

"That's rather a difficult question to answer, as you may not believe what I'm going to tell you, Colonel."

"Tell me and let me be the judge of that."

"Sir, yes, sir. I haven't put in everything that happened during the mission because some things happened on different versions of the same day…"

Explaining as best I can what happened on different versions of yesterday's operation, I include: getting out and brushing against the pillars, getting lost off-world, and the numerous times I died when blown up by the bomb we'd retrieved.

"I can see why that wasn't in this report, and your story is rather hard to credit if it weren't for some of the corroborating evidence. So why do you add more to your story, Sergeant?" asks Colonel Philmore.

"Because it happened to me, sir. I've lived through the same day twelve times, seeing different outcomes as I changed my choices about the things to do and say, sir. It might sound crazy, but it has to be something to do with the pillars, sir. I think when I touched them the first time it created a link, and when the bomb went off it caused me to remember what had happened before, sir."

"Colonel Philmore, I would like to say something if I may?"

"Go ahead, Mr Anderson, I know you are quite excited by the report."

"Thank you, Colonel. In short I believe Sergeant Tachikoma. I'm not at liberty to disclose why I believe her. But the reason this mission was given the priority to go ahead is because we at the Agency received information about another country having access to a similar device. The confirmation of all the various bits of intelligence from Sergeant Tachikoma's actions during this mission will mean the security of our country can be maintained."

"As per our previous conversation, Mr Anderson, I will take it on good faith what you've told us does all make some kind of sense in the bigger scheme of things."

"I can assure you it does, Colonel. However, there's one question Sergeant Tachikoma hasn't answered, which I would like clarification on. How did you know to use the code name RED SLIPPERS?"

"You told me to, sir. You won't remember the conversation we had on one of the previous days when I wasn't at my best where we sat and talked. It was you who told me to include the name

RED SLIPPERS in my AAR, sir. As plans go, it seems to have worked, sir."

"That it does, Sergeant Tachikoma."

"Unless there's anything more to add or anyone else has any questions," Colonel Philmore pauses, "then I would like to say well done. Sergeant, I wish you all the best for your Officer Candidate School, as it seems to me it is a well-deserved commission."

"Thank you, sir. I couldn't have done it without my Marines to support me, sir."

"Don't ever forget that and you'll go far as an officer. Meeting dismissed."

47. UNKNOWN TOMORROW

Only the dead have seen the end of war.

— George Santayana

Sergeant Tachikoma
First Combat Armor Suit Reconnaissance Company
CSN *Hornet*
Saturday, July 4, 2071

The next day we all get to enjoy a barbecue on the aft lower-hangar deck fantail. The sun is shining, and the taste of salt is in the air as the white wake of the *Hornet* trails out behind into the distant ocean. Off our port stern is the *Tortuga*.

Everything's right with the world. To my surprise, I see Mr Anderson on the fantail talking to Captain Johanson.

I'm talking with the survivors from my platoon. The conversation is one of joy for being alive, and commiserations for the comrades we've lost. A mix of denial, anger, and sadness permeates our chit-chat about giving it back as good as we got.

Delgado is coming to terms with Gentle's loss. Jackson's death has hit Rodriguez worst of all, though.

The truth is, we're all taking the loss of our friends hard. But on the whole, Marines understand the price they might have to pay to defend our country. And I know it could've been so much worse.

Washington and Thompson let me finish talking to the survivors of my platoon and wave me over to where they're standing next to the barbecue. The aroma of steak being cooked reminds me I'm hungry.

"You holding up OK, Tachikoma?"

"I'm good, I may and go see the doc for something to help. And you?"

Washington replies, "I'm peachy, we had it easy. Thompson here, not so much."

"Nah, I'm just out of sorts because I was promised beer if we didn't end up using the ordnance we took out." Thompson smiles, but behind the eyes, there's the loss of the lieutenant and two good men under him. It has hit him hard. "I failed the lieutenant, Schwartz, and Jackman. They were good Marines. I'll miss them," he says.

"You didn't fail the lieutenant," I say.

"She's right, and you brought the platoon back," says Washington.

"Seems to me you're potentially officer material, Thompson."

Thompson swears at me. "Wash your mouth out, Tachikoma. Just because you're going don't mean I have to take being called a bastard by you."

Washington laughs. "She's still got your number. So what's this I hear about you eyeing up the spook, Tachikoma?"

"He's easy on the eye and listens when I tell him stuff, unlike you two."

"Well, you be careful to hide the body once you've finished

with him is all I'm saying. The Agency doesn't take kindly to its personnel being eaten up and spat out by feisty Marines looking to have some fun," says Washington.

Then I smile and laugh out loud; my friends laugh with me. Friends I will miss when I leave, but at least they're alive.

"Remember, the Agency always find the bodies, doesn't matter how good you hide them. We'll leave you now," says Thompson pulling Washington along with him. "Have some respect and give the woman some space to maneuver."

Across the hangar Mr Anderson is now standing by himself on the deck, and I wave at him to come over. Everyone else around me moves away, leaving us to talk alone. If I was paranoid about such things, I would suspect I've been set up.

"So how's everyone, Sergeant?"

"Angry, pissed off with the Agency for telling us shit, but more pissed off with the Chinese for shooting at us. I see you knocked your head on something."

"Yeah, I had to go to med-bay to get a couple of stitches put in. I'm fine though. How are you feeling?"

"I'm OK, just wondering what you were talking about with my commanding officer, though?"

"He was wondering what the heck you saw in me. I didn't know what to say."

"He cares about his people, and the Agency has a reputation of seeing us as expendable, which means we're all glad to be alive despite your best efforts. I'm also wondering: Does this mean the Agency is sponsoring off-world travel?"

"I couldn't comment. But I'm confident we won't be exploiting the Afghani pillars anytime soon."

"Does that mean there are other pillars?"

"I can neither confirm nor deny the existence of other pillars," he says, smiling at me.

"I'll take that as a yes then, shall I?"

"You can take it any way you want to, but I can't possibly comment on the existence of other pillars. Just to change the subject: when I was a kid, I always wanted to fly. My grandfather use to tell me stories about Spitfires dog-fighting Messerschmitts and other tales of derring-do and adventures during the Battle of Britain."

"Derring-do!?"

"He was old, he used to speak like that."

"Ah I see."

"When I was sixteen he paid for an introductory flight in a glider as my present. I was both thrilled and scared on the day. I have this memory of being catapulted into the air and hearing the rush of the wind."

"This sounds like a long story, do you want something to eat and drink?"

"Sure, why not, assuming you're not bored?"

"Not bored, just hungry from standing next to the barbecue and smelling the cooking." So we go and stand in line to get steak, onions, and fries, and pick up sodas. "As you were saying, Mr Anderson."

"Oh man, you had to be there when the pilot tipped the wing up and I looked down to the ground. It terrified me, but I knew that I wanted to be a pilot."

"So why didn't you enlist with the Air Force then?"

"Funny you should ask, but I went to a recruiter and asked about joining up. She told me that fighter pilots were all cubicle jocks. Still, I'll give her credit for telling me all about the astronaut programme. She inspired me to study hard and get a commission."

"So how's that working out for you?"

"Not going according to plan."

"No plan ever does."

"You've got that straight. I got a commission in the

Confederated States Air Force in intelligence because I could train to be a mission specialist for NASA."

"Didn't work out, huh?"

"Real life got in the way. Got married, got out of the service because the wife didn't like all the moving, got divorced."

"Sounds sad."

"More for her. I loved her, but she couldn't stop drinking. So I reapplied to get back in. Turns out I was now too old. They were looking for younger people. Go figure. Anyway the CIA offered me a chance to come work for them as a science and technology analyst."

"Shit happens."

Anderson laughed. "That's one way of putting it."

"So you've been spying on everyone ever since?"

"No comment. If I told you, I'd have to kill you."

"Yeah right, you could try," I say, smiling at him.

"You always play hardball?"

"Trust me, this isn't me playing hardball," I say and then laugh.

"I guess not, given what I know about you. Anyway the point is I want to thank you for reigniting my dream of humanity going to other worlds."

"Sure, whatever. I have a question for you?"

"Go ahead and ask. I'll answer if I can."

"Why couldn't everybody else move around when the pillars activated? I mean they're not much use to anyone if no one can walk through them when they open."

"I don't have a clue, but I'm going to do my best to find out. First thing I'm going to do is put in a request to have you tested to find out what makes you different."

"You sure know how to chat a woman up."

"Sorry?"

"Nothing, carry on."

"Anyway, my point is that I always wanted to travel to other worlds and now we can…I missed something here, didn't I?"

"You did. The Corps likes to call it *situational awareness*."

"So this isn't the conversation for chilling out on the Fourth of July with burgers and a drink?"

"About sums it up, Mr Anderson."

So we change the subject to the weather, the food, and stuff. Glen asks me if we can exchange addresses and catch up later. I say I would like that very much. Later on my Marines rib me for being all soppy around a spook. But it's all right by me. They're alive, and soon I will be off to become an officer and a lady. Not something I would ever have imagined myself doing before the mission.

Ooh…Rah!

DRAMATIS PERSONAE

Mr Glen Anderson is a CIA representative whose request to retrieve missing Special Forces operatives leads to Operation Clean Sweep.

Second Lieutenant Ayesha-Imani Beckford is the leader of the 1st CASR Fourth Platoon, operation call sign Cerberus Four Papa, Company handle Lobo. She is fourth in the company chain of command. Her operation call sign is Cerberus Four-Six and her company handle is Lobo Six.

Second Lieutenant Joshua Bergeson is the leader of the 1st CASR First Platoon, operation call sign Cerberus One Papa, company handle Hellhounds. He is fifth in the company chain of command and acts as the S2 Intelligence officer. His operation call sign is Cerberus One-Six and his company handle is Hellhound Six.

Private First Class Charles Brownlee is a member of 1st CASR First Platoon Bravo Squad and in Hellhounds Fire Team 3. His operation call sign is Cerberus One-Eight and his company handle is Hellhound Eight.

Lance Corporal Daniella Luciana Gonzalez Delgado is a member of 1st CASR Second Platoon Alpha Squad and the Fenris Fire Team 2 leader. Her operation call sign is Cerberus Two-Three and her company handle is Fenris Three.

Lance Corporal María Fernanda Gentle is a member of 1st CASR First Platoon Bravo Squad and the Hellhounds Fire Team 3 leader. Her operation call sign is Cerberus One-Seven and her company handle is Hellhound Seven.

Private First Class Jorge Falto Hernandez is a member of 1st CASR Second Platoon Alpha Squad and in Fenris Fire Team 2. His operation call sign is Cerberus Two-Five and his company handle is Fenris Five.

Private First Class Terry Jackman is a member of 1st CASR Third Platoon Alpha Squad and in Wulfgang Fire Team 1. His operation call sign is Cerberus Three-Two and his company handle is Wulfgang Two.

Private First Class Bjorn Jackson is a member of 1st CASR Second Platoon Bravo Squad and in Fenris Fire Team 4. His operation call sign is Cerberus Two-Ten and his company handle is Fenris Ten.

Captain Poul Johanson is the commander of the First Combat Armored Suit Reconnaissance (1st CASR) Alpha Company of the Hound Dogs Battalion, operation call sign Cerberus. 1st CASR is deployed as part of the Confederated States Marine Corps Thirteenth Marine Expeditionary Unit, otherwise known as the Fighting Thirteenth. His operation

call sign is Cerberus Six and his company handle is
Big Dog.

Private Morgan Jones is a member of 1st CASR Second Platoon
and in Fenris Bravo Squad Fire Team 3. His operation call sign is
Cerberus Two-Eight and his company handle is Fenris Eight.

Corporal Samuel Knight is a member of 1st CASR Second
Platoon and the Fenris Alpha Squad Fire Team 1 leader. His
operation call sign is Cerberus Two-One and his company handle
is Fenris One.

Lance Corporal Jan Kowalski is a member of 1st CASR Second
Platoon and the Fenris Bravo Squad Fire Team 3 leader. His
operation call sign is Cerberus Two-Seven and his company
handle is Fenris Seven.

Lance Corporal Catherine Langford is a member of 1st CASR
First Platoon and the Hellhounds Alpha Squad Fire Team 1 leader.
Her operation call sign is Cerberus One-One and her company
handle is Hellhound One.

Gunnery Sergeant Jacob Locklear is Alpha Company's senior
NCO. His operation call sign is Cerberus Four and his company
handle is Growler.

Private First Class Juan Padilla Lopez is a member of 1st
CASR First Platoon and in Hellhounds Alpha Squad Fire Team 2.
His operation call sign is Cerberus One-Five and his company
handle is Hellhound Five.

First Lieutenant Jack McCarthy is the leader of 1st CASR
Second Platoon, operation call sign Cerberus Two Papa, company

handle Fenris. He is also the company XO and is second in the company chain of command. His operation call sign is Cerberus Two-Six and his company handle is Fenris Six.

Second Lieutenant Miguel Ramirez Perez is the leader of 1st CASR Third Platoon, operation call sign Cerberus Three Papa, company handle Wulfgang. He is third in the company chain of command. His operation call sign is Cerberus Three-Six and his company handle is Wulfgang Six.

Colonel Alan Philmore is the commander of the Confederated States Marine Corps Thirteenth Marine Expeditionary Unit, otherwise known as the Fighting Thirteenth. Operation call sign Birds Nest Six.

Sergeant Emilio Jose Ramirez is 1st CASR First Platoon's senior NCO and the Hellhounds Bravo Squad leader. His operation call sign is Cerberus One-Four and his company handle is Hellhound Four.

Private First Class Alejandro Marquez Rodriguez is a member of 1st CASR Second Platoon and the Fenris Bravo Squad Fire Team 4 leader. His operation call sign is Cerberus Two-Nine and his company handle is Fenris Nine.

Lance Corporal Eric Schwartz is a member of 1st CASR Third Platoon and the Wulfgang Alpha Squad Fire Team 1 leader. His operation call sign is Cerberus Three-One and his company handle is Wulfgang One.

Private First Class James Spader is a member of 1st CASR First Platoon and in Hellhounds Alpha Squad Fire Team 1. His operation call sign is Cerberus One-Two and his company handle is Hellhound Two.

Sergeant Lara Atsuko Tachikoma is 1st CASR Second Platoon's senior NCO and the Fenris Bravo Squad leader. Her operation call sign is Cerberus Two-Four and her company call sign is Fenris Four.

Sergeant Jeffrey Thompson is 1st CASR Third Platoon's senior NCO and the Wulfgang Bravo Squad leader. His operation call sign is Cerberus Three-Four and his company handle is Wulfgang Four.

Private First Class Stephanus Vosloo is a member of 1st CASR Second Platoon and in Fenris Alpha Squad Fire Team 1. His operation call sign is Cerberus Two-Two and his company handle is Fenris Two.

Private First Class Patricia Ward is a member of 1st CASR First Platoon and in Hellhounds Bravo Squad Fire Team 4. Her operation call sign is Cerberus One-Ten and her company handle is Hellhound Ten.

Staff Sergeant Henry Washington is 1st CASR Fourth Platoon's senior NCO and the Lobo Bravo Squad leader. His operation call sign is Cerberus Four-Four and his company handle is Lobo Four.

GLOSSARY

AAR After Action Report, which is a written description of what has happened during a mission, and can sometimes be referred to as a "mission report."

Aries A suborbital space-plane that is launched off the top of a rocket booster. Retrieval is done by using a MULE. See MULE.

ARG Amphibious Readiness Group that describes a group of Navy warships known as an "amphibious task force" with an attached landing force of Confederated States Marines and support units.

Bán Chinese squad.

BENT Brevity code word for equipment inoperative.

BigDog BigDog was a quadruped robot created in 2005 by Boston Dynamics in conjunction with Foster-Miller, the NASA Jet Propulsion Laboratory, and the Harvard University Concord

Field Station. Its development led to the creation of the first driven combat armor suits.

BGB Big Gray Boat, appellation describing any large Naval ship.

CEASED Brevity code word for "subject emitter has stopped radiating."

ChameleonFlage An active camouflage system that mimics the surrounding environment. It's an integral part of the feedback system for the sense of kinaesthesia that makes driving combat armor suits through the surrounding environment intuitive for the pilots.

Chicken Nickname for the V-32 Thunder Hawk. See Thunder Hawk.

CAS-C4P Combat Armor System Dash C4 (Command, Control, Communication & Computer) Patrol. Informally called a Buster because of its size. The active LIDAR array is pivoted to allow the suit to remain hidden behind terrain, and the Buster bristles with aerials for its primary role of controlling Human Operator Surrogates a.k.a. surrogates or combat androids. See HOS.

CASE-2X The Marine Corps Combat Armor System Environment Dash (Mark) 2 Extreme is driven by its operator, unlike its lighter counterpart MARPACE suit that is worn. It can operate up to three days before needing to be refueled. See FM51-CASES and TO-2051-16-02-1U for further details. Command variant CASE-2XC has enhanced C4 suite.

CBI Confederation Bureau of Investigation, formerly known as the Federal Bureau of Investigations, also known as the Bureau, a change of name that arose after the second American Civil War of 2037 and the formation of the North American Confederation.

CIA Confederation Intelligence Agency, formerly known as the Central Intelligence Agency often referred to as the Agency.

CIC Combat Information Center or operations room is where the tactical decisions are made on board a warship.

Coffin locker An under-the-mattress storage place for clothes and personal items.

CSAF Confederated States Air Force is the name of what was previously known as the United States Air Force, also known as Chair Force, a disparaging appellation to describe how they do their job.

CSGS Confederated States Geological Survey is a civilian agency that researches water, earth, biological sciences, and mapping services.

CSMC Confederated States Marine Corps is the name of what was previously known as the United States Marine Corps. The change of name has not mellowed the attitudes of the Corps, or its creed, and as a result they are still badasses that you do not want to mess with.

CSN Confederated States Navy.

CYCLOPS Brevity code word for a UAV, unmanned aerial vehicle. Commonly incorrectly referred to as a "drone."

DARPA Defense Advanced Research Projects Agency, now

defunct and replaced by Global Dynamics Corporation Defense Industries.

Dog Widely used nickname given by Marines for their CASE-2X suits. It stands for Dispersed Operation and Guidance System, which is the name of the near AI/expert system interface, and it also has the advantage of resonating with the historical tradition of Marines being called Devil Dogs by the Germans during World War One.

ECM Electronic Counter Measures provide a means to deceive or counter radar and other electronic sensor systems.

ECCM Electronic Counter-Countermeasures are part of the defensive measures taken to reduce the effect of ECM upon a vehicle's operating system.

EMP Electromagnetic Pulse that causes interference in electronic systems, and can be used as a weapon to disable a vehicle. EM pulses can be generated by nuclear explosions at high altitude or by non-nuclear electromagnetic pulse (NNEMP) weapons.

ETA Estimated Time of Arrival.

FOD Foreign Objects and Debris, which are loose items that have fallen onto the flight deck of a carrier that can have an adverse effect upon the effectiveness and success of flight operations.

FRAGO Fragmentary Order, or warning order, which notifies personnel that there has been a change in the plans for an operation.

FREAK Frequency hopping.

GECAL 50 The GECAL 50 GAU-19/A is a three barrel rotary autocannon from General Dynamics that fires the 12.7 x 99 mm fifty cal BMG round.

GEOINT Geospatial Intelligence derived from the analysis of geospatial imagery.

HOS Stands for Human Operator Surrogate a.k.a. a Surrogate or android, which are semi-autonomous robots with a hybrid expert system artificial intelligence operating system. This allows the operator to effectively multi-task by distributing themselves across a network and act as a force multiplier. Global Dynamics Corporation Defense Industries sales pitch calls them An Army of One.

HUD Heads-Up Display, a system that allows the user to see instrument data overlaid on their main screen without the need to open another window.

HUMINT Human Intelligence acquired from clandestine espionage operations.

IFF Identify, Friend or Foe.

INTEL Intelligence gathered through spying or monitoring of signals. See HUMINT and SIGINT.

KRISS Vector Compact submachine gun firing a .45 ACP round that is issued to CASE suit crews as part of their survival gear.

Lián Chinese for company.

Lie Bing Chinese rank equivalent to private.

LIDAR Alternative name for the acronym LADAR, which stood for Laser Detection and Ranging. LIDAR uses a short pulsed laser to illuminate a target to determine the distance to an object, thus providing a 3-D image of the target at the same time as determining the distance.

M21-A8 A 40 mm Gauss rifle with an eight round cassette magazine/powerpack firing 10mm discarding sabot rounds.

M41-AC230 The General Electric Company M41 is a long-recoil autocannon that fires a 20 x 170 mm round with a range of 5 kilometers, and it has an inbuilt Mk 30 40 x 53 mm underbarrel grenade launcher effective out to one kilometer. The M41 standard load-out is four magazines, each holding ten armor piercing tungsten-steel penetrators, and two magazines, each with ten High-Explosive Air Burst (HEAB) warheads, and five rounds of High-Velocity Canister Cartridge (HVCC) for the grenade launcher.

M240LC General purpose machine gun using the 7.62 x 51 mm NATO round that can be used in the sustained fired role to suppress the enemy without overheating, which has been modified for use on combat armor suits.

MACE suit Shortening of MARPACE. See MARPACE.

MAP Magnetic Anomaly Project. Financed by the Confederated States Geological Survey and the Confederated States Air Force to study geological phenomenon that led to the discovery of the pillars.

MARPACE Marine Corps Power Armor Combat Enhancement suit that is modified to operate in marine environments, a.k.a. MACE suit. See also PACE suit.

MOS Military Occupational Specialty training, which takes place after attending recruit training camp. All officers and enlisted Marines are then assigned a four-digit code that denotes their occupational field and specialty.

MULE Medium Utility Lifting Envelope. A hybrid lifting body transport airship.

NOE Nap of (the) Earth. Flying low to the ground to be below radar detection.

NBC Nuclear Biological and Chemical. Used as a descriptor for environment, threat level, or ability of a unit.

NNEMP Non-Nuclear Electromagnetic Pulse. See EMP.

OODA loop Observe, Orient, Decide (and) Act. A recurring cycle used to get inside the enemy's decision-making cycle by making decisions quicker.

OPFOR Opposing Force, a.k.a. the enemy.

OPSEC Operational Security.

ORBAT Order (of) Battle. Those units from a formation that are actually deployed in action. For example the First Combat Armored Suit Reconnaissance Company ORBAT runs with four platoons, each with two squads of five combat armor suits. With the addition of the commander and senior NCO this makes for a total of forty-two personnel. See TO&E.

ORP Orbital Reconnaissance Platforms, more commonly referred to as spy satellites.

Oscar Mike Phonetic alphabet for On the Move, as in "moving now."

PACE suit Power Armor Combat Enhancement suit that is worn and reacts to users' body movements in a naturalistic manner, a.k.a. PACES. The suit has NBC resistance built in and has facilities for handling bodily waste. The suit can operate for up to twenty-four hours before requiring a stop for recharging depending on environmental variables. See FM51-PACES and TO-2051-08-08-1R for further details.

Pái Chinese platoon.

PAD Personal Access Device. A wearable computer interface that can be accessed by various means depending on the sensors and accessories worn.

POD Plan Of (the) Day. Every day in the military has a plan for what is happening that day. This generally ranges from repetitive to banal, except when it doesn't.

POG POG or pogue is an abbreviation meaning Person Other (than) Grunt that is less pejorative than REMF, which stands for Rear Echelon Maintenance Force, if being polite. The less polite version should be obvious.

RIPPLE Brevity code word for two or more munitions released on a target.

RPG Backronym for Rocket-Propelled Grenade, which stands for Ruchnoy Protivotankovyy Granatomyot, a handheld antitank grenade launcher.

Shàngwèi Chinese rank equivalent to captain.

Shàowèi Chinese rank equivalent to second lieutenant.

SIGINT Intelligence gathered by listening to communication traffic. This can be as simple as studying the amount of data flowing between stations to identify headquarter units or decrypting intercepted messages.

SITREP Situation Report.

Space-plane A colloquial expression referring to any craft that enters orbit as part of its flight plan. See Aries.

Thunder Hawk The V-32 Thunder Hawk is a heavy-lift tilt-fan aircraft. Commonly referred to as a Chicken by those who fly in them due to their ungainly looks.

TO&E/TO & TE Table (of) Organization and Equipment (Army); Table Organization and Table Equipment (Marines). This lays out the composition of each unit at every level, and is driven by the forces' doctrine. For instance the First Light Armored Reconnaissance Company, when at full strength, consists of four platoons and a headquarters squad of two CASE-2X Dogs. Each platoon has three squads with four combat armor suits, split into six fire teams of two. The platoon is commanded by a lieutenant with a sergeant. This makes for a paper total of fifty-eight personnel. However, field strength is less due to sickness, training, and vacant slots. See ORBAT.

UAV Unmanned Aerial Vehicle commonly referred to in casual conversation incorrectly as "drones." See CYCLOPS.

Xiashi Chinese rank equivalent to corporal.

Zhongzhi Chinese rank equivalent to Sergeant.

AFTERWORD

I ended up writing a military SF story as my debut novel quite by happenstance. I was writing another story, just before Christmas 2012, when a phrase popped into my head, *It's all Big Dog's fault that I died yesterday under a mountain in Afghanistan.* I wrote the phrase down, and put it to one-side, so I could carry on with my other novel.

My good intentions didn't go as planned.

The ideas encapsulated in that sentence wouldn't leave me alone. It kept nagging at me. The idea literally forced me to start writing a new novel, driving me to run with the random phrase, morphing more and more ideas, until I ended up with creating the Bad Dog novel you are reading now.

But one thing became obvious, I wanted to write a story where the concerns of the character are driven by their desire to do their duty, and that her solutions came from military doctrine. The scope of the problem in this story is very much about tactics, but tactics are driven by doctrine and what is called the OODA loop: observe, orient, decide, and act. The decision cycle was developed by the military strategist Colonel John Boyd of the United Staes Air Force. Boyd applied the concept to the combat operations process, and the Unites States Marine Corps took his ideas to produce their book on doctrine called, *Warfighting*, that I talk about in this novel.

For those of you interested in the science behind Bad Dog you'll all have to thank Professor Max Tegmark, for his ideas about us all living in a mathematical based multiverse, and Professor't Hooft for developing the idea about living in a holographic universe. Both of these men were the inspiration behind the pillars and how they work. Any mistakes in the physics are of course attributable only to me.

Finally, every story written owes something to previous stories written by other authors who have gone before them. I would acknowledge that in the greater scheme of things that I stand on the shoulders of giants. Bad Dog is no exception to this observation, because no novel is written in isolation. Without the support and encouragement from Susan Parker, my Alpha reader, I would never have completed Bad Dog. It was her feedback and enthusiasm that drove me to write more. I would even go so far as to say that she is the person who should be thanked most for the story you have been reading.

I am also indebted to my Beta readers too: Clive Rushen, Roger Bell-West, and especially to David Barrow, Brian McCue and Alix McFarlane who all went beyond the call of duty in giving me constructive feedback. Those who have read my first draft can all attest to the differences between what they read and the novel that you have read.

Thank you one and all.

Ashley R Pollard
London, UK
December 2017

ABOUT THE AUTHOR

I am a cognitive behavioural therapist with a background in mental health nursing. My working career has ranged far and wide from civil servant to sales assistant.

I've written for *Battlegames* and *Miniature Wargames* magazines, and I was both a reviewer and columnist for Games Master International. In addition, I was a freelancer for FASA Corps working on the *3055 Technical Read Out*, and I wrote the *OHMU War Machine* wargame rules. My current non-fiction writing is a monthly column for *Galactic Journey*.

I've been told I have more interests than most people have dinners, which include: cycling, aikido, iaido, photography, miniatures wargaming, and painting.

I am unashamedly a starry eyed dreamer.

Want to know more?
https://ashleyrpollard.blogspot.co.uk/
ashley@ashley-pollard.com

Lightning Source UK Ltd.
Milton Keynes UK
UKOW04f0555260118
316881UK00001B/23/P